Flipping the Record

Heather J. Bennett

With huge thanks and gratitude to
The Plano Texas Writing Group, Guild of Unwritten
Words, my Beta Readers, and my family for their
endless encouragement and support.

1976

Chapter 1

"Hello? Do you *mind*?" an impatient voice grumbles beside me.

Looking down at my magazine on top of the reception desk, I pay no attention.

He claps twice and I lift my gaze to be greeted with glassy blue eyes amid a very stern expression. "Yeah, *hi*. So, do people just stand around here waiting for assistance or…?" He snaps and I smell the alcohol on his breath.

I realize he's speaking to me after glancing into the empty lobby of the recording studio. "Excuse me?"

"Ah-sis-tance," he enunciates with a hint of a Southern twang.

He's on such an ego trip, I'll be surprised if he doesn't need a TWA flight to get back from it. No wonder the receptionist is MIA. He stretches his neck forward, keeping his gaze on me, and snaps again, swaying as he reaches out to grab the reception desk to steady himself. His eyes are such an incredible blue, I'm almost distracted until he opens his mouth again. "Do you want to keep your job?"

Crinkling my forehead, I drop my chin, trying not to snort. "My… job?" I'm three weeks in working with Country-Rock legend Curt Parents on his fifth album as a session musician. I don't think this guy has a say over whether I keep my job, even if he is friends with Curt. "Look, I get enough sass from the guys I work with," I begin.

He squints, probably trying to get me in focus, and interrupts. "Do you know who I am?"

Wow, the 'do you know who I am' line? *Seriously? Yeah, bub, I know precisely who you are. Everyone in the music industry knows who Jeff Kingston is.*

"All I'm doing is trying to take a break." I press the air between us with a flat palm. "I think you're confused…"

Before I have a chance to explain, the receptionist returns, hurrying to her desk with a string of apologies. I step aside to let her sit and blink at Blue Eyes before I open my palm and turn to her. "Oh, he's *very* important and needs ah-sis-tance *immediately*."

He presses his lips together and blinks in my direction before turning his attention to her and mutters something about takeout menus. Instead of the attitude, though, he's almost flirty with a playful smile and reaches over the counter to tug an end of one of her long blonde pigtails. When he finishes, he nods, looking back and forth between us with his gaze landing on me. "*Do* you work here?"

"She's in Studio B with Curt," the receptionist answers for me. "Remember? I told you yesterday."

Why would she tell him where I was working? Why would he care?

Walking past the reception desk, he stops to squint at me, poking my *International Musician and Recording World* magazine. "Ignore page thirty-two—band's crap."

As he wanders down the hallway, cowboy boots with worn heels scuffing as he goes, I flip the magazine to page thirty-two. His face, with the rest of his band, Expedition, stares up at me. Even in black and white, I can see how blue his eyes are. From down the hall, he looks over his shoulder, setting wire-rimmed sunglasses over his eyes. He's a mess, quite frankly, but I don't know if I've ever seen anything, or anyone, more rock-n-roll.

Later that night, I'm the only one left in the studio, ready to lay this guitar in traffic and be done with it. *Ages* ago my guitar teacher told me, "if you can sing it, you can play it," since the brain controls both functions. This week, I doubt him. I've been singing what's in my head for *days*. I can hear it, but there's one section where my fingers refuse to play it. Curt loves what I've done, so he doesn't care what I hear in my head. I'm the one that's not satisfied.

The studio door opens, and I don't think twice about it, figuring it's one of the other session guys. They know how focused I've been, so I appreciate that they don't interrupt. I keep working, running through the section a few more times. After the third attempt, I glance up to see who came in, intending to bitch about this riff still not working.

Instead, it's Rude Blue Eyes, looking much more sober, wearing threadbare light denim jeans with a slightly fraying flair at the bottom.

"Do you need another menu?" I ask.

"You're good," he says, ignoring my comment and pushing away from the wall.

I fiddle with one of my strings, tightening it back into tune. "Thanks," I mumble, and I lift my head. "Did you need something?"

"I heard you playing and wanted to check it out."

"How did you hear me playing? I'm in a soundproof room."

"I was looking for one of the techs in there." He motions to the booth with his chin. "We're just down the hall."

"I know. I bumped into you earlier, remember?"

He reaches behind his head and rubs his neck, his eyes narrowing as he winces—possibly with embarrassment. "Shit," he mumbles, and a Southern twang trying to break free makes me snicker. "I'm a belligerent asshole when I drink tequila."

Smirking, I arch an eyebrow. "*Just* tequila?"

He tilts his head side to side, pursing his lips and wincing again. "You may have a point, but tequila makes me particularly crotchety. Sorry if I was an asshole."

"Apologize to the actual receptionist." I turn my head to glance at my guitar. I'm using my sunburst Gibson Les Paul and notice a new scratch on the back with a sigh. Choosing one guitar is like choosing your favorite sunset, but this one is well-loved and well-worn and by far my favorite at the moment.

"Oh, *trust* me, I've kissed Jackie's ass several times over. Unfortunately, she knows me well," he says with a playful grin, like that's enough to get him out of trouble. Stepping across the studio with a long stride, he stretches his hand to me. "Jeff Kingston, by the way."

"Cassandra Taylor." Shaking his hand, I notice it's as torn up and calloused as mine.

"Curt's told us all about y'all. He's impressed with his new crew. You been a session player long?"

"Long enough." I don't mind being a session player. It's long, weird hours, and you need to be up for and ready to play whatever music they hand you. The pay is decent when I get the gigs. Competition is crazy, though. I mean, there are only two or three other females in the pool, but we're wrestling against guys going for the same jobs. Working with Curt adds to my credibility and experience, however, being the only girl in the band means I need to play twice as well at half the price while they expect me to clean up after them and take the lunch orders.

I want to do my own material, maybe even have my own band someday, like Linda Ronstadt, only with my songs. There are boxes of material stored under my bed waiting for me.

"My name's finally out on the circuit enough that I'm getting actual paying-something-worthwhile rock gigs." I run a finger along one of the scratches on my guitar before looking back at him. "I lose a lot of jobs because they think girls can only play that acoustic folksy-type stuff."

"Well, Joni Mitchell's done okay," he says with a chuckle, crossing his arms over his chest before rubbing the back of his hand over the stubble on his chin.

"Yeah, Joni Mitchell is cool. So are Judy Collins and Carole King, but who wants to be compared to them constantly? Do you want to have people ask you to be more like REO Speedwagon or the Stones all the time?"

"Well…" He lifts a shoulder. "We aren't quite the same kind of band."

"Joni Mitchell isn't quite the stuff I'm interested in playing, either—but I am thankful she's at least got the doors cracked open for the rest of us to try to squeeze ourselves through."

"Well, you keep playing like that?" He lifts his chin and grins. "I don't think you'll have anything to worry about."

"For the time being." I shrug. "Unless I can't get this damn line down."

"Sounds pretty good to me."

"It's not where I want it to be." I lift my hand. "There're a bunch of notes in there that don't want to come out here." I wiggle my fingers as if that's supposed to help break up the logjam.

"Well, I'll leave you alone then to work it out," he says, taking a few steps back offering a smile. His entire demeanor changes when he smiles. He looks approachable with eyes that crinkle at the sides. "Feel free to come hang out later if you want a break or something." Tugging his sunglasses from his hair, he points over his shoulder. "Studio C."

I nod before I return to my guitar, but lift my chin when I don't hear him leaving. He's paused by the doorway, listening again. I arch an eyebrow at him, and he sticks his sunglasses over those beautiful faded denim eyes before ducking out of the room.

"So, you'll never guess who came into the studio today." I laugh, dumping some veggies into a strainer. "Jeff Kingston."

Leo, my boyfriend, stops melting the butter in a different pan and blinks at me; his eyebrows arched. *"Jeff Kingston?* Expedition's Jeff Kingston? Stopped into your guys' studio? He's friends with Curt, right?"

"Well," I shrug, "it was just me by then. He said I was good." I shake the string beans to drain them.

"Wait, *Kingston* said you were good?"

I step over, adding the beans to the butter, curling the corner of my mouth. "Yeah. So?"

"Babe, that's a big deal!"

"He's a rude, obnoxious asshole." I take up the stirring as I nudge Leo out of the way.

"He's allowed to be an asshole," he tells me, folding his arms over his chest. "You know who he is, right?"

I cock my hip to the side and tilt my head at him with a straight face. "No. Never heard of him or his band's multi-million-selling albums that're constantly on the radio. Who is he again?"

Irritation flickers to life in the pit of my stomach. *Is he serious?* I'm the one who's bringing in the steady paycheck working in this industry. I'm the one working with dozens of icons and wanna-be's alike, that's in the studio listening to what's being done—and by who—and he's going to stand there and question my industry knowledge?

Of *course*, I know who Jeff Kingston is. It kills me he's allowed to be a jerk just because they've made some fantastic albums. I look over to the stack of records by the stereo where Expedition's first album is displayed, knowing their following three are behind it. Half of the bands in America are trying to sound like them, Leo's included. And because of my experience, I know it's why Leo isn't making any splashes. The industry doesn't need the copycats when they have the real thing. But, since I'm only some *lowly session player*, he doesn't listen to me.

Leo leans over and kisses my nose. "You're allowed to be an asshole when you're a member of Expedition."

I roll my eyes and grab a bowl. "No, you're not."

He takes the bowl from me and nods. "Yes, you are. And if he said you were good? Baby, you're on your way!"

"Not if I can't get that damn riff down." Irritation ignites a little more as I serve a portion of rice and string beans over some chicken for myself. "And I don't need some arrogant drunk's opinion making my reputation."

Leo laughs and drops onto the couch, pulling his dirty bare feet up and crossing his ankles. "I'm sure he was a lot more than drunk." He chuckles. "He probably thought you were cute, but that isn't gonna hurt you any, that's for damn sure." In his eyes, I'm just some chick who 'gets it' and 'plays guitar' but I'm the one who's making connections and getting the steady work with it while he bartends and plays in local dives with his friends.

I sit at the little table tucked in the corner of the living room. This place is tiny, but we've managed to make it work. Half the time, only one of us is home to use it. "So, you're saying I should have taken him up on his offer to drop by his studio?"

"Seriously? Are you insane? Go! Put that down, put on something slinky, and go. Now!"

I know stopping in their studio won't hurt. Connections are how you make a career in this industry, but I've made a point not to make them because I have breasts. "I'll stop by tomorrow."

"What time? Maybe I can meet you at the studio," he asks over a mouthful of food as I shake my head. "What? Why not?"

"Because you know the rules. You made them, remember?"

"Yeah, but that was different," he says with a lift of his shoulder.

"Why? Because it was you meeting the famous people at trendy bars?"

"It was more that the famous people I met would want to steal you away from me, babe." He gives me a soft smile and cocks his head. "And I didn't know if you'd run off with them. I mean, you can't run off with Jeff…"

"Oh, *Jeff*, is it now?"

He crinkles his nose at me. "He's got a girlfriend."

"I know. There was a picture in the paper a few days ago. Someone doodled all over his face. Gave him devil horns, pitchfork, and a tail. Put a halo around her head with wings, and stuck it up at the reception desk. Everyone got a huge kick out of it."

"My point is, I don't think Jeff would care if I was in the room or not. But you already got his attention because you're cute."

But it's my *playing* he complimented, not my looks. I stir the rice around in my bowl with my fork and literally bite my tongue.

"Let's go by tonight. Say you forgot something in the studio."

"Leo, no. I've had a really long day, and I just want to eat dinner and go to bed. Stop, okay?"

"He's probably not there anyway," he says with a dismissive sigh. "Probably at some party you don't know about because you didn't stop into his studio for him to ask you to it."

"I'd still be here if he told me about it." I lean back into my chair.

"You could have come home to tell me we were going to some really exclusive Hollywood party and we could have gone together."

"You weren't supposed to be home. You were supposed to be working tonight. Besides, he was an asshole. He'll be an asshole to you, too."

"You don't know that. Maybe he'd like me. I'm likable." He gives me a wide, goofy grin, looking like he's twelve. With his blond curls and summer tan, he makes me think of a kid hanging out at the beach. It makes me miss the days we'd spent all day on the beach, playing in the surf and kissing on the blanket.

"You're so dopey," I chuckle with a shake of my head. "I'll see if I can give you a heads-up tomorrow and have you meet me or something. *No* promises." I take a bite of food and roll my eyes at him as he grins wider. "Since when are you such a huge fan of Jeff Kingston, anyway?"

"It's more Teddy Derricks. If Kingston is around, Derricks can't be far behind." He glances over at me after finishing his dinner. "You know who Teddy Derricks is, right?"

"Can you please stop treating me like I live under a rock? You *do* know what I do for a living, right?"

"Yes, and you'd probably get a lot more gigs if you played up those tits a little more. Man, if *I* had tits like that, you could be sure every guy in the studio saw them so *I* could get the job."

My head drops to the side and I stare at him. "*Nice*. Thanks."

He furrows his eyebrows and shakes his head. "What? That's a compliment."

"My tits getting me work is a compliment?" I do my best to keep my voice even and calm.

"Having them doesn't really hurt you."

"Hang on, you know how hard I have to fight to prove myself. Do you really think it's my tits getting me work?"

"Oh, babe, no, that's not what I meant. Sure, you can play." He's saying the words, but I don't hear the conviction behind them, accented by his shrug and nonchalant tilt of his head. "Besides, you don't get excited by your gigs. You just treat everything like a job."

"That's not true!" My mouth drops with an exasperated breath. "I don't drool and become some teeny-bopper fan that needs to squeal about it. If I'm going to *keep* my job, I need to act accordingly. Believe me, I am plenty excited to work with Curt. I have every album he ever wrote. I'm not going to blow this by being stupid and giddy. And besides having all of Expedition's albums, Derricks' guitar solo in '*Rushing Water*' was the first thing I taught myself on guitar. I'm as much a fan as you are. You used to know that about me."

"Oh, I do, babe." He reaches over to rest his hand on my knee. "It's just you don't seem to be all that excited by it anymore. All the people you meet, the places you get to play. I'd give my eyeteeth to play in some of the venues you've been to. I mean, sure, it's not like you're part of the band or anything."

Enough of the band to play the venues, I want to say. *Enough of the band to be asked to be part of it when they take it on the road sometimes, but I say no because* you *don't like it when I'm gone for long stretches.*

"You're closer to the life than I am right now even if you kind of sold out"

"I *what?*"

"... and, you know, he's not really my bag, so I'm not as impressed by him as you are," he finishes.

"Yeah, I can see how being successful could hurt your credibility." I stand up and put my bowl on the counter. "And I *haven't* sold out. I'm *paying* our bills. I'm going to bed."

"Are you mad at me or something?"

I lean over to give him a quick kiss and shake my head. "Just been insulted enough for one evening."

"What do you mean, insulted? Who insulted you?"

I'm too tired to explain it to him.

The phone ringing jars me awake. It takes me a second to reach over, but I lift the receiver, on the verge of speaking, when I hear him say, *'I told you not to call me here, Sandy.'* I open my eyes, cover the mouthpiece, and hold my breath. My heart beats faster as I listen, my brain unable to keep up with my thoughts. What's happening? Who's Sandy?

She responds in that annoying girly whine. "You were supposed to meet me. What happened?"

"I got her schedule messed up, babe. She's home," he whispers. "I couldn't get out. Wish I could have, though." His voice becomes silky. "I'd be having a lot more fun with you, foxy lady."

"Don't let me stop you," I say into the receiver before slamming it down and kicking the blankets off. By the time I get into the living room, adrenaline floods my brain. I'm shaking with anger. "Get out."

"Oh, now, baby...."

"Get the *hell* out." I point to the doorway.

He stands up and puts his palms out to me, patting the air between us. "I can explain, Cass."

"You can *leave*, is what you can do." I open the front door for him. Picking up one of his shoes, I toss it onto the grassy lawn. I pick up the next one and throw it at him. "Go!"

"Come on, now, Cass," he says, fumbling with catching the shoe, "let me explain."

"Out!" My heart pounds against my chest. My hands shake, gripping the open door.

Pointing down the hallway to our bedroom, he starts, "what about my stuff?"

"Oh, your *stuff*?" I pick up an ashtray and throw it out the door. "That's yours, right?" It lands on the sidewalk and shatters. "This is yours, too, right?"

I pick up a picture frame from one of the end tables and chuck it at him. "How about that? Yours, right?" I pick up a candle and toss it. There's a magazine that gets thrown next. "What about that?" I'm becoming one of those crazed women parodied on television, but I pick up another frame. This time, I aim for him. He fumbles again. It hits his chest and drops to the floor, breaking at his feet. "How about this?"

"You're acting nuts, Cass!" he tries, still trying to pat the air between us, his eyes wide. "Calm down!"

"I'm not even *halfway* to nuts, Leo!" I scream, hoping the neighbors turn their lights on so it can be even more embarrassing. "Get the *fuck* out of my house!"

"Babe..."

"My father put *my* name on the lease! I've paid the damn rent for the last six months."

"Come on, baby..." He steps over the broken frame and reaches his hand out, his head tilted to the side as though he's going to try and reason with me. As if there's some reasoning to him being a cheating bastard.

I step forward and pick up a dirty, empty ashtray, ready to take aim. "You haven't been getting as many hours, huh?" I hurl the ashtray at the curb. "Band practices have been taking up more time?" I cross the room to grab his transistor radio from the table and lodge it. It shatters on the sidewalk next to the ashtray. "How much do I want to bet that both of those things can be called *Sandy*?" I'm enraged even more and hurl the empty dinner bowl at his head.

By now, he's in front of the open door and ducks. As he stands erect, I shove his chest to force him to take a step back and slam the door, swiftly locking it. "I'll let you know when your shit's on the curb to pick up!" I scream.

As I'm turning off the lights, he begins knocking, trying to talk to me through the door. I go to the bedroom and take several deep breaths, which soon dissolve into sobs as my rage drains. Sitting on the side of the bed, I grab a pillow and bury my face to mute them. I don't want to give him the satisfaction of hearing me cry.

I don't fall back asleep, of course. All I had to do was look around the bedroom and see his things to work myself up into another fury. I stomp to the kitchen, grab a trash bag, and start tossing his things inside it, tears slipping down my cheek. When I fill a bag, I dump it out on the curb. Once his stuff is out of sight, I rearrange the living room, and follow that by doing the dinner dishes because, of course, Leo didn't. Then, I take a shower, hoping that might calm me, but instead I spiral, remembering when we first met, how he used to respect me, that he was impressed with my talent and drive.

I knew things weren't perfect between us. God knows there's no passion between us after three years, but I figured it was because we got comfortable and our schedules were getting in the way. We've just been passing each other in the hallway. We hadn't even slept in the same bed, much less had sex, in at least a month, but I thought it was a temporary thing. How could I have been so blind? So stupid?

After my shower, I try to eat something, but can't swallow anything and cry again, staring at one of his shoes sticking out from under the couch. He's not worth this, damn it! So, I decide to go into the studio to work on that riff to keep my mind busy.

"Good party?" Jeff asks, coming in the opposite direction at the studio. He's still wearing the same Hawaiian shirt decorated with surfers and palm trees he had on yesterday. His hair looks pretty run-through, too, with over-grown curls pulled into messy waves. He's playful, and I suppose he meant to be funny, but nothing is funny. I just curl a corner of my mouth up, drop my chin, and keep walking. As I pass, he places a hand on my elbow, and we turn to face each other. "You okay?" His eyebrows furrow and his voice lowers.

"Peachy." The tears return to my voice, and I shake my head, pulling my arm back. "Thanks." I swallow and offer a quick nod before I start toward my studio without even glancing back. Once I get to the door, I know he's still standing there because I haven't heard the scuff of his boots on the floor. I slip inside and close the door behind me, praying I'll be left alone for a few more hours so I can get my head together.

Half an hour later, Jeff comes in with a brown paper bag and paper cup. I glance at him, but all he does is nod as he puts the bag and cup on the folding chair next to me without a word. The cup is filled with black, strong coffee. Inside the bag are some little creamers, sugar packets, a stirrer, a chocolate glazed doughnut, and a neatly rolled joint.

I glance over at him by the studio door, a hint of a smile crossing my lips. He nods again, returning my grin, and closes the door behind him.

So rock-n-roll.

Flipping the Record

Chapter 2

Later in the evening, I'm a little more in control. I managed to finally get the riff I wanted and kept playing it, so it's committed to muscle memory now. I *can* do it, and Curt was floored once I got it out. I feel like it's helping me work through some of the emotions, anyway.

On my way out, I slip into the booth at Studio C to see who's still hanging around. Jeff is in the studio behind his kit. Teddy Derricks stands in front of him on his guitar, and they are honed in on each other, playing something fantastic. It's fast and light, and Derricks is shaking his head with the beat as Jeff nods his chin along, his entire torso grooving with it. Gary Baker, their bassist, has his head dropped back, and his head sways as he plays within the groove. Opposite him, Darryl Thompson, their other guitarist, bites his bottom lip and shakes his head along, his notes dancing over top of it. They're all wearing headphones to hear each other over the instruments. A few more bars and everyone starts singing 'ooohs' into their mics as Jeff begins belting out a lyric, eyes closed tight. The mix in the booth is *amazing*. It's crisp and light as they finish up. Jeff finishes with a soft drum flourish, and light hit on his crash and opens his eyes to smiling faces all around the room.

"Please tell me we got that," Derricks says, turning to face the booth.

"I'm smelling another gold record, boys," Stan says, clicking the button to be heard over the studio speakers inside. "I got it all."

"Can we put this one to bed yet?" Thompson whines as he bends his fingers. I know how he feels.

"You're Curt's girl," Derricks says, pointing to the booth, spotting me. I nod and blood rushes to my cheeks. "Outta sight," he says with a grin. "What'd *you* think?"

"From the little bit I heard, it was damn funky." I grin.

"Ha!" Derricks triumphs. "Take *that*, Michael Grayson! Who's laid back *now*?"

"Ignore him," Jeff says with a wave toward me and a grin. "He's been bitching about that article Grayson wrote in *Rolling Stone* all week." He takes the headphones off, drapes them over the mic stand in front of him, and shakes his head, reaching up to fluff his curls so he doesn't have headphone hair. "Can we get a dinner break now?" It's not like he has to ask anyone's permission, is it?

Stan waves for me to go inside, and I do, feeling awkward about it. I'm not the one that goes to other studios. I was just being nosy and wanted to see how they worked. No one gives a crap if I show up or not, but when I step inside, Derricks puts his guitar in his stand and comes over to shake my hand, introducing himself—as if any of these guys need an introduction. I try to smile and be polite and not make a complete fool of myself as the rest of them come over, too.

Jeff comes to stand beside me and winks with a little, playful grin crossing his lips. "You hungry?" he asks, nudging me with his elbow. I am pretty sure he hasn't left the building since yesterday, still in the same Hawaiian shirt, a lot more wrinkled now. He's grown well beyond a five o'clock shadow, and it's full scruffy stubble, but his blue eyes are playful and teasing, and little crinkles appear around them with his smile.

I shrug and rock my head from side to side a little. "I could eat." What else am I going to do? Go home to the empty house to cry again? The more distractions, the better right now.

"Cool." With another nudge, he turns me around toward the studio door and guides me out with his hands on my shoulders. "We'll be back!" he calls over his shoulder as we leave.

In the hallway, he pats his pockets and pulls out his wallet and keys. "Just makin' sure. Come on," he says with a decisive nod, taking hold of my hand and leading me out the back way to his cute baby blue Porsche parked in the lot. It's a convertible, but the top is up. He actually opens the door, waits for me to get in before closing it, and heads around to the driver's side. When was the last time *that* happened? I think it may have been my date at the high school prom. The car smells like leather from the bucket seats and there isn't a speck of dust on the dash or dirt on the floor mats. It distracts me momentarily from the panic bubbling up from my stomach about going to dinner with *Jeff Kingston*. How the hell am I supposed to play it cool?

Then, he gets in and revs the motor to life. The 8-track blasts initially, but he reaches over to turn the dial way down before sticking the gear in reverse. We fly back before he slides it into first, and tears out of the parking lot. Jeff Kingston distracts me from being with *Jeff*

Kingston.

I look over at him with an arched eyebrow. "In a rush?"

He releases a comfortable laugh and confidently maneuvers his way around the slower cars. Moments later, we're free of traffic and on the open highway.

"Thank you, by the way, for the coffee and, uh, *doughnut.*"

He glances at me with another easy smile. "You looked like you might have needed someone to be nice to you."

I take a deep breath and look out my window, willing the tears to go back. "Yeah," I nod, "you could say that."

"Anything I could help with?"

I press my lips together and try to smile at him. "Not really. I threw my boyfriend out last night."

"Oh…" He furrows his eyebrows at me. "What'd he do?"

"I didn't really let him stick around for the details after overhearing his conversation with some girl who called the house after he told her not to." I look over at him as he keeps his eyes on the road. "You look like someone who might understand how he feels right about now."

He nods and grins into the streetlights that pass.

"Yeah, don't take this the wrong way," I say, squinting and crinkling my nose, "but I'm not surprised."

"Funny that," he says with a chuckle and a little twang lingering. "Pretty sure all of L.A. knows I'm no angel by now, don't they?"

"Yeah, well, I didn't know *he* wasn't. And now I'm wondering how long he's been fucking around. We were together three years!" He glances over at me with widened eyes. "I know. I'm an idiot."

"Guys are assholes," he says with a shrug. "I don't know what to say. I gave up trying to make excuses. We're all assholes."

"Especially when you drink tequila?"

He laughs and nods broadly. "*Especially* when we drink tequila!"

"Stick to beer or something tonight, then, okay? I've had my fill of assholes for the week."

So much for sticking with beer. We *both* do shots of tequila and it evaporates any possible nerves I may have had about having dinner with him, and then some. We end up making out in the car in the parking lot outside the restaurant. He's very good at this kissing thing, soft and tender, thorough and attentive. His hand caresses my jaw as it slips into my hair, and I rest my hand on his chest, my palm between his unbuttoned shirt. He leans in a bit more. I drop back against the car door as the kisses grow more intense.

My God, when was the last time someone was this interested in kissing me? When was the last time *I* was interested in kissing someone? His stubble scratches my chin and lips, and I pull back a bit to take a breather, twirling one of his curls around my fingers with a huge grin on my lips. "Just… give me a second. You're scratchy." I touch my fingertips to my chin.

He chuckles and comes back in with a delicate kiss, running a finger along my cheek, brushing my hair over my shoulder. His eyes are so intense, even in the dim light from the parking lot. His grin is self-assured and playful. Even his lips are good. Do people even notice *lips*? But his lower lip is fuller and so elegantly kissable. I lean forward and bring him back to do it all over again, chin scratch be damned.

"Do you want to go somewhere and continue this?" he asks after another round. This time, his mouth found places on my neck to kiss, along my collarbone when he brushed my shirt aside as his other hand discovered my breast. I let him continue as my brain whirls. I haven't been with anyone other than Leo in three years. Do I want to be with someone so soon? Am I ready to get naked in front of a complete stranger, even if he looks this good, and can kiss this well? Someone I'm going to be seeing a whole lot more of if we're in the same studio?

And what if I say no? What happens when we see each other in the hallway?

What happens if I say yes? Am I ready for this kind of fling? Am I willing to be the girl for 'right now?'

Then he kisses me again, and my entire body answers for me.

Alright, it's the tequila talking. But if he's half as good as how he kisses, I'll let tequila talk more for me.

Back at his place, he offers me another drink and lights up a joint—and it's the good stuff. We start making out again on the couch before he takes my hand to lead me down a short hallway to the bedroom. My head spins with the alcohol and weed, and every touch sends shivers down my spine. We undress and meet on the mattress beneath soft, white sheets. He's more slender than Leo, physique-wise, and it takes some getting used to, especially his chest as I run my hands over it, and his arms, along his torso. Not an ounce of fat on him, most of him is muscular, well more muscular than I'm used to, anyway.

His hands rest on my breasts before his mouth lays over them. With his mouth busy on top, his hands get busy below and come up between my legs to begin caressing me. I moan, pressing my head back into the pillow with how amazing I feel right now. He doesn't rush, takes his time, but it doesn't take me long. I call out as the pleasure spreads through me, coursing through my veins like ice water on a hot day.

Before I can relax with it, he climbs between my legs and guides himself inside. I gasp again, still turned on from the orgasm. I take hold of his hips and lift mine to greet his strong thrust, initially slow and deliberate, but soon hard and fast as he moans above me, biting that lower lip that is so damn kissable. Sweat forms around his forehead and he cries out quick and short with his own release, dropping his body down against me, head burying into my neck.

I feel his heavy breath over my skin before he starts kissing me again, shifting to lay beside me. I turn so we're facing one another and we keep kissing and touching bare, sweaty skin until we come together again, a little more prepared for how each of us moves, and how to guide each other to pleasure. When he comes and drops beside me, I close my eyes and let him lay behind me with a deep, contented breath. His arm drapes over my waist and we drift into an exhausted sleep.

I open my eyes when I feel someone on the mattress and pull back with a stretch and yawn. It's still dark outside. I don't think we were asleep very long, but I'm not the one who has studio time booked and needs to get back. He's put a mug on the nightstand for me and smiles, brushing my hair off my face before coming in with a quick kiss. "I'm gonna jump in the shower while I'm here for more than five minutes." He rests his hand on the mattress behind me and comes in for another kiss. "You're welcome to join me if you're so inclined, or you can stay here." He tilts his head toward the nightstand. "I only have tea right now, and the milk's gone sour. Sorry."

"What time is it?" I lean up to grab the mug, resting back against the headboard. Since when don't I care about being naked in front of people? The sheet drapes around my waist and I can see his gaze glance at my bare breasts while I sip the tea.

"About 2:30. I gotta get back, unfortunately."

"No, I figured."

"All right," he says, hesitating for a bit before he pulls away from me and heads to the bathroom. I watch his muscular, bare butt and skinny hips.

Am I that person that joins him in the shower? I hear the water turn on and take another sip of the tea, looking to the bathroom with the door left wide open. *Tonight*, I'm going to be that person. What the hell? With another sip, I slip from the mattress and peer around the shower curtain. "Room for one more in here?"

He breaks into a smile. "I think I can accommodate that." He reaches his hand out to help me over the lip of the tub before pulling me against his wet skin and begins kissing me. I end up on my knees giving him one hell of a blow job, which is so out of character for me, but this whole night is out of character for me.

Once he's come, he draws me against him, my back against his belly, and he runs the soapy wash rag over my body, lingering around my breasts and groin, more than anywhere else. With a step back, he places long, sensual kisses between my shoulders and along my neck. I close my eyes to his touches, never knowing my back could be this sensual. His fingers slide between my legs. I lift my chin with his touch, inhaling the hot, steamy air, letting my body fall into the passion. Once I moan with my pleasure, he steps up close behind me again and wraps his arms around my waist as I pulse with it. He chuckles into my neck. "I got you," he whispers.

I can only nod against him and try to breathe.

He turns the water off and wraps me in a towel with soft kisses before he wraps a towel around his waist and leads me back to bed where we have sex, *again,* on the wet towels. There's no lingering afterward, this time. He slips on his jeans and goes over to a chest of drawers to pull a tee shirt over his head.

I finish drying off and get dressed. We both keep glancing back at each other with silly, little grins. He goes back into the bathroom. I finish the cold tea sitting on the side of the bed and wonder whether I should attempt to straighten the sheets, but he returns before I can. He takes my empty mug and I follow him out of the bedroom. He's cleaned up our drinks from before and now puts my mug in the dishwasher—either he's very tidy or hiding evidence. I am certain it's the latter. When he comes from the kitchen, he's smiling and reaches his hand out for mine, grabs the keys from the little table by the front door, and we're back out into the early morning air.

Turning the radio up, we drive back to the studio without speaking. I keep waiting for this to feel weird and awkward, but he is so relaxed and casual that he puts me at ease about all this. Is it ironic? Hypocritical? I broke up with my boyfriend because he was cheating on me, and the following night, here I am in someone else's bed as the other woman. My entire body is singing, though. I shudder thinking of his touch and take a sharp, quiet breath and grin, looking out the window with it.

"Cold?" he asks, reaching over to turn the heat up a bit.

"A little." I mean, I am only in a shirt and jeans. It's not like I was planning on being out.

He reaches over and takes my hand, resting it on his thigh as he drives. When he needs to change gears, he releases it, places it on his thigh, and leaves it there. I feel his muscle and warmth through the denim as he shifts and comes back to wrap his fingers through mine. It's as though we've been doing this for years. Inside, my body is tight and amped up, energized. Even I'm dismayed at what's transpired. Outwardly, however, I am the picture of casual ease. Once we reach the studio, he walks around and opens my door for me, helps me up, and pulls me against him for another kiss, long and deep.

"Thanks for coming out. I had a good time," he says with an easy smile.

"Yeah, me too," I reply as if I do this kind of thing all the time. I lean back against the car to find the keys for mine and he waits and walks me to it, kissing me again.

"I'll see you at work in a few hours, eh?" he says with a wink.

"It's a good chance, yeah."

"All right. Get home safe." He closes the car door behind me once I'm in. I start my engine and watch him head inside through the rearview mirror, then shift my eyes to blink at myself.

What the hell just happened?

When I pull into my driveway, Leo is sitting on the front stoop with a bouquet of flowers between his feet. As my headlights hit him, he stands, and I release a tired exhale. He crosses the little yard between us; the flowers dangling from his hand. "Where the hell have you been?"

"That's none of your business." I saunter past him.

"It's 4:30 in the morning! You weren't at the studio. I went by after my shift. You weren't *there*."

I turn, my house key poised for the lock, and shake my head. "Well, where I go, who I see, and what I do is no longer your concern.

Did you get your things in time, or did the trashmen take it away?"

"I got them. Your care putting them in garbage bags was breathtaking."

"Imagine that." I unlock the door. "You have five minutes before I call the cops on you. Good night."

"Oh, come on, Cassandra!"

I turn to him. "Or you can keep yelling and the neighbors can call them for me."

"I came over here to talk to you… to explain." He steps up on one of the steps and I put my hand out. "I've been sitting here for hours waiting for you. No one knew where you went off to. I was concerned."

"Be real. You went to the studio so you could pretend to bump into Expedition. I was fucking Jeff Kingston after we had dinner." His entire body jerks in either shock or disbelief, and he blinks at me as if he's trying to catch up to the words. "Now, I'm going to sleep so I can go to work in a few hours. Go away. Don't come back. Tell Sandy how concerned you were for me."

"She didn't mean anything to me, babe."

"Then, wow, you really screwed up." I open the door and step inside. "And by the way, just so you have all the information? I never realized sex could be *that* satisfying." I offer an angelic grin as his mouth drops open. I don't know that he believes me, but it seems to have at least gotten his attention. "Good night." I close and lock the door.

"Can you at least hand me my car keys?" he sighs through the closed door.

"They're in one of the bags," I reply, "minus the house key. You've been sitting here all night for nothing."

I turn off the porch and living room lights and sit on the couch, listening to him curse for a few minutes. He knocks until a neighbor calls out their window to tell him to shut up or they're calling the police.

As I sit in the dark, I drop my head back on the couch. What world did I enter tonight? Who's this chick who wanders off with rock stars to have dinner and sex? Climbs into the shower with a man and leaves pre-dawn as if all of that were a common occurrence? I'm not even remotely embarrassed by it. I don't even remotely regret it. Hell, I had *fun*! Jeff was pleasant, attentive, and interesting to talk to. He could kiss like nobody has the right to know how. He knew his way around my body, which made me feel amazing pleasure. He *smiled*.

He opened the car door for me? If it weren't so random, and I didn't know any better, it was almost *respectful…* aside from it being a one-night stand and knowing that he's cheating on his girlfriend.

Up until yesterday, I thought I would end up marrying Leo eventually. Today, I'm taking pleasure in letting him know this random guy I met is a better lover. Maybe it's still the tequila speaking, although I am not even tipsy. It could be adrenaline. I'm buzzing. My body hasn't felt that kind of pleasure or attention in *years*.

Tonight may be some kind of declaration. I'm taking my body and my life back. I can sleep with whoever I want to sleep with—and did! The fact that it was Jeff Kingston from Expedition was a lot of pink, fluffy, sugary sweet icing. And man, do I love icing.

At the studio the next morning, a lanky brunette is standing with her arms folded at the end of the hallway. Her mouth is tight and her head cocked to the side as she blinks at Jeff. He's standing with his back against the wall and his hands stuck in his back pockets with one shoulder lifted, his mouth twisted. It doesn't look like it's a *good* conversation. She flips long, brown hair over her shoulder and straightens her top over her form-fitted white pants. Whatever she says, he nods. A moment later, she stomps down the hallway in her wedge heels, breezing by me without so much as a glance. I'm used to that. I'm not one of those model types. I am zero threat to any of the beauty queens. I tend to dress like one of the boys since I'm hanging with them all day, plus at any moment, I could be asked to work with cables or fiddle with amps. It helps keep everyone focused on the music and not whether the *girl* can play rock'n'roll.

Jeff stays against the wall and curls a corner of his lip in a weak smile when he sees me. "How was your night?" He glances past me toward the model.

"Fine. I take it that's the girlfriend?" I also glance back.

He lifts his chin. "Yeah."

"Did you screw up?"

He nods, but grins. "I was so focused on putting the dishes in the dishwasher, I forgot to go back and straighten the bed."

I wince and pucker my lips. "Ooops."

He shrugs again. "I'm an asshole."

"She's…?"

"Pissed. She'll get over it."

"You sound pretty confident about that," I snicker.

"Oh, darlin', we're not in this for love," he tells me, shaking his curls. "It's perception at this point. She makes me look good. I'm not supposed to make her look bad. It's not about love at this stage of the game."

I take a step back and furrow my eyebrows at him. "That's…" I pause and watch him look back down the empty hallway after her, realizing what he just told me is bullshit. "A shame." The words seem to catch him off guard. He rubs his fingers over his mouth, blinking at me as if he's not quite sure how to respond. I don't wait for one. I smile and brush my hand over his shoulder before I enter the studio. "I'll see you around."

"We need to hijack a guitarist." Teddy bursts into our studio a few hours later, still holding onto the knob. With his other hand, he points and curls his finger at me. "You. Come. Now."

As I blink in shock at his beckoning, Curt bursts into a laugh. "Do I get her back?"

Teddy furrows his eyebrows together and nods emphatically. "Oh, yeah, tomorrow? That work for you?"

I glance between them both. "Excuse me? Do I…?"

"Tomorrow's cool," Curt agrees, talking over me. He looks over and motions with his head toward the door with a wink. "You don't mind, do you?"

"Oh, I get a *say*?" I scoff with a short breath.

"No," Teddy says, shaking his long brown hair and stepping backward. "Bring your guitar." He taps his foot, glancing behind him and then at me as I finish and pack up.

I shake my head in dismay at Curt, my mouth opening and closing.

"We'll pay you double what he's paying you for the day," Teddy adds, and I turn my head to look at him. "Come on! Come on!" He steps back inside and takes hold of my guitar case, but I dig my heels in, stop, and don't let go.

"Don't touch my guitar," I warn him. He releases the handle and looks taken aback a moment before he nods in appreciation, lifting his hands and making Curt bust into a laugh. The other guys laugh, too, just a little lighter. It's obvious Curt and Teddy are better friends. Curt can get away with that kind of thing.

"I apologize," he says, as if he understands how I am about my guitar. "I meant no disrespect. We're just in the middle of something...."

"All right. I'm coming." I collect the rest of my things. "I feel like I just got swapped, like a baseball card or something."

"Just for today," Curt promises with a lift of his chin and a warm smile. "You're still on my team."

I follow Teddy back to their studio. It's only down the hall but feels like a marathon trying to keep up, both with his long strides and the thoughts whirring in my head. What does Expedition want *me* to do? Why did Teddy choose me when there were two other guys in Curt's studio he could pick? Am I going to be able to do what they want? Keep up? My palms are already sweating.

When we barge into the studio, everyone is standing around Jeff's kit. Jeff taps out a light beat on the high hat, and the other guys nod along. Darryl strums a choppy chord, with Gary playing steady. They look over at us coming in, and Jeff breaks into a smile, still keeping the beat. He nods a greeting and closes his eyes briefly with it. Darryl turns to me and breaks into a grin. "Set up," he says as his long blond strands fall in front of his shoulder, so he has to shake it to get it out of his way.

Teddy picks up his guitar as I plug into the amp and play a few chords to make sure I'm in tune with them. As soon as I hear the chords come to life, I settle a little. Chords. I can do chords and progressions. I know theory. I can play guitar.

"We need you to do this," Darryl says, turning to me, playing a funky, choppy progression. I watch his hands a moment, studying the chords as I nod and pick it up, playing along with him.

"Outta sight," Teddy says and starts strumming a completely different progression within the same rhythm, complimenting mine. I don't know how long we groove, but each of us takes the lead at some point and when we finish, I stand back, flushed with adrenaline, grinning like I've discovered I'm a woodland faerie with magical powers. *I just rocked out with Expedition.* I want to stomp my feet and do a little dance, but stand still and wait for my next cue.

They're pretty pumped, too. Teddy and Darryl high-five each other, and they both turn to high-five me at the same time while everyone laughs. Teddy lets out another holler and walks in a small circle with his hands on his hips, grinning broadly. "See? Now that's what I'm talkin' about! That's what I was goin' for... that richness, that extra layer, man!" He punches the air and looks around at the rest of us. "Yeah!"

Darryl comes to stand across from me and extends his hand. I slip mine into it with a laugh as he slightly bows. "I heard you had chops. Nice job. Where'd you learn to play?"

"Older brother's bedroom. He had good albums." I nod my head toward the door. "And hours, and hours, and hours, and hours, and *hours* of studio work," I laugh. He takes hold of my wrist, flips my hand to look at my palm, and then feels the tips of my fingers. "Yeah," I say, "sandpaper. Ain't nothing girly or dainty about 'em. My poor mother is horrified."

"But we're impressed," Darryl says, releasing my hand. "You got talent."

"That means a lot coming from you," I say with a smile, and now I feel like the goofy fan, feeling my ears burn in a blush. "Thank you."

"Don't thank me. You put in the work."

"All right, are we ready to go again?" Teddy asks, coming back from the sound booth wiping his nose. I'm pretty sure I know what he was doing in there. He has more detail about what he wants me to do, and I nod along, moving my hands along the neck of my guitar with his instructions.

They stop and start, and we pick it up, and stop and start again, and stop. Sometimes they laugh when they screw up, others, there's a string of curses and growling, stomping feet, and tossing picks across the room. It's not very different from Curt's sessions, but these guys seem closer. These guys are a band, and Curt is very much a solo artist using musicians he's familiar and comfortable with. The teasing is more personal; back-talking and making faces behind one another's backs are more sibling-like. I'm dragged right into the teasing and mocking and feel like a little sister. I can also dish it out, and when I do, I crack them up. It earns more respect.

I am shocked to find out we've been at it for six hours, and it's almost midnight. The entire day is gone. I take a long, deep breath and release a slow, quiet exhale.

"Hey," Jeff says, coming up behind me, nudging his shoulder into mine.

"Hey, yourself," I say with a smile.

"You okay?"

"Sure." I shrug, slipping my guitar strap over my head. "Why not?"

He lifts a shoulder and glances at Teddy and Darryl. "I don't know."

I get the sense he's feeling a little left out with all the guitar work going on, and I didn't have the chance to talk much with him. I'm still on an adrenaline rush and brush my hand over his forearm, feeling pretty brazen doing so. I mean, is that considered professional?

He glances back at me and smiles. "Know what? Never mind. You were awesome today. Thanks for helping out."

"It was pretty amazing to be part of this. Trying to keep up!" I widen my eyes. "Ever have one of those days where you think you still have so much to learn?" I laugh.

He grins before he puckers his lips and shakes his curls back. "Don't sell yourself short, Cass. You managed just fine." I can't help but brighten my smile. "You got plans? Wanna grab dinner with us?"

"Is that...? I mean, I don't want to crash..." I bumble, but my stomach is growling.

He smiles and motions for me to follow with another shake of his head, reaching out to grab hold of my fingers. Maybe it's still the adrenaline, but I like when he does that. "Hey, wait up," he calls after everyone as they head out, tugging me along behind him.

After a long dinner, Jeff drives me back to my place. It was only polite that I invited him in, right? I roll over and stretch out in my bed as my elbow nudges him sleeping beside me. Holy crap! Jeff is still sleeping beside me, bare-chested, scruffy, and beautiful. We fell asleep with the bedside lamp on, and I'm confused about what time it is until I lift onto my elbows to squint at the clock on my nightstand: 4:16 am. It's only been three hours—and a good one and a half of that was screwing around with Jeff.

I don't know what this is. I don't really care. I'm usually not this nonchalant about sex. Maybe I'm trying to prove something to myself—that I can be fine without Leo? That sex can be fun? Maybe because, damn, he's good at pleasing me and making me crave more because he enjoys himself and is so confident in what he's doing. There is no meaning to this aside from some fun and feeling a whole lot of pleasure having it.

"What's up?" he mumbles, squinting in the light.

"You need to go?"

"Not really," he breathes, turning onto his side to face me, still squinting. "You kickin' me out?"

"Nope." I reach over to turn out the light. "Conserving energy. Don't need the light on all night."

"I like feeling around in the dark," he murmurs as I lay back down beside him, my back against his furry chest. His hand rides slowly over my belly to my breast, and he palms it softly.

"Again?" I sigh with his touch, stretching out along his torso with my eyes closed.

"Too much?" he asks, his mouth against my neck.

"Just checking to see if you're going to be a tease or not."

He shifts. I roll onto my back as he brings his mouth against mine. "How about a bit of both?"

When he reaches between my legs, I could melt into the mattress and moan softly against his mouth as he kisses me. Grabbing onto his wrist, I guide him a little more to what I like. He murmurs, "like this?" into my ear, soft and low. I moan a response as my pleasure builds even more. Just as I'm on the verge of orgasm, he guides himself into me. Initially, I'm crestfallen because I was so close to release, but if he keeps this up, I might just...? Is that *possible* while he's on top of me like this...?

"Don't stop," I inhale quickly, throwing my head back into the pillow and shifting beneath him. "Just... don't...." I grab onto his waist, closing my eyes as he fills me over and over, deep and steady.

It might be the first and only time I've ever achieved an orgasm while someone was screwing me. I cry out, my eyes squeezing tight as it happens, and I let my body fall into it. He concentrates on his fulfillment. I open my eyes with a shaky breath to watch him sink his teeth into his bottom lip and lift his chin with his release. Moments later, he withdraws and drops beside me with an exhausted, satisfied groan, rolling onto his back and laughing. His hand drops over his head as he brushes sweaty curls back and catches his breath. "I love when that happens," he says to the ceiling before turning his head to grin at me.

"I didn't know that was possible." I exhale deeply, blowing my cheeks out. My entire body buzzes. I want to kick my feet and shake my hands and run around the block.

He laughs harder, and it seems to brighten the room. Dropping the back of his hand onto my belly, he turns onto his side. "Well, then, you're welcome."

"I thought that only happened in pornos."

"I don't think it's quite realistic in pornos."

"That's why I didn't think that was *possible*." I turn my head to blink at him in the shadows and take a deep breath. "My God."

He laughs again.

I draw in to kiss him, long and deep, as if I'm craving it. I pull him closer, just to feel his body against mine, to know it was a real thing, to know he was real and solid. "I'm putting a gold star on this day."

"Does this count as one day?" he teases, his mouth against mine again. "Are you counting calendar days, or…?"

"Shut up, and take the damn star," I tell him before accepting another sensuous kiss.

I wake to knocking and lift onto my forearms, squinting over in the direction of the front door. Jeff lifts on his elbows, his eyebrows furrowing together in confusion. "What time's it?" he asks, and *wow*, he has quite a drawl when he's not paying attention to squashing it.

I glance at the clock and sigh. "10:37," I grumble. "Fuck. I need to get into the studio."

There's knocking on the door again.

"Maybe answer that first," he says and falls back into the mattress with a yawn, running his hand over his bare chest. My eyes follow the movement, and I can't help but grin. "Yeah, after you stop that knocking." He nudges me with his knee before giving me a wink.

"I won't have time," I tell him, slipping out of bed and into a pair of shorts and a tee shirt. I disappear down the hallway, running my fingers through my hair. I'm not expecting anyone and hope it's not the building maintenance as I peer through the peephole.

Leo's back on the porch. He lifts his fist to knock again as I open the door a few inches and stick my foot behind the door to keep him from entering. "For the love of all things holy, now what?" My voice sounds groggy and hoarse.

"I went by the studio to talk to you, and you weren't there again," Leo says, attempting to put his hand on the door to push it open, but I manage to hold it firmly. "I got concerned. You always go to work when you're scheduled. Are you alright? Is everything okay?"

"Fine," I sigh. "Do you need something?"

As Leo starts answering, Jeff comes down the hallway in his jeans with the top button undone, scratching the back of his head with his hand. After a loud yawn, he asks, "Hey, babe, where do you keep your towels?"

Okay. I'm petty. I move my foot. The door seems to yawn itself, swinging wide to reveal Jeff. It's pretty damn obvious what he's doing here. Obvious enough even for Leo to figure out. His mouth drops, torn between wanting to freak out because Jeff Kingston is standing shirtless with bedhead *in my living room* or because *Jeff Kingston* is standing shirtless with bedhead in my living room.

"Babe?" Leo asks, peeling his gaze from Jeff to look at me.

I lift a shoulder.

"Oh, sorry," Jeff says, oblivious to what is happening. He smiles at Leo with a quick wave and disappears back down the hallway.

"Jeff fucking Kingston?" His gaze lingers over my shoulder, blinking in disbelief.

"No. *Fucking* Jeff Kingston." I move to close the door.

He points into the house, at this moment realizing I wasn't making up stories just to make him jealous. "Wait, are you for real?"

"You really think I'm going back to this?" I ask him, motioning between us. "After that?" I point down the hallway. I laugh, this time just closing the door as he opens his mouth.

Jeff sits on the edge of the bed with a broad, wicked grin. "So? How's that?" he giggles, that flat 'a' lingering on his tongue. He leans his hands back on the mattress.

"Oh my God!" I cackle, crossing the room to straddle his lap and kiss him. "You did that on purpose?"

"Hey," he sits up a bit to wrap his arms around my waist, "every now and then, it pays to be Jeff *fucking* Kingston, doesn't it? That was him, right? The ex? I didn't just...."

I kiss him. I kiss him between loud laughs and sheer gratitude for making his presence known. I also thank him in other ways and am very late for work.

Later, after my shower, standing next to my bed, I pull a tee shirt over my head and sit to grab my socks off the mattress. Jeff folds his hands behind his head and knits his eyebrows together, watching. "So...." He draws out the word before taking a breath and licking his lips.

"So... what?" I glance over my shoulder at him. It's really not fair. If something that delicious is in my bed, I should be able to enjoy it.

"I don't know how to put this, but," he says with a hint of hesitation, "do you dress like a girl sometimes?"

"What's that supposed to mean?"

He laughs. "I told you. I didn't know how else to say it."

"Yes, I dress like a girl sometimes. Not at the studio."

"Why not?"

I put my hands on my breasts. "Because having these, and looking like I have them, usually equates to boys like you asking me to make them a sandwich and answer the phone. So, I draw as little attention to them as I can so that maybe, just maybe, someone might take me seriously when I pick up my guitar. Boys seem to think that unless there's something hanging between your legs, you can't possibly rock."

He nods, puckering his lips in consideration, his hand coming out from under his head to rub the hair on his chest. "So, if I were to, say, ask you to go with me to a party?"

"Right," I scoff, going back to getting dressed. "You do that; I'd actually look like a girl."

"Well, this is my ass-backward way of asking." I turn to find his eyebrow arched and a grin on his face. "There's a thing down at the Roxy."

I laugh, shaking my head. "Um, you have a model girlfriend. About this tall?" I lift my hand over my head. "And this thin?" I lift my pinkie finger. "Remember her? She's that chick from the hallway a few days ago."

"Yeah. We were breaking up." He curls his upper lip and tilts his head against the pillow.

I stop and turn to face him. "What?"

"Yeah." He nods, a faint, sad smile on his face. "We broke up." He shrugs, pressing his lips together. "She's heading out of town, and I've been asked to collect my things."

"Oh, Jeff," I sigh, "I'm so sorry. I wouldn't have teased you like that had I known."

He shrugs again and takes a deep breath. "I wasn't surprised." That smile still not quite reaching his eyes, regardless of how laid back he's trying to be. "So, what do you say? Want to go to this thing with me at the Roxy Friday night?"

"Ah, sure. How girly should I dress?"

He grins. This time it reaches eyes. "Knock my socks off."

Chapter 3

"What the hell am I supposed to wear?" I whine Friday afternoon, flopping across my bed. Curt's going to the party, too, so we didn't have any sessions scheduled. I spent the morning staring into my useless closet and called my best friend Hannah to rescue me. "I've never been to a party at the freaking Roxy! I'm not cool enough to be allowed inside the place. Now, I'm supposed to show up next to Jeff freakin' Rock Star, who's used to having some model on his arm?"

"First of all, breathe." Hannah laughs with a bright smile. "That's why I'm here. I know you have something, and if not, I brought some of my stuff. We'll figure it out."

"Did you hear the part about a model?"

"Yeah, and you've slept with him how many times? If he wasn't attracted to you, he wouldn't keep coming back now, would he?"

I sit up, resting my palms on the mattress behind me. "I'm about the only girl in the building. It could be plain old accessibility or laziness."

"He's Jeff Kingston. All he has to do is blink at a pretty girl on the sidewalk. You never try to be girly to know how pretty you can be with a little effort. You're always too busy trying to blend with the boys."

"It's worked for me." I smirk. "I'm sleeping with Jeff Kingston."

She wags a finger at me. "You got a point." She nods, crinkling her nose. "Show me what you have."

I open my closet door, push half the clothes on the rack aside, and step back. "It's not much."

"You don't need a lot, just one." She steps up beside me, pulling some hangers over one by one until she reaches a red satin dress. "What about this one?"

"Oh God," I say, widening my eyes. "I haven't worn that in ages."

"Try it on." She pulls the dress from the hanger and shoves it into my hands.

I sigh without any enthusiasm and give her a doubtful look. Tugging my tee-shirt over my head, I slip the dress on. It's backless and ties behind my neck, so I just reach back and hold it.

"Okay, no." Hannah shakes her head. "When I say try it on, I mean wear the damn thing. Take your jeans off so you're not all bulky around the middle. Tie the strap. Take off your bra. Let's see how it *fits*." I sigh again but do as she says. "Bingo!" She reaches over to adjust the front, exposing a lot more of my chest than I think is necessary.

I readjust her adjustment, but it doesn't matter. My boobs are going to be on display regardless of what I tug or pull. "It feels tight."

"It's supposed to." She steps back, nodding with a wide smile. "My God, Cass, you have an amazing figure, and this shows it off perfectly."

"I feel naked."

"I think we figured out why he keeps coming back." She folds her arms over her stomach and tilts her head. "I think I'm actually jealous." She has no reason to be. With her natural blonde hair and bright, California sunny-blue eyes, she's the one the boys usually hit on when we go out. She twists her lip and squints at me. "You need a belt." She turns back to the closet and finds nothing suitable, apparently, but goes to her bag of goodies. When she returns, she's got a pair of gold sandals and a thin gold belt. Dropping the shoes in front of me, she wraps the belt around my waist. "Try these on." She nudges the heels toward me. They're a good four-inch heel with a little ankle strap that matches the belt. I give her a doubtful look but slip them on because I know I can't wear my flip-flops and don't have anything suitable for a disco. "Perfect. Go look." She points to the full-length mirror on the back of my bedroom door.

I take a reluctant breath, go to stand in front of it, and stop short. I mean, I'm no model, but there's a *girl* in the mirror, all right. There are soft curves, a lot of boobs, and long legs showing through slits that go up my thigh through the folds of the skirt. "I don't think it looked like this last time I wore this."

"When was that?"

"Three years ago, maybe?"

"Well, I don't know why it didn't. You look foxy now. How are you going to do your hair?"

I give her a helpless look. "I was thinking of just pulling the one side back?" I lift my hair as an example, and she nods.

"And make-up?"

"That's why you're here. I don't do the night on the town stuff. You have to show me how."

She beams and presses her palms together. "Oh goody! I was

hoping you'd say that!"

By the time she's finished, I've got different shades of pink eyeshadow on my lids and a shiny pink gloss on my lips. She's done nothing but gush about my complexion and how flawless it is. I guess that comes from not wearing a whole lot of this crap on a daily basis. She's added eyeliner and a bunch of mascara. I have lashes I never knew existed. My cheekbones have contour blush and blush-blush. Who knew there were this many options and layers for blush? Thanks to Hannah's hot rollers, my long, dark brown hair gently curls down around my shoulders. The one side is pulled back with a barrette attached to a long, thin, satin red ribbon that drapes in my hair. When I look in the mirror, I barely recognize myself. My brown eyes seem a little brighter with the pinks around them, my lips look full, my cheekbones high. I glance at Hannah, blinking, and back to the mirror. "It's not too much, is it?"

"For the Roxy?" she laughs. "*No*. You look amazing."

I grin at her through the mirror. "I kind of do, don't I?" I laugh. "How did you do that?"

She rests her hands on my bare shoulders and leans in to rest her chin on one of them. "I didn't do a whole lot. You just need to try a little bit more." She pinches her fingers together. "You need to stop seeing yourself as one of the boys for five minutes and see yourself as how the boys see *you* sometimes, because Cass? You're really pretty if you'd stop trying to hide it."

I smile at her again through the mirror and take a deep breath. "Thank you."

"He'll be here in half an hour. Get your shoes on. Put the lip gloss and blush in your bag." She rushes around the house and finishes me off, tossing a shiny gold wrap around my shoulders as the finishing touch for the so-called night air. Kissing my cheek, she tells me to call her tomorrow to tell her all about it and flies out the door like a fairy Godmother.

Before I have a chance to not know what to do with myself, Jeff's at the door in a pair of rust-colored corduroys with a plain white button-down and dark blue blazer. He's cut his hair so that it now curls around his face in a neat halo, and trimmed his beard, too. When I step back, he comes inside and pauses. His eyebrows lift, and he blinks, breaking into a wide smile. "Hot *damn*, lady," he whispers in his slight drawl.

I smile and curtsy. "So, this is me dressed like a girl."

His eyebrows stay lifted, and his smile stays wide, but he nods. "You look..." He exhales and blinks at me.

"I feel like Cinderella."

He steps forward, wrapping an arm around my waist before kissing me. "I'm not letting you out of my sight come midnight or any other time. You're coming home with me."

"Is that so?" I feel my cheeks prickle with a blush and wonder if he can tell with all this makeup on. "Does that make you my Prince Charming?"

"It certainly makes me one hell of a lucky bastard," he laughs, leaning in to kiss me again.

"You're gonna mess up my lip gloss."

"All night long," he drawls slowly, messing up my lip gloss.

Playing with the big-boy rock stars is *fun*! Jeff has a car and driver for the night, so we sit in the back of a roomy Towne car with the partition pulled over and fool around most of the way there. He has champagne and strawberries, which he tries to feed me, but I keep laughing. I never understood the whole 'feeding' someone being sexy. I lean in to kiss him instead, which seems to be more the end goal anyway, right? He tastes like cigarettes and strawberries, smelling spicy and earthy when I kiss below his ear. His hand slips between the material in the front of my dress and fondles my breast. When we're close to the Roxy, he pulls back and winks at me, so we start behaving. I triple-check that I'm covered—well, as much as I can be, anyway. Pulling up to the nightclub, there are photographers on the sidewalk taking pictures into the car window.

He gazes out the window for a moment before turning to grin at me, taking hold of my hand with a deep breath. "Rock star reporting for duty," he mutters with a tilt of his head. "Ready?"

"Show me the way."

The driver opens the door. Jeff slips out and offers his hand to help me from the car and then rests it on the small of my back. His palm is warm against my bare spine, and his thumb brushes over my skin. I can't decide if it's because he's nervous or isn't thinking twice about all this. He gives me a look as cameras flash from different directions. I wonder if our picture will be in the paper and whether I'll get the doodle treatment. He pays no attention to any of it and heads down the walk.

Inside, we are bombarded with loud music, flashing neon lights, and a hostess to guide us to the VIP area. Already there are a bunch of people, most I recognize, between my studio work and rock magazines. There's a long, low black couch curved around the perimeter of the VIP section. A dark table that's the same length as the couch is covered in a variety of alcohol, ashtrays, and mirrors with white powder lines. He's greeted with handshakes and hugs. The girls all get kisses on the cheek. I half expected to be left behind or forgotten once he gets around his friends. Instead, he steers me beside him with his hand on my lower back, politely introducing me to the people I don't know.

Teddy keeps blinking at me as though he can't quite believe it's me. He leans over, kisses my cheek, and pulls away, shaking his head. "You look fantastic as a girl."

"I'm always a girl, Teddy." I laugh.

"Yeah, but not like this." He arches both eyebrows.

I rest my hand on his arm and laugh. "And that's precisely why I don't," I chuckle, reaching up to tug at the halter material to make sure I'm covered and swallow heavily. I'm not used to people looking at me like this, like I'm something to look at and not passed by. I smooth my skirt again and do everything in my power not to cross my arms over my chest to hide.

He nods, looks me up and down again before his gaze levels with mine. "I completely understand, but you won't be able to hide it anymore. Not now that we know you look like this underneath."

"Let's just keep it our little secret, then." I scrunch my nose at him.

He laughs and shakes his head. "No chance of that after tonight. Your secret is out… that lucky bastard."

Jeff turns his attention to me, leaning in and sliding his hand over to my waist. "What're you drinkin', darlin?"

"I'm good with a beer, really," I say in his ear to be heard over the music. He nods, tells the scantily clad waitress, and we make room for ourselves on the couch.

"I suck at these places," he says in my ear over the noise. "I mean, I don't dance."

I laugh. "Neither do I." When I pull back, he kisses me. It's not long and drawn out, but it's long enough. I feel like he's staking his claim on me for everyone lingering around. I pull back and run my thumb over his very kissable lower lip and look him right in the eyes with a grin. We have more pretty, scantily clad waitresses, more people visiting, more alcohol, and food being brought out.

Jeff leans over at one point and offers me a bump of cocaine.

I look at it, then at him.

"You never did it?" he asks, again leaning forward to speak in my ear over the music.

I shake my head.

He nods and does the bump himself, like he's showing me how before he looks back over at me, barely lifting an eyebrow in an offer.

I nod in return.

He offers me another chance. What the hell? Since I'm playing with the big boys, I may as well play along, right? This time, I do as he did and close my eyes, expecting a burn or pain, but it doesn't. It's kind of numb at first, and then I feel *alive! Awake!* My heart thumps in time with the music. My breath catches and wants to inhale and exhale at the same time.

Jeff bites his lower lip as he looks at me and cracks up into laughter with my response. He leans over and kisses me, letting his hand run up my bare back. It's like I suddenly have a million pleasure points on the surface of my skin where his fingertips touch. I want to find a room somewhere and screw him inside out.

"Okay?" he asks, chuckling at me.

"Oh my God," I mumble breathlessly. My heart races, and there's a flush of warmth spreading over my skin. "How long does this last?"

He grins and runs his hand along my jaw, leaving more magic dancing on my skin. "Not long enough." He tilts his head, taking a sip of his drink. "Enjoy it while it lasts."

"I don't know what to do with myself," I laugh, looking wide-eyed at him.

"I have an idea." He smirks at me, putting his drink down on the table. We kiss like kids in heat with hands wandering everywhere. I love the way his chest hair feels beneath my fingertips. His hand touches bare breast beneath the top of my dress, and it's intense and sensual. I want to climb onto his lap and screw him right here. I don't even care how discreet it is. It's dark, aside from the flashing disco lights and mirror ball. We're tucked into the curve of the couch, out of the way. Pretty sure no one here gives a shit what we're doing. Around us, others keep talking or laughing, doing their lines, and partying. It's like we're part of the furniture.

It isn't long until this wears off and my breathing and heart rate return to normal. It's disappointing and sad in a way, but my chin feels raw from his beard, so maybe taking a break from being a horny teenager is a good thing. It's decreased for him too, and we pull apart. He gives me a curious look, checking in.

I offer a smile, reaching for my drink as if nothing happened, but my hand is shaking. I check to make sure my clothes are still covering me, which thankfully they are, and pull back a bit more to lean against the couch and catch my breath. He takes hold of my hand and squeezes before releasing it, lighting up a cigarette. I take it from between his lips and start smoking it myself, cracking him up. "So, you're that kind of girl, huh?"

"What kind is that?"

"Quiet little partier s'long as no one is looking too closely."

I lift my eyes and stick my bottom lip out.

He leans in close, his voice deep and seductive in my ear. "You're just full of surprises, aren't you?"

"You'll need to stick around to find out." I blow a stream of smoke over his head and curl my lip halfway in a tease.

He laughs, lighting his own cigarette and shaking his curls. "I *need* to go be famous for, like, five minutes," he tells me. "You okay hanging out here or do you want to come?"

"I'm just gonna sit here and watch you be famous."

He rolls his eyes and gives me a quick kiss before pushing himself up and going to join a small circle gathered by the VIP entrance. He's calm and smiling, shaking hands, and laughing. He makes it look so damn easy.

I take another drag of the cigarette and drop into the cushions. I don't think I'd be able to stand just yet. All of me feels shaky, and I'm not sure if it's from the coke or Jeff or just being part of all of this. This isn't my life. I can't afford to do this kind of thing… ever. I'm practical. I save my money. I don't take chances. I don't draw attention to myself. I am not this person. It's been so long since I've been flirtatious. Right now, it's exciting to be greeted with smiles and kisses, and yeah, even have someone want to cop-a-feel when I've been invisible for so long. I know it's not love, but my God, it's a whole lot of fun for a change. It's *fun* having someone flirt and be charming. If I want to be playful and flirty in return? I *can* because he doesn't know any different.

By the time we are ready to leave a few hours later, I'm tipsy, my feet hurt, the back of my neck hurts from the rubbing of the tie on this dress, my hair is annoying by getting in my face constantly, and I am ready to grab Jeff's hand and show him how turned on I am—maybe ask him for another bump of coke to see how sex feels when I'm that alive.

We start making out and groping at each other once we're in the backseat of the car. I'm busy unbuttoning his shirt—well, what little is left to unbutton. He has the first four undone already. I undo the next two down to his navel so I can finally put my whole hand on his chest. I read one of the street signs as he's kissing my neck and realize we're not heading toward my bungalow. "Where are we going?"

"Teddy's place," he says, his kisses now between my breasts before feeling me up and bringing his mouth to my neck. "Afterparty. Why? You got somewhere to be?"

"We keep groping like this? *Yeah.*" I drop my head back onto the seat and moan as he kisses along my collarbone.

"Trust me," he whispers in my ear before drawing my earlobe between his lips and tugging. He releases a long, hot breath into my hair.

"Not a chance, but I'm along for the ride," I tease, my hand gripping between his legs, feeling his arousal. He groans in my ear, pressing his hips against my hand.

The car stops in the driveway of a large, Spanish-style hacienda with lights burning throughout, loud music playing, and lots of people milling around. He's untucked his shirt to hide his hard-on. Smoothing my skirt, I tuck 'the girls' back into my dress and leave my shoes in the backseat because they hurt too damn much to even pretend that I'm going to put them back on. Both of us laugh as he carries me over the gravel on the driveway. Stopping at the open doorway, he sets me down and takes hold of my hand to lead us inside.

It's a beautiful place with high ceilings and 1920s Art déco accents throughout. It's obvious he knows his way around by the way he guides me down the hallway into the back. The yard and pool are lit up. More people mill around drinking, snorting, and talking. I'm catching bits and pieces of conversation as we weave our way through.

"… *I heard he was signing with Geffen again with a four record deal and more of the royalties….*"

"… *If you want a better sound, go to Record Plant. Talk to my guy! He'll set you up….*"

"… *Did you hear who she was with? Like any of those suits know how to be loyal! Who is she kidding? Her contract is lousy, too….*"

"… *great, primo Acapulco Gold, dude. I know a guy! I can hook you up….*"

Jeff shakes a few hands, kisses a few cheeks, but we don't stop to chat with anyone. He shakes Teddy's hand when he sees him, grabs a bottle of champagne from one of the ice buckets scattered throughout, and leads me around the pool to the little cabana.

"… *but why doesn't he love me…?*"

"… *I'm telling you, it goes from zero to sixty in, like, three seconds! Pretty cherry red….*"

"… *no, your chords are off. You should go from a C to an A then the G….*"

He knows where the key is and unlocks the door, flicking the switch to a room decorated with white wicker furniture with blue pillows. Dark blue towels are piled on a white wicker table near the door.

He locks the door and puts the champagne down on the table before standing in front of me. Pulling the tie at the back of my neck, finally, he draws the halter material through his hands to free my breasts, once and for all, coming in for a long kiss.

I busy my hands with the last remaining buttons on his shirt, letting my palms run over his chest and slide his shirt and jacket off his shoulders. He has to stop to unbutton his cuffs but shakes himself free. He undoes my useless little belt when he comes back, lets that drop to the tile floor, and then undoes the button holding the rest of my dress in place. It cascades down my legs, creating a red satin pool at our feet. I start working on his belt and jeans, and they end up in a crumpled pile next to my dress.

We step to the lounge and lie down. He places kisses along my neck, shoulders, breasts, belly, and thighs before pulling away. Grabbing the bottle of champagne, he tilts it, splashing my naked body. It's freezing, and I cry out, but he leans down, his warm tongue licking and drinking it off my skin before splashing some more. My breath is shaking, aroused even more between the cold of the fizz and the warmth of his tongue. The next time he splashes, it drips between my thighs, and he goes down to drink me in. My head floats with pleasure until I cry out with an orgasm that pulses through my entire body. He sits up and drinks some champagne from the bottle, and shares it with me through a kiss.

I take the bottle from him and draw a mouthful. Before I swallow, I push him onto his back and go down on him. It's his turn to feel the little bubbles as I slide the tip of him through my lips and play my tongue against him. I get a surge of satisfaction when I hear him suck in his breath, followed by a low guttural moan. Working his length between my hand and mouth, my tongue darts and swirls, listening for his breathing, moans, and gasps. His hips rock against me, and his hand holds a fistful of my hair as he groans with pleasure.

I release him, and he shifts me onto my back, sinking himself deep inside with a long, hungry groan. He doesn't lose a bit of the rhythm I started with my mouth, and grooves into me, finally feeling his own release as he arches his back and swallows a cry. Dropping beside me, breathless, his hand settles on his stomach, and he turns his head, sweat or champagne, making his curls stick to his forehead. "I wanted to do that all fucking night," he laughs, his shoulders lifting off the cushion with it.

I laugh, my entire body still reeling. "Me, too! You said we were going somewhere else, and I wanted to cry. I just wanted to get you alone."

He rolls onto his side to kiss me, long and deep, his hand resting on my breast. "But now we should go back out there and let someone else have the room. Satisfied for the time being?"

I pull him back to me. I want to do this all night. We don't leave until I've had him once more, and we drain the last of the champagne.

The party still rages when we emerge. I'm pretty sure it's gotten bigger, even. People spill onto the lawn, naked in the jacuzzi, or skinny dipping in the pool. Some are in the pool fully clothed, too, like that's normal. Music blares from the speakers and some people are dancing near the bar set up by the house. I glance around to see if the neighbors would care, but there aren't any neighbors to see, although you may hear the party echoing through the canyon. I've never seen anything like this.

We grab more champagne from the ice buckets scattered around and start mingling. Jeff does more introductions, but most everyone is drunk or stoned and I'm not going to remember their names, either. When we find Teddy, he eyes us up and down with a playful smirk hanging on his lips. "Nice of you to join us."

"Looks like you're doin' just fine without us," Jeff replies with his own smirk, taking Teddy's joint and doing a hit before offering it to me.

"I think you two might have been having a little more fun than the rest of us," he teases.

I take a hit off the joint before handing it back, trying not to blush because, hell, what Jeff and I were doing was downright tame compared to what's going on around me. Behind me, I hear Darryl bellow, *"Geronimo!"* Seconds later, there's a huge splash from his cannonball into the pool. People squeal. Drinks are spilled and splashed. I wonder what all that's going to do to red satin.

I took the next day off to recover, not just for a hangover. After sharing all the details of my night with Hannah, she said my lack of sleep may have been from the coke, even though I didn't feel its effects anymore. I understand why everyone seems to have and use it now, though. It was quite a kick, but I expected it to last longer. I'd think it'd get annoying having to maintain that high for any length of time, not to mention expensive. I did like it, but I don't see myself going out of my way to do it again.

Today, though, it's back to reality. Before heading to the studio, I brought the dress to the cleaners, with champagne, chlorine, and I don't even want to know what other stains. It's probably a complete loss. However, when I got dressed this morning, I stood in front of my closet and stared at the cute little dresses I never wear and the pile of worn, shapeless tee shirts and chose a cute dress. I mean, it's nothing crazy, too revealing, or anything, but when I wear it, you can't deny I'm a girl. I still pulled my hair back into a ponytail because I can't have it falling in my face when I play guitar all day. Then, I do a quick coat of mascara and dab blush over my cheeks.

My God, who *am* I?

Some of the guys tease me when I come in wearing a dress, but when I strap my guitar on, not one of them asks me to get lunch or answer the phone. They all talk shop and music skills with each other, and going by the looks I've been getting, I think the word is out that Expo chose me to lay down some tracks. Or they heard about the Roxy thing… or Teddy's afterparty. I don't know that I'm comfortable with all this speculation. It might be easier to be an invisible session player, after all. I don't know what people are thinking anymore… maybe I don't know what I'm thinking anymore. I try to keep myself focused on laying down the tracks Curt needs for most of the day, but I keep looking over at the studio door during our break.

Should I drop by their studio? Will he come by to say hi? Neither one of us talked about this being a regular 'thing.' I haven't heard from him since he left at the crack of dawn after the party. For all I know, it's over. He's had his fill and set his sights on the receptionist or something. Immediately, an ache rushes through my chest. I'm not ready to move on. I may not be anything special to him, but I'm having way too much fun for it to be over.

When we finally break for lunch, I start down the hallway and walk just a bit slower past their studio, wondering if they're in yet. Should I just pop my head in? Curt comes trailing up behind me and wraps his arm around my shoulder. "D'you have too much fun at their going-away party?"

I feel my breath catch.

"I figured we may have lost you when you didn't come in yesterday."

"Way too much fun," I falter. "Yeah. Sorry about that."

"Oh, no worries. I probably should have taken the day, too. My God, Teddy can throw a party, can't he?"

"Crazy." I force myself to sound light and cheerful while my head whirls. *Going-away party*? How come I didn't ask what that party was for? Why didn't he say what it was for? Did I miss people talking about them going away? I feel like a complete idiot.

Curt keeps walking a few steps ahead and turns to point at me as I pause by the restroom. "Want me to grab you something?"

"Umm… coffee," I manage with a smile, but my insides are weeping.

Going-away party…

Where'd he go?

Why can't I breathe?

Chapter 4

About a month later in my new place, I'm in bed after a long day at work when the phone rings, waking me up. I reach for the receiver, push myself up from under my blankets, and answer with a mumble.

"You moved."

Immediately, my heart skips a quick beat, and I'm awake. "I did. You disappeared."

"I went on tour. That's not disappearing. I was pretty easily found. Usually up on a stage under a spotlight somewhere. There were posters about it even." He laughs.

I take a quiet breath and grin into the darkness with the sound of it. "Well, some of us were in a studio and maybe didn't *see* those posters."

"Really?" He sounds surprised.

"Really."

"You didn't know...?"

"No."

"Well, shit, sorry, darlin'. I just figured you did."

Do I nag about him not calling for a month, either? I mean, it's not like we're dating or anything, so it's not like he was obligated. But it would have been nice. I don't want to push though, now that he's finally called. Which reminds me; "how'd you get my number?"

He chuckles. "People talk in this town, darlin'. Where are you? Can I see you?"

I give him directions to my new apartment, hop out of bed, and into the bathroom to shave everything that needs shaving. Then I slip into something a little sexier than an oversized tee shirt. I also brush my teeth and run a brush through my hair because, sure, doesn't everyone look this put together and perky at midnight?

When he knocks, I peek through the little peephole and bite my lips to keep from giggling. He's a hairy monster on the other side. His hair is all frizz and too big to even curl. It didn't just grow out; it grew *wide* and defies gravity. His beard is a shaggy mess, as well. I know it's him under there because I recognize those beautiful blue eyes.

He smiles as soon as he sees me. When I close the door behind him, he embraces me, pressing me back against it in a kiss that even my toenails feel.

"Welcome back," I say, wrapping my arms around his shoulders.

"Thanks," he says into my hair, his arms sliding up my spine in the embrace.

"Hungry? Want something to drink?"

"Not right now." His fingers comb through my hair as his mouth finds my neck. "Maybe later."

"Oh," I sigh, cocking my head to the side, "good."

His face is furrier, but that doesn't change his artistry in bed. Once we finish, I go back to the oversized tee shirt and push myself up on the mattress. My hand runs over the soft trail of hair beneath his navel, leading to the sheet covering him. His eyes close, but there's a broad smile on his lips. I watch his chest rise with a deep breath.

"So, did you forget to pack your razors before you left? Lose a bet?"

"Couldn't be bothered," he chuckles, eyes kept closed.

"Obviously." I laugh, my fingers playing with his hair now, twirling it to see if it could be curled. It does, sort of, but doesn't hold a shape very well. "When'd you get back?"

"Today." He sighs.

"Nowhere else to go?"

He opens an eye to peer at me. "Plenty of places. I'll take that drink now if you got it."

"What would you like?"

He pushes himself up to rest against the headboard and takes a deep breath. "Whatever you have. The plane was pretty dry. All that canned air, you know."

After slipping out of bed, I flick the light on in the little galley kitchen with my brain whirring. Sure, he could have gone to Teddy's or some other guy's place. Does he even have his own place? Did he find something after he moved out of his girlfriend's pad? He could have gone to any number of hotels or probably any number of girls' places. I probably just answered my phone first, right?

By the time I get a glass and pour some iced tea, he's leaning in the doorway in his faded, worn jeans. He grins at me with pale skin and dark circles under his eyes. Even his cheeks are colorless. "Here you go."

He takes the drink and goes to sit on the couch in the living room, draining half of it in one swallow.

I sit across from him, still not quite believing he's here. "So, how was it?"

He nods and takes a breath. I watch his gaze glance around the room, lingering over knick-knacks and photos before they land on me. "It was good. Crazy. Busy. Long. Boring. Hilarious. Repetitive." He lifts a shoulder and offers me a tired grin. "You know, the usual."

"I don't know. I've never been on the road. I do the studio work, but don't get asked to do the tours. A girl can do it on the album, but they don't want her to do it on the road because it hurts their cred or something."

He furrows his eyebrows. "Not even Curt?"

"I've turned down one or two of his offers because Leo didn't like me going out, which probably didn't help. Did a few rehearsal dates, local stuff." I offer a simple smile and shrug, pretending it didn't bother me—but it does. How much did I give up for that jerk?

"Man, we gotta fix that." He slouches further into the couch, taking another drink.

"So, how long are you home for? When do you disappear into the dawn again?"

He gives me a sideways look. "I'm telling ya, I *didn't* disappear. It's not like the damn tour was a secret. You were at the going away party."

"I didn't know it was a going-away party." I laugh. "I was too busy trying to keep my boobs in my dress."

He laughs and tosses his head back with it. "Yeah, that failed."

"No thanks to you."

He laughs again, a little lighter. "Yeah, well, I didn't hear a whole lot of 'no, please don't' coming outta you." His drawl is back, and I don't know if he's using it to flirt or too tired to try to control it. "Quite a lot of 'yeses,' breathless, and in quick succession, for that matter." He winks playfully at me. "Not a whole lot of 'no."

"Yeah, well…." I think I'm actually blushing. "I'm easy. What can I say?"

He gives me another look and grins. "I don't know about that. You make me work—not that I'm complaining." His lip curls up just a bit to the side, and he arches an eyebrow. My God, he's so good at that rock star thing.

"So, how long are you home for?"

"We've got a month before the next leg. Teddy wants to head into the studio to try and finish the album and get that put to bed.

What about you? What're you up to?"

"Between jobs at the moment. Possibly something coming down the pike next month."

"What're you gonna do in the meantime?" he asks, pushing himself up a little.

"I waitress."

He sits up, and turns to face me, horrified. "What?"

I laugh. "What? A girl's gotta eat, Jeff. I have rent and food and stuff to pay for. There's a reason I moved. This place is cheaper and more affordable on one salary."

He shakes his head. "Well, alright, but waitressing? No." He shakes his head and sits back. "No, we gotta get you a better gig."

"Working on it." I brush my hand over his thigh. "Trust me."

He just keeps shaking his head. "No, like… tomorrow. You're too damn good to be waitressing. What about your own stuff? You said you had a bunch of songs."

"What about them?"

"Do them. Do your own music, get yourself out there, not be a session player."

I grin and pat his thigh again. "Silly boy, you're adorable. You think anyone can afford to record an album? That kind of thing costs more than food and rent. You've been a rock star too long."

He grabs my fingers and looks at me, those bright blue eyes catching mine and not letting go. "We'll make it happen. One of the few things I really have is connections, Cass. Leave it with me, okay?" He finishes his iced tea and puts the glass on the floor at his feet. "Tomorrow, quit your job… or wait, today. It's today, isn't it? Later, quit your job." He shakes his head and gives me a sideways look again. "Waitressing?"

"It's honest work."

"I agree." He stands up and puts his hand out for mine. "But you're a musician and too talented to sit around and wait for an opportunity to find you. Hi, I'm Opportunity. You've been found. Let's make a record. Well, tomorrow or later… after we sleep. Because I need sleep. Maybe the day after tomorrow. You have plans? Can I crash?"

"Feel free."

Is he really this homeless—or does he not want to be alone? Is it that hard of a transition after being on the road with all that activity and people around to go back to an empty house and silence? Regardless of the reason, with all the other options he had, he called me. I slip my hand into his and turn off the light in the hallway, letting him lead me back to my bedroom. This time, he climbs into bed, drapes an arm around my waist, and pulls me close against him. There's a gentle kiss against my shoulder before he's dead weight and asleep in less than a minute.

A few hours later, he squints in the light, furrowing his eyebrows together, and exhales. "What're you doing?" he mumbles, closing his eyes with a deep sigh.

"I'm going to work. I can't leave them short-handed. Go back to sleep."

He takes a deep breath and runs a hand over his chest, nodding into the pillow.

"I'll be back before you're awake, probably, but just in case, eat whatever you find. I left clean towels out, too," I whisper, as if that's somehow not going to disturb him.

He nods again, stretching his hand across the mattress and curling his fingers. He peeks over to me and wiggles his fingers again, so I sit on the side of the bed in a pair of stockings, still buttoning my white blouse. He tugs at my sleeve, so I lean onto my elbow and smile. "What?" I whisper.

"Have a good shift." He reaches to draw me closer for a kiss, then rolls onto his side, away from the light. He's asleep by the time I sit up.

I drag the sheet over his shoulder to another one of his mumbles. I don't even bother trying to make it out. Oh, how I'd love to screw my shift and climb into bed with him, but I can't do that. They've been so understanding of my erratic schedule. I can finish this one shift.

My mind is already thinking about the songs I have, which ones are ready, which might need a little more work. Is he really going to do this? Can this really be happening? I wonder, though, will he be here when I get home?

I take my fifteen-minute break at the restaurant when Hannah comes in for lunch. Tugging at her elbow, I pull her outside and lean in closer to talk with my eyes dancing. "He showed up last night."

"Who? *Leo*?"

I widen my eyes and shake my head, continuing in an excited ramble. "*Jeff*! Called me at midnight. He's at my place now. Mentioned helping me do my own songs! As in, quit working here to do my own music."

Her mouth drops open, and her head comes forward as she widens her eyes. "Are you serious? He just showed up?"

I nod and laugh. "I have no idea what to make of any of this anymore."

"Cass, I'm going to be *that* friend but, please, don't get too involved," Hannah says, gripping my forearm, a warning in her voice. "I've seen this type of guy before. I work for a lawyer in Los Angeles and see this kind of thing all the time. He'll eat you alive if you swim in his tank."

"How the hell can I not? I mean, I know this means nothing to him. He's only passing the time until his next model, or tour, or something, but Hannah... out of anyone in the world? He actually could help me get my stuff heard. I could find out if I'm really any good or good *for a girl*. If he wants to use me—which, by the way, I'm not going to complain about because the sex?" I widen my eyes and look around again. "He can use me all he wants."

"He is," she says with discernible clarity, looking worried and tilting her head, still gripping my arm. "You're not just playing with fire. He's a complete inferno. I mean, I love you, but...."

I rest my hand over hers and squeeze. "Han, I *know* he not sticking around."

"Exactly. Is Jeff getting your hopes up about your music and then flying off and leaving you halfway done? What's to say he's not going to go off without a word again halfway through the thing, keeping you on the hook to finish it? What if you can't afford to finish it?"

There it is: reality. It's just slapped me in the face with a cold, wet rag. He could disappear on his next leg of the tour without saying a word again, and then what? What's to keep him from starting all of this and then get distracted by his own career or the next chick he bumps into? Where does any of this leave me in the end, besides well fucked—both figuratively and literally?

I shouldn't get my hopes up about all of this. I need a more detailed discussion once he's not half-asleep or trying to get in my pants to see how realistic all of this is. I need to slow it down. Remember who I am—and who he is. I'm still a nameless session player in the fantasy playground he lives in. He's a rock god. I'm still a girl.

"I don't want to dash your hopes and dreams, Cass." She rests her forehead against mine with a sigh. "I haven't met him. You know him better. I just don't want to see you get left holding the bag and having to pay something off that will take you years to do when he promises the moon and then gets distracted. I'm so excited someone like him recognizes your talent. I want him to actually recognize it, though, in writing or something. It's just my sensible law school self talking." She wraps her arms around me and squeezes. "Just be careful."

Reality has kicked my ass by the time I get home from the diner. Tips stunk, my feet hurt, my legs are tired, my back is sore, and my paycheck is a joke. It's enough, added to the rest I've saved, to make rent this month. Jeff's on the couch with my acoustic guitar when I unlock the door, strumming something soft and quiet. There's an empty plate sitting on the cushion and an empty glass by his bare feet. He still has dark circles under his eyes, though, and his hair is a huge, wild mess. When I close the door, his smile warms, and damn it, I want to believe it's for me, and not just for 'the girl for right now.'

"Hi, honey, you're home," he teases, the corners of his eyes crinkling as his smile softens. He continues strumming the guitar, not really playing anything. There's an attempt at fingering some chords, but it's not solid. "How was your day?"

"Exhausting." Kicking my shoes off, I send them halfway across the room before dropping beside him on the couch. I rest my head against his shoulder. "Must be a full moon or something because people were insane today."

He turns his head to kiss the top of mine. "Thought we could order in for dinner. Figured the last thing you'd want to do is think about dinner, and I didn't see a whole lot to make anything. Did you give your notice?"

I groan. "No."

"Why not?" He slides to the side a bit.

I sit up. "Because you were delirious last night, and I didn't know if you were serious or not."

He shakes his head. "I wasn't delirious. I was completely serious."

"But, I mean, you only have a month, and you're going to be recording your own album." I furrow my eyebrows.

"I already talked to Jace."

"Who's Jace, again?"

"Our manager."

"Expedition's manager?"

He shakes his head. "No, *ours*, yours and mine."

"Hang on..."

"You need a manager, Cass, or one that's going to actually work harder than the one you have now so you don't get stuck waitressing between jobs."

"I don't have one now. I couldn't find one that...." I pause. "He's willing to take on a girl? You told him I play guitar, right? Not acoustic Joni Mitchell, Judy Collins stuff, right?" He nods. "And he was okay with taking me on?"

"He trusts me."

"How many people has he taken on on your word?"

"Three."

"And where are they now?"

"One of them got a recording deal with Columbia," he starts. "She's recording her second album. The first made it into the Top 50. You may have heard of her? Jamie Reynolds?"

"Yeah, Leo loved her. We had that album."

He nods and puckers his lips. "There was this other singer named Fiona May. She had a few singles chart."

"You know Fiona May?" She doesn't do the kind of music I do, but he's being modest when he says she's had a few singles chart. She's been compared to Linda Ronstadt and selling out venues for a year.

"We've, um, crossed paths a few times, yeah," he says with a subtle nod and fingers a chord on the guitar.

"I see." Maybe someday he'll tell another of his young conquests that we've 'um, crossed paths,' too. "And the third?"

"Time'll tell," he says, setting those denim-blue eyes on me. "You've got an appointment with him tomorrow afternoon to discuss goals and plans, so I hope you're not working."

I blink at him. "I'll find someone to cover. You're serious? You're for real? You want to do this?"

"I wouldn't be doing it if I didn't want to, Cass. I think you have something. You're talented, and when you dress like a girl, you knock people off their feet. That's not gonna hurt you."

"Oh, yeah?" I ask, pulling back to lean into the arm of the couch. "That's all it's done, Jeff. People see a girl with an electric guitar and think some poster teenage boys will drool over. They don't see talent or credibility, and if that's what you have in mind...."

"I didn't say *model*, did I?" He shifts to turn toward me. "I didn't say pin-up. *You* need to get over the fact that you're a girl that can play, Cass. Maybe once you start believing it, others will follow your lead. You proved yourself to us. Darryl didn't see you as just a girl.

Teddy didn't see you as just a girl. Curt doesn't see it. The rest of the guys he's been working with? Who was the last guy who asked you to answer a phone or make him a sandwich?"

"Well, there was that one guy who wanted to fire me for not getting him a menu…" I arch an eyebrow.

"Yeah, and where's that guy now? Turned ass around backward and making introductions because you proved yourself to him." He's not playing with me. He seems almost angry. His eyes even change to a stormy blue. "And it wasn't because I took you home and got laid. So, *you* need to get over it and go in there like you're a talented musician, *not* a girl."

I look at him with wide eyes and nod. "Okay."

"Okay," he mutters, turning back to the guitar fingering.

"Thank you," I add, "for making introductions, for helping."

He gives me a sideways look, but there's a smile in there. "You're welcome. We'll work on living arrangements next."

"What do you mean?" I look around my apartment. "What's wrong with where I live?"

"No privacy," he replies with a shake of his hair. "That neighbor across the way keeps peering through her door all day."

"How would you know unless you were peering through yours?"

"I left to pick up some cigarettes and got some groceries in. Your fridge was empty."

"Yeah, well, I eat at the diner, usually. She's a little nosy, but she doesn't bother me or anything. It's not that big of a deal."

"Well, there's not enough room for two people, either."

I swallow a gasp and blink at him again. "Oh? Who's moving in?"

He lifts a shoulder, strumming a quiet chord. "Be easier if we moved in together."

"Easier how?" I try to hold on to something because my entire world has gone from zero to one hundred-ten miles an hour without a crash helmet.

He responds with another lazy shrug.

I bring my knees up onto the edge of the cushion, close my eyes, and take a breath. "What are we doing, exactly? Because I feel like I'm missing, like, six steps in between from when I went to work and came home." I open my eyes to see him smiling at me and nodding in agreement. "So, what are we doing?"

"Jumping in with both feet, I suppose." He leans the guitar against the couch cushion. "That's a nice guitar, by the way." He points to it.

I nod, resting my hands on my shins. All of my guitars are nice guitars. They're the only things I allow myself to spend real money on.

"Look," he continues, "I don't really have a whole lot of time to do things slow, take my time, go a-courtin' as they say." He's turned on his playful twang. God, the charm just oozes from him when he chooses. "I guess I figured this is going pretty good. Why sit around and do the I stay here, you stay with me, we go back and forth, pretending we're not living together when it's really what we're doing? It's not like I'm home a whole lot, anyway."

"But what about the other girls?"

"What other girls?"

I arch an eyebrow and tilt my head. "I'm one of the other girls, Jeff. There're other girls out there... aren't there? I can't be the only girl you're interested in."

He blinks and sort of snorts a laugh. "Why not?"

"Because you're Jeff Kingston, and we got together because we both had nothing better to do that night. Didn't we? You didn't know me to be interested in me."

He cocks his head to the side and keeps smiling. "Why not?"

"Because that's not how this happened."

He shifts, bending his leg, and rests his hands on his calf. "How did this happen?"

I open my mouth and close it with a breath. I don't know what this is to answer him.

"Does it really matter all that much? If you'd rather not...."

"I just have a problem getting my head around the fact that you're interested in me when there are so many other more fashionable... beautiful... established girls out there that are maybe more your scene?"

"My *scene*?"

"Success-wise, I mean. You know, more used to your kind of recreation, the parties, the nightclubs, the fame, the drugs."

"Oh." He nods and crinkles his nose. "So, I'm not a real person? Is that it? I only go to parties and nightclubs. I don't go home nights and want to unwind and just be with friends? I'm only ever famous?"

"*No!* That's not what I mean. I mean, more like I don't want to embarrass you. When you have to be seen or do something out in public...."

"How about we leave the public out there," he waves his hand toward the window behind us, "and go by who's in this room? Since, you know, who's in this room is who's actually going to be in the thing."

I tilt my head to the side and take a breath, my cheeks burning. He called me after all when he came home. He's still here when he could have easily gone elsewhere all day. He's made phone calls to help me, and here I am giving him a star trip when he's not even acted like he wanted one. I lower my knees down and scootch forward with a smile, leaning in. He meets me halfway so I can kiss him.

"So, does this mean you'll call me when you disappear out on tour if we live together?" I reach out to attempt to curl that mess of frizz on his head.

He arches an eyebrow. "I called." He lifts a shoulder. "I don't remember specific dates, but I called a few times. Figured you were in the studio and didn't want to bug you there. Honest, Cass, I don't know what you were thinking, but I didn't just disappear. Dates and time get really twisted out there, but I *did* try to reach you."

"Oh." I have no clue what I'm doing or getting myself into. I only know that I want to. I stifle a laugh, considering Hannah told me not to get involved, but didn't I already know I was? Going by how crushed I was when I found he left after that party; crushed, like a penny on a railroad track. "Where'd you like to live?" I ask.

"I kind of like the beach," he answers.

"The beach?" I murmur and watch his face with a smile breaking over mine. "I could do the beach."

And another penny is laid on the center of the track, with a train coming, picking up speed.

Chapter 5

Two days later, I trudge into Expedition's studio after my second meeting with my new manager, Jace, and have a bunch of curious faces looking hopeful in my direction.

Great. No pressure.

"Cass? How'd it go?" Jeff asks.

I force a smile. "We'll see." I shrug, feeling as fake as I sound. That only draws more curiosity, and Jeff narrows his eyes in quiet question to explain. Being on the other end of that skeptical stare is unnerving. I'm nervous and uncomfortable and not quite sure what to do with my arms, so I cross and uncross them, trying to get my shoulders to relax and unclench my jaw. "He… didn't quite have as much faith in my work as you do."

"What the hell is wrong with him?" Jeff drops his drumsticks into the holder and comes around his kit.

"Seriously?" Darryl adds, hands on his hips. "He deaf?"

Darryl is a prime example of getting a chance because of having a dick. He's a great guy, very funny, and one of the most talented guitarists in the business, but he doesn't have a great singing voice. He harmonizes fine, but his mic isn't turned all the way up when they're performing live. He's done two solo albums, though, and even had a top ten hit. I'm one hundred percent sure I can sing better than him, but….

"He didn't say I didn't have a chance, but he didn't quite hear it. We're going to do a few demo tapes. He'll see what he can do." I cock my head to the side toward my raised shoulder, trying desperately to play all this off as 'no big deal' and failing. I'm embarrassed. I want to go hide in a cave.

"Aw, babe," Jeff says, making his way over to wrap his arms around my shoulders and pull me close. "He'll see it. Don't worry."

I'm trying hard not to be disappointed and bawl into his shoulder, and it's really, really difficult. I let my cheek rest against him and slip my arms around his waist, but they stay limp.

"Come on," he says, pulling back and slipping his hand into mine.

He doesn't even say anything to the rest of the guys. We just head out of the studio and down to another one that's not being used. Leaning on one of the consoles, he folds his arms. "What'd he say *exactly*?"

"Exactly?" I lift my shoulders and release a breath, but this time, tears fill my eyes. "He said I can play guitar, but he's not so sure about my voice. Which is pretty much what most everyone says. My stuff needs some polishing—which isn't a surprise. Maybe once it's cleaned up, it'll be more suitable for my voice or something, but basically, he's doing you a favor." I attempt to smile. "Which I, kind of, prefer he didn't."

He shakes his head and exhales with a huff.

"But thank you for making the introduction, at least."

I'm back under that skeptical eye, and he furrows his eyebrows, dropping his arms. "You're giving up?"

"Jeff, he's not the first one to say the exact same thing. It's all I hear." I shake my head and grasp my fingers together in front of me. "I'm good on guitar. I'm not a strong singer. I can hold my own, enough for back-up. They like my songs, just not me doing them. If I can sell my songs, though? If he can get my songs in front of some artists? I'll take it. I *can* write. I don't have to be center stage. I just want them to be heard."

"What's your best one?" He puckers his lips in thought, squinting at me.

"Best song?"

"*Yeah*. That's what we're talking about, isn't it?"

"I don't know. I have, like, forty of them."

"Go get me what you showed Jace," he says with a quick flick of his chin.

I'm already getting a sense of what he's aiming to do, and my stomach drops. "Why?"

"Just go get them." He pushes off the console and starts toward the door.

"I won't let you do one because you feel sorry for me."

He stops and turns around, folding his arms across his chest, and those eyes are a dark, stormy blue, swimming in arrogance. "Oh, darlin', trust me, if we don't like 'em, we don't do 'em. We don't take pity on anyone that much. Our name's gonna be linked to it. If we do it, you can be damn sure it's because we can do it justice. Go get what you have. We'll see if there's anything we like. You may be saving us a week in the studio because we're coming up dry in there. This may just be an opportunity we both need."

As I head out to my car, I keep shaking my head, uncertain if I want to do this. *Is he taking pity on me? Do they really need songs? Expedition? What if they don't like what I have? Can I sit in the room listening to them pick my songs apart? Maybe I should just get it over with now, so I can go learn how to type or get married. Maybe I can be a music teacher.*

I realize how defeatist I sound, even in my own head. I let myself get my hopes up again, only to be told the same thing other agents told me. I'll bounce back when a lyric forms in my head or I hear another melody form while washing dishes. Right now, I'm disappointed and fed up. When I come back with my folder and tapes, I hand them to Jeff in their studio. "If it's all the same to you, I'm going to leave these and head home. My ego is shot for one day."

"Come on, Cass," he says with a slow blink and quick shake of his head, "what if we like them?"

"Surprise me when you get home." I lean in to kiss him, the tears back in my eyes. "I'm done for today."

He gives me a look, squinting and pulling his head back. It's almost as if he wants to say something but decides against it with a rise of his chest, trying to not roll his eyes at me. It's not necessarily a tender or understanding gesture. "You need a thicker skin, babe."

"I do. But it's not going to happen in a day." Of course, now the tears start slipping down my cheek, damn it.

He arches an eyebrow and takes a deep breath before leaning over to give me a peck. "See you later." He taps his fingers against the folder. "All these up for grabs?" He's losing patience with me. I see it in his face, the tight corner of his mouth pulled back, and a dismissive shake of his head. "I'll see you later," he says with a breath and turns.

I rest my weight on one foot and drop my shoulders with a sigh. "Would you rather I stay?"

He glances at me over his shoulder. "You mean *participate* in your career?"

I close my eyes and take a breath before glancing around to see who, if anyone, is listening. The other guys seem to be keeping their heads down or working on something else, and not really paying attention to us. Maybe they're being polite, but that doesn't mean I have the patience to be.

"I'm *not* feeling sorry for myself, okay? I hope you find something. But I don't know that I can sit by and listen to more criticism after hearing it all morning." *Especially from a band I've admired, and that's inspired me,* but I don't dare let them know that. I'm still supposed to be professional, and I am failing on all fronts today.

All he does is glance over his shoulder and curl the corner of his mouth back again. He's not impressed by me today, either.

I drop my hands to my waist and cock my head to the side. "You know, I never asked you to do this."

He turns and drops his chin. "*There* you are."

"What are you talking about?"

"You think you only have to work when you *feel* like it in this business? That you get some criticism and get to go home and pout? You think we," he hooks a thumb over his shoulder, "don't hear how much we stink all day, every day? Not just critics, but random strangers who think it's okay to tell us how much we suck when we sit at a restaurant or go out to get our car washed even? We have critics all over, the worst in this room, among ourselves. But we don't go home and *sulk.*

"You show up. You do your fucking job. If you're going to be a musician or a songwriter, get used to hearing people criticize, wanting to change the things you wrote. They may just make it better. It's called collaboration. And really Cass? If you're not going to fight for your work, who the hell do you think is going to do it for you?"

Damn it! I feel like a child berated in front of the class. It's worse because I know he's right. Licking my wounds is a luxury I can't afford to have. *Suck it up, buttercup.* I can cry later when I go home. I grab the folder out of his hand. "Who's singing or are you doing harmonies?"

"None of that has been decided yet," he snaps. "We haven't seen the music."

"Well, do you have an *idea*?" I glance up at him before shuffling through the folder. "Because this suits your voice." I shove a piece of paper at him. "This would suit Teddy's." I hand him another. "But if you're looking to do harmonies, if we rewrote some bits, this might work for all of you." I shove another at him.

He skims the papers, shuffling through them. Without looking up, he asks, "you stickin' around?"

"Yes. I'm going to go have a smoke first." He looks up at me, arching his eyebrows. "What? You think you own the market in weed?"

He tries to hide a grin, but it sneaks out anyway, almost as though he's laughing at me. "No, but I could join you."

"So could I," Teddy suggests from across the room.

"Me too," Darryl adds, looking up from his guitar.

"I'd be willing," Gary pipes up with a nod.

"Betcha we have better shit," Jeff adds.

"Betcha you don't. I took what I have from you." I smirk, cracking him up.

He reaches out and wraps his elbow around my neck loosely, pulling me against him. His other arm wraps around my waist and holds me tight. "Fight for this, Cassandra," he says into my hair. "Don't let anyone tell you you're not good, not even yourself. Prove 'em all wrong."

"No, no, no!" Teddy cries out, shaking his mane of hair out of his eyes, acoustic guitar slung over his shoulder. We've been in the studio forever… okay, maybe twelve hours. But we've been working on one segment for eternity and they're still playing with the harmonies. "I do that part. You sing the third. He's got the fifth." He looks over to Jeff, widening his eyes in exasperation, and picks at the b string, trying to make his point. "I can't hit that fucking note. That's yours."

"Then we need to fix that transition because what's here ain't gonna work."

"I thought you could fuckin' sing anything," Teddy says.

"You fuckin' thought wrong," Jeff answers with an annoyed shake of his head. He runs a hand through the mass of hair and shakes it out again. "We need to clean that up."

"Again? Can we do it tomorrow?" Darryl asks, dropping back into the cushions with a groan, staring up at the ceiling.

"Why?" Teddy snaps.

"Because it's 4:15 in the morning," Gary says with a yawn.

"Let's just get this one verse down," Teddy continues. "We're almost there."

"You already put the composer to sleep," Darryl says.

I assume he thinks I'm asleep since I'm lying on the floor. "Just resting my eyes. I'm here." I lift a hand into the air and wave. We've rewritten the verses three times now. The chorus is still a work in progress. When they actually do sing the right harmonies, it's luxurious, like a river of melted chocolate. My entire body takes a deep, comforting breath when I hear it.

I can barely contain myself that these are my words, my melody they're working on. One of my inspirations for even attempting to be a musician is singing my lyrics and music. If I had half an hour of sleep, I'd be giddy, but right now, I'm just exhausted. "One of you sing a B, one does the G, one does the D, and one of you do an F. Make it a G7 chord."

"This is why she stuck around," Teddy says with a laugh.

"She wants to finish this and go to bed," I mumble with a deep breath. "We can finagle the rest later today after we sleep."

"We would have figured that out." Gary yawns again.

"If any of us were awake," Jeff finishes.

"All right," Teddy sighs, "let's leave it for now."

"*Hallelujah*," Darryl says.

Someone nudges me with the toe of their shoe and I open an eye, finding Jeff leaning over me with a tired grin. "Ready to go home?"

"Can't we just stay right here?" I whine. "I'm too tired to move."

"You don't want to sleep on the floor." He nudges me again and reaches a hand out to help me up. "Come on, baby, let's get you home."

Once I stand, I drop my head forward to rest on his shoulder and close my eyes again. "I'm so tired. How can you guys sing?"

He reaches into his pocket and pulls out a little vial. "Chemicals," he says, opening it, shaking a little bit out, and sniffing. He shakes out more and offers it to me. It's not like they were hiding this from me. I could hear the hard sniffs on occasion, but I didn't consider doing it myself to keep up with them. I don't hesitate now and sniff, almost instantly feeling more alive and, at least, like I'm going to make it home without falling asleep at the wheel. I also remember how fantastic it made me feel when I kissed him at the going-away party and lean in to do so now. It's still pretty awesome.

"Let's get home, okay?" Jeff brushes his hand through my hair and kisses my forehead.

The coke lasts long enough to get us to the house, but not much longer. Maybe because we are so tired. Maybe it's the sound of the ocean when we drive with the windows down along the street with the sun starting to rise. Maybe it's all of it. In the house we go directly to the bedroom, stripping clothes as we go and fall onto the mattress... so much more comfortable than the floor. He drops an arm over the small of my back as I lay on my stomach.

"I can't believe you're doing one of my songs," I murmur into the mattress.

"Told you," he says, running his hand along my spine, "you have to fight for it, or no one else will."

When we walk into the studio the following afternoon, Teddy hands me a piece of paper. A cigarette hangs off his lips as he looks at me through slitted eyes. "See if you can come up with something," he says before walking away to tap ashes into an ashtray, then slings on his guitar.

Jeff peers over to look at it, drops the corners of his mouth, and nods, arching an eyebrow in consideration. Releasing my hand, he rubs his together, walking further into the studio to get the session started. They have worked together so long it's instinctive. They know what's next without even discussing it. By the time Gary comes in, they're back around the couch working on the harmonies like we never even left. I don't think Gary even did since he's wearing the same open shirt and bell bottoms he wore yesterday. It all happens so much smoother than it did last night or this morning, or whenever it was, now that they've rested. I sit on a stool, holding this sheet of paper with their words and music on it, being asked to add to their work. It's surreal.

I'm distracted when they stop talking, and their voices come together, blending in that sound they have. It's not the Beach Boys or Eagles or CSNY, but it's a kind of blend that makes them immediately distinguishable from any other group. When you hear it, you know it's them. This time, they're singing my song. I feel the notes swirl around in my head, and my chest fills with it. I actually have tears in my eyes when I look over at them.

Teddy glances over at me with a wide, toothy grin. "Whadda you think, song writer? Is that what you had in mind when you wrote it?"

"Um…" I stammer, blinking at them with a grin, "you guys might have exceeded my expectations."

He gives me a nod and turns around to the booth. "I think we're ready to give it a go, Stan." He glances around at the rest of them.

"What about instruments?" I ask.

"I want to try it a Capella first and see what it sounds like."

I nod, grinning down at the floor, trying to hide the silly enthusiasm I'm feeling about this whole thing. I hope I remember this moment for the rest of my life. Even if nothing comes of it. Even if it never makes it on the album. I want to remember what it feels like to have these guys standing in a circle, so focused on my music, their voices blending so impeccably as they sing something that came from my heart and spirit. It's hard maintaining my professionalism and composure. I want to giggle and jump up and down like I'm six. Jeff looks over, knitting his eyebrows together, but I grin, straightening my shoulders, and shake my head, pretending to be an adult. I head into the booth and sit as they check levels and echo. About five minutes later, they begin with Teddy tapping his foot for the beat and a snap for when they come in. It's incredible, and in here, seamless. You can hardly hear one voice over the other, and that trademark sound of theirs is in stereo.

I catch Jeff looking over into the booth, and he grins, winking at me as he sings a verse harmonizing with Teddy. He drops his chin just a little as if he's saying, 'I told you so.' I can't help but smile back and stifle a laugh. They do a few more takes, and we rework one of the verses again, but by the end of the day, *I'm Always at Home, my* song, is officially recorded by Expedition.

I'm a credited songwriter.

Once they finally take a break, Jeff comes into the booth and stands behind me, wrapping his arms around my waist and dropping his chin on my shoulder. "Hungry?"

"Possibly," I say, dropping my head back against him, feeling the warmth of him envelop me. When he lifts his chin, I slip my hand into his. "We need to make a pit stop first."

In the hallway, I push him back against the wall and kiss him, my hand burying into the mass of curls to pull him against me and not let him pull away. Thankfully, he doesn't try. His hand slips into the back pocket of my jeans, and I feel his fingers press against my ass, drawing me against him. His other hand rests on the small of my spine and pulls me in tighter.

I hear the studio door open, and Darryl and Gary come out. We don't even pretend to stop. Darryl tells us to 'carry on' as they walk by as if I had plans to do anything else. By now, I've unsnapped 3/4 of Jeff's shirt, and I'm running my palm over his chest.

"We're not going to make it home, are we?" he laughs in my ear with a heavy breath.

"Nope," I reply against his mouth, taking his hand, leading him down the hallway.

One of these rooms has to be empty. After trying the studio across the way and two offices, we finally find one. I drag him inside, locking the door, and finish pulling the snaps open on his shirt as my mouth lands on his collarbone. He pulls back to start undoing the buttons on my jeans. We continue losing items of clothing, groping, grabbing, and kissing. I don't know which of us is more turned on. As soon as I'm free of my jeans, he presses me back against the door and lifts my leg, grabs me by the waist, and enters me with a hard, fast thrust. The door rattles with it as I hold on to his shoulders and drop my head back with the next.

I'm already aroused and gasp when he enters me again, my hand pressing against the back of his neck and drawing his mouth against mine. There's not much time for it as his urgency grows harder and faster, the door shaking with each thrust. He comes with a heavy groan and tries to catch his breath, but that's when I grab his wrist and guide him between my legs to continue what we started. My fingers press against his shoulders as I fall into my pleasure, dropping my head back into the door with a low, satisfied moan and heavy breaths.

"Better?" he whispers into my hair.

I nod and whimper, still feeling the pulse of my pleasure.

"We gotta do more of your songs if that's how you respond."

"Like you haven't gotten lucky before now." I press my mouth against his in a kiss he can't back out of.

"This was more than lucky, babe," he says, kissing me in quick succession. He runs his fingers through my hair and comes in for another, my turn not being able to avoid it until there's a knock on the door.

I jump with a yelp. He busts into a laugh.

"Uh, I need my office," the voice on the other side says.

I drop my forehead into Jeff's shoulder and crack up for a second. After putting ourselves back together, he looks over to make sure I'm dressed, one hand on the doorknob. I nod to him, smoothing my shirt and checking my jeans are zipped. He leans back over his shoulder to kiss me and opens the door, grabbing my hand.

"Thanks, man," he says to the guy leaning on the wall across the way with a nod. I drop my head to look at the floor, trying not to bust into another laugh, knowing I am beet red. Jeff slips his arm around my shoulder as if this is just another daily occurrence and part of the job. I risk a glance over my shoulder, but the guy's already in his office. I suppose it's a risk you take working in a studio, though, isn't it? And probably why the other doors were locked.

Later that evening, when we get home, there's a large box leaning in the vestibule by our front door. Jeff hangs back, pretending to get something out of the car, so I'm the first at the door to see it. I glance at the label, and my name is on it, but I haven't ordered anything, much less have anything ordered for delivery. I unlock the door and glance over my shoulder to see Jeff coming up the walk.

"What's that?" he asks, but there's a slight smile on his face.

The door is open, so I flick on a light inside and return to the box. "Possibly a short body? I don't know."

"You should maybe open that, then."

I lift the box. It's not heavy. I know it's a guitar by the shape, but I am *certain* I did not buy a new guitar. "Do *you* have an idea what it could be?"

He walks past me with a twinkle in his eye and a grin on his lips. "Not a body."

I pick up the box and bring it inside, asking, "what did you do?"

He's standing in the living room with his hands on his hips and his head cocked to the side. I rest the box on the couch and get a knife to slit the tape, holding it closed carefully, giving a sideways look to Jeff as I do. He sits on the other couch, clasping his hands together expectantly. There's a plain black guitar case inside. Lifting that out, I unclasp the buckles, open the lid, and step back with a gasp.

Inside is one of the prettiest acoustic guitars I've ever seen, an Ovation Patriot. I know this by the stencil of the drum and American flag on the lower corner of the body. Around the sound hole is more of a stenciling inlay of what looks like tiny abalone leaves and abalone inlay on the neck. The body itself is a dark nutmeg color, and it has a rounded back. It's easily one of the most gorgeous guitars I've *ever* seen.

"What do you think?" Jeff questions almost in a whisper.

I look over my shoulder at him, hands covering my mouth, and back to the guitar. "What did you do?"

"It's a limited edition," he says, moving to the end of the couch. "Only 1776 were made for the bicentennial. The stencils were destroyed after they used them. It's supposed to have a full, bright sound because of the body shape." He points to it. "Teddy said it was good."

I snap my head back to him. "Teddy…?"

"I'm a drummer. I don't know much about guitars. He had to help me pick it out. This is where we disappeared to before lunch. We weren't at the record label. Do you like it?"

My hands shake as I reach out to stroke the dark wood and finger the leaves around the sound hole. "I... but..."

He motions with his chin. "There should be a card in there. You might have to actually pick it up, though." He chuckles.

"It's *so* pretty, Jeff." I sit beside the case and lift the guitar, resting it on my lap and strum gently. Of course, it's tuned perfectly. At the bottom of the case is a small white note card. I pick that up, keeping the guitar nestled on my lap.

Congratulations on becoming an official songwriter. Keep fighting. Can't wait to see what's next. He put his initials beneath the words, '*I'm Always at Home,*' and yesterday's date.

I lean over and kiss him, resting a shaking hand against his jaw while the other holds onto the guitar neck. "I don't know what to say." I'm almost breathless with the shock and sheer generosity.

"Tell me you like it?" he suggests with a nervous grin.

I strum a few chords before caressing the body and run my fingers over the strings. "I love it. It's gorgeous." I lean over and kiss him again. "*Thank you.*"

He smiles, reaching out to run a finger along my jaw, those blue eyes staring into mine. "If you ever doubt your talent, just grab this and remember I believe in you."

Now there are tears in my eyes. I smile through them and look down at the guitar and caress it.

"I think you're supposed to play it, not pat it. That's what they tell me, anyway," he whispers.

"It's one of the sweetest presents I've ever received," I tell him, my gaze holding his.

He sits back into the couch cushions and folds his hands over his stomach. "You're welcome." He lowers his chin and gives me a soft smile. "Play for me."

Chapter 6

I'm home, expecting Hannah for dinner after working all day with some new guy Jace thinks has potential. New guy thinks he's already a superstar and doesn't need anyone's help and that he's doing me a favor by using my song. I was this close to taking it and walking out to let him flounder, but stuck it out because regardless of the assholes, I have to remain a professional. I probably could have walked and no one give a crap, but I would. I'm paying my dues, I guess, and the sooner I pay it off, the sooner I can be choosy about who I want to work with. At least, that's the grand scheme in the back of my head. Right now, all it means is that ass got to feel superior and think he's helping some chick make her rent. I don't think Jace told him who I live with. I got the sense that if he knew, he'd have been much nicer and a lot less condescending... maybe.

While Expedition was on their European leg, Jeff left it up to me to find a place on the beach for us to live. It didn't take long with the budget Jace gave me to work with. All Jeff's expenses flow through Jace, it seems. It's easier for the office to keep on top of what needs to be paid and what they're allowed to expense the record company this way. Plus, things get paid on time when Jeff's not around to write the check. I found a fully furnished two-bedroom ranch with a sunken living room, a dining room, and an eat-in kitchen with a deck that sprawls along the whole back of the building. Steps lead right from it onto the beach. By the time Jeff returned, he had a place to return to.

In an attempt to clear my head, the back patio doors are open to the deck and I light a bunch of candles in hurricane lamps. Lavender incense burns in the living room. Outside, a lazy Pacific Ocean rolls up onto the shore and the hills overlook the beach in the twilight. All around me are simple sounds—birds calling, ocean waves, no cars on the street, no voices, nothing. It's peaceful and I suppose now I understand why Jeff wanted to be on the beach. After being around so much noise, it makes sense. I crave this after a day of work and my life isn't even a quarter as hectic as his.

Hannah walks in and snickers, handing me the brown paper bag of Chinese food. "Look who's gone Hollywood," she teases.

"I'd be burning patchouli if I was Hollywood. This is more Bohemian, I think," I return with a sarcastic crinkle of my nose.

"Whatever you say," she groans with a shake of her head. "Can we eat? I'm starving."

We fill our plates and head out onto the corner of the deck, where there's a faded wooden picnic table off the kitchen. I turn my chair, facing the beach and the hills that hug it. Resting my feet up on the railing, I slouch in my seat, holding my plate in front of me. She chuckles and shakes her head again. "Now, what?"

"You got used to this pretty quick," she says with a grin.

"Look out there. Why would I stare at a picnic table when there's an ocean to look at?"

"You've got a point." She turns her chair to mirror me.

"See? Not very difficult to acclimate, is it?"

"Where's Rock Wonder?"

"At the studio. I saw him for a whole half an hour the other day."

"I heard him on the radio for longer than that on Tuesday."

"Yeah, this album is taking a lot out of them. Then, they have to go back out on their East Coast leg. I don't know how they do it."

"I do." She sniffs sharply, wiping beneath her nose, and arches a knowing eyebrow at me.

I chuckle and roll my eyes. "Well, yeah, that's part of it. But I feel bad for them. They're all exhausted."

"It's their job. He can always become a car salesman."

"With that hair?" I laugh.

"Well, maybe not, but he's got that charm thing down."

I take a bite of food and look out to the beach for a second while I chew. "You really don't like him, do you?"

"I really don't know him," she answers as I glance over at her. "I never actually met him. He's always off somewhere or in a studio. I work business hours and only see fleeting glimpses of him. I don't have the stamina to go to your parties and go to work the next day."

"They're not my parties," I tell her. "They're other people's parties, and I happily invite you to them."

"I couldn't keep up. I met him in passing once. I don't trust him."

"Why not?"

"Because, Cass..." She exhales and shakes her head. Her eyes flick away and she keeps shaking her head. "It all just happened so fast. Why?"

"Why what?" I put my plate on the table and sit up to face her. "Why *me*?"

Her eyes dash in my direction and she shakes her head more fiercely. "No! That's not what I'm saying. I'm just worried that he started this so fast, he'll end it faster, and you're going to be heartbroken. He's swept you off your feet and into this." She opens her hand out to the beach house. "And yes, he has helped you and opened a lot of doors for you, but you're talented. Don't let yourself think that any of this couldn't have happened without him."

I arch a doubtful eyebrow and snicker.

"It might have taken longer, but you'd have gotten noticed. I've watched you do this before, that's all. You think you're doing your thing and being independent."

I open my mouth, but she continues with a tilt of her head.

"You end up putting what you want on hold while you take care of your boyfriend, so they can take advantage of you. There. I said it. I'm sorry, but I'm scared of what he's capable of doing. You put so much of yourself aside for Leo, and he didn't give you a quarter of this. You gave up your job and your apartment. You're gonna feel sorry for him and want to take care of him because he works so hard and is so tired." She uses my words against me, and her eyes drop to the deck beneath her feet as she bites her lips.

"I know," I sigh. "I didn't start off being Leo's doormat, though." I inhale a deep salty breath and try not to roll my eyes. When we first started dating, he actually thought it was cool that I could play guitar. Somehow, my talent became the stability while breaking his band became the priority. "I let it happen, though." I want to say I'm fierce and independent, but I've never given myself a chance to find out if I am. "I mean, I'm less of a dishrag than I was with Leo, anyway. I think. At least now I'm actually working on my own career—more than I've ever been able to—and Jeff *encourages* it. He's made so many introductions. I wouldn't have had access like this before." I glance back to Hannah and my chest rises with another reluctant breath. "I don't want to question it so hard."

"I want you to be happy, truly happy, Cass. I'm just leery. He's cool. He's a freakin' rock star, for crying out loud. How could you not get swept up in his wake? I'm just over here holding your life preserver, asking you to *please*, be careful."

I turn my head and look at her with tears in my eyes, feeling a little silly, but it's pointless trying to hide from her.

"Oh," she sighs, her shoulders dropping and her hand reaches across the table to me. "Oh, honey, you're already off in the deep, aren't you?"

I nod and take her hand for a quick squeeze. "How could I not be?" I turn my head to the ocean and hills and swipe at the tears. I have no real reason for them. Maybe because I do get the same sense of fear when I stop for a moment and let myself take a good look around, wondering how the heck I got here, too.

But there are mornings when I wake up and he's slipped into bed during the night, sleeping so hard nothing wakes him. I wrap one of his curls in my finger and run a finger down his jawline, feeling the stubble light against my fingernail. He drapes an arm around my waist and holds me against him like I used to do with my stuffed animals to comfort myself. In those moments, I get the sense that it's *me* he's seeking comfort from, that I'm offering something *he* needs and he lets himself take it. His ego is so asleep he's left vulnerable for just a little while and he reaches for me. I bite my lips together and release a deep breath. "I can't help it. I can't explain it. I just..."

"Well, I'm going to hold on to your life preserver for you in case you need it. Just do me a favor? Look back every now and then. Let me know you're okay?"

I nod and give her a thankful smile. This is why she's my best friend. She tells me what she thinks. She doesn't look around at all of this and think I've got it made. She looks at me and wants to make sure I'm being taken care of instead of me doing the caretaking. Maybe, this time, I am. The quiet ocean breeze caresses my cheek, and I want to believe this can have a happy ending.

A few days later, I'm working on a song at the kitchen table, waiting for him to come home when the phone rings. It's the third night this week Jeff's called after eleven o'clock to ask if I could bring a change of clothes for him in the morning. "When do you think you'll be home?" I ask, looking into the darkened living room. "This is crazy."

"I don't know," he grumbles. "Is my Hawaiian shirt clean? Can you bring that by in the morning with a tee-shirt and a pair of boxers?"

"Anything else?" I sigh, doing my best to ignore this sense that there is no way they're working seventy-two hours straight. He can't get half an hour to come home and shower? No matter how many clean clothes I bring him, he's going to need to shower. Which, of course, means my mind wanders to how it was we met and wonder who's working in the studio that he's taking out to dinner… and where he's taking her for sex and a shower. We never discussed being exclusive or anything. It's not like he's not taking care of everything for me. It's not like he's neglecting me. It's just, I can't help but feel like he's not neglecting others, too, and I'm not a hundred percent sure I'm comfortable with it. I don't have any proof, though, so then I feel guilty for not trusting him. They have barely ten days before they have to go back on the road, and they don't have a whole lot of time to get this album finished. With the help of some coke and other things, they *could* be going seventy-two hours straight.

"Babe, this is how this works," he says, almost as if he's reading my mind and not talking about the recording process. "It's not forever. It's not all the time. It's just how it all works."

"I know." I'm not quite sure how understanding I sound, though. "But then you're going on tour again."

"Who's to say you're not going to be able to come along for some dates this time? Why do you need to stay here?"

"If I pick up some work…."

"Then don't complain that you won't see me, Cass. It's not like you need to do that." Now, he sounds annoyed.

"How about we have this discussion another time when we're both not tired and cranky? What else do you need me to bring besides a change of clothes? Where are you showering?" I'm curious to see how he responds. "Don't you need to shower?"

"They have bathrooms here," he snaps. "Why? You think I've got a bunch of spare time to run home with someone? Is that what this is about?"

"No! Geez, it was a question. You like to be clean. I live with you, remember?"

"I gotta go. See you tomorrow."

"Sure." I sigh.

"Hey, Cass?"

I roll my eyes at the ceiling. "Yeah?"

There's a second of hesitation before he says, "I love you."

My breath catches and I look straight ahead as if the words might be hanging in the air for me to catch them, to make sure I actually heard what he said. But I know I did because my heart beats just a little quicker and I have a goofy grin on my face despite the shock of hearing it.

"I love *you*," I reply, trying to breathe the words out.

I blink at the refrigerator in front of me, at a little snapshot stuck to the front with a magnet. It was taken at Teddy's house a few weeks ago. I actually look tan now that we're living on the beach. I'm laughing, not even looking at the camera, wearing a little white summer dress with a daisy in my hair. He picked it and stuck it behind my ear for me from Teddy's yard when I commented they were my favorite flower. My hand rests on his chest and my head on his shoulder. He's got his arm hooked around my neck, looking right at the camera with bright, pale denim-blue eyes smiling. I'm happy, and it's all caught in that photo.

Knowing all that I know. Doubting absolutely everything, questioning his motives, and my sanity, at the end of the day, when it's just us, and he turns his attention toward me, he can bend and roll me like silly putty. Now, on top of everything, he goes and says, 'I love you?' Oh! How I *want* to believe him.

I want to be the person on the end of the phone that he's going to come home to... eventually. I want to be the person he wants to see after a leg of a tour, after a long day at the studio, takes to a party, and gets his picture taken with. I'm safe. I'm cared for. I'm protected. He's introducing me to a bunch of people who are looking over my work and putting it on their albums. I'm working, and it's not as a nameless session player on someone's album anymore. He's given me no reason not to believe him, but I can't shake the doubt nibbling at the back of my brain. But even so... I love him.

Dear God, help me, but I do.

A few nights later, I lean my shoulder against the paneling in the darkened hallway, watching Jeff on our couch with a guitar. He's looking at papers on the cushion in front of him, attempting some kind of fingering. At least, I don't think what he's playing are the actual chords. He's proven himself a better drummer than a guitarist, but I give him points for trying. I step out from the darkness into our little dining area, and he turns his face toward me. His eyes are wide, and I can see the repressed frustration pressing on his lips.

I soften my smile and try not to laugh. "Need some help?" He takes hold of the guitar by the neck and shoves his arm out, stiff and straight. "It didn't sound that awful."

"You haven't seen what's actually written here to know what it's supposed to sound like," he says with his little Texas twang.

I take the guitar and sit opposite him, glancing over the notes on the paper he's turned toward me. Fingering the chords initially, I play what's before me as his eyes hone in on the guitar neck. I can see his fingers attempt at making the movements on an imaginary guitar neck. I play through it a few times and hand him the guitar again.

"Aw, no, really? You're gonna make me?" His laugh more a stuttering breath.

"Come on. I'll walk you through it."

He takes a deep breath, lifting his chest and shoulders with it before taking the guitar from me. "You got your work cut out for you."

"You're not that bad."

He arches an eyebrow at me.

"You're a drummer playing guitar. I know what I'm working with. Go ahead, start with the first chord."

We amble through the progressions. He reads the notes, fingers the chord, and looks up at me for silent approval. I reach over and fix his fingering when necessary. He gets frustrated easily but, to his credit, he sticks with it. After about half an hour, he sticks the guitar back onto my lap, rolling his eyes and shaking his head with a breath. I start playing the chords again, improvising a bit here and there as I go.

He crinkles his nose and curls his lips at me. "Show off."

"You've never seen me behind a drum kit." He chuckles, but his eyes still follow my fingering. I turn the guitar to hand it back to him, but he puts his hands up and shakes his head. "Oh, come on, you need to work more than half an hour to get it down, babe."

"I'm going to need more than a month to get that down," he says with a sigh as I bring the guitar back and keep playing. I play what's on the paper, already memorized, so he can pick up on what's there. "Why're you playing guitar, anyway?"

"Teddy wants us all on guitar for this one, acoustic," he grumbles. "He forgets that I don't really play. I get *by*. This is pushing it."

"Do you want me to try and simplify it for you?"

"Can you?"

I smile and nod, already changing some things around.

"Geez, why didn't he do this in the first place?"

I hand the guitar back and we start again. This time, he picks up on it a little easier and is more relaxed. That, right there, is his battle. He stiffens up and tries too hard. When he's playing the chords more fluidly, I see his shoulders relax as it comes to him. After he's gained a bit more confidence, I tell him to change up his fingering until he's playing what Teddy had down. It's a little more effort, but he's not nearly as daunted by it.

"You're sneaky." He grins when he realizes what I've done.

"I'm a professional." I offer a wink and a nod.

"Well, Teddy and Darryll thank you because now they don't have to sit there and teach me. You're a lot better teacher than they are. Smell better, too."

"Wow, you flatterer." I reach over to fix his fingering again. "Don't get lazy, now." I tap his finger with mine.

He rolls his eyes at me. "I don't have to have it perfect right now, tonight, you know. We're going to practice it a gazillion more times tomorrow. Can you come in with me so when they fuck things around, I can play it?" He stops playing and leans forward. I meet him halfway and accept his kiss. "Be my tutor?" he croons.

"Oh, I would, except this guy I sometimes live with, you know, when he's actually around and not working? Well, he's got me doing a bunch of errands for him. I've got a laundry list, and come to think of it, laundry, to do for him tomorrow."

"He sounds like an asshole. Tell him to take a hike."

"He has his moments." I giggle. "Easy on the eyes, though."

"Well, I sure hope he knows what he's got goin' for him." He shifts just a bit closer.

"Me, too." I accept a deeper kiss. "I'll give you a call if he bails or has to work or something."

"Seriously," he says, dropping back into his arm of the couch, "*can* you come tomorrow?"

"Well...." I take a breath. He never asks me to help him with his guitar work. He has Darryl and Teddy, so why would he? But he asked me. I mean, all I have is a hair appointment and lunch with Hannah. It's a crappy thing to do at the last minute, but his request is actual work. My hair needing a trim is more frivolous. "I can probably rearrange the thing I have," I hesitate. I smile back but feel disappointed. It's just a haircut. I can do lunch some other time with Hannah. She understands my music thing.

He glances up from looking at his fingering and grins. "Thanks." He goes back to the guitar but glances up again. "You'll be able to get the laundry, though, right?"

"It's already done." I push myself up off the couch.

He looks up at me and smiles, those blue eyes bright. "What the hell would I do without you?"

I start back down the hallway to call Hannah and cancel lunch.

"Your own laundry," I mumble to myself.

The following afternoon, I take Jeff's car. I'm almost as adept as he is at zipping around traffic now. Usually, I enjoy driving it. Right now, I'm annoyed and take it out on the stick shift, blasting the radio with the top down and ignoring the looks I get at the stoplights. Fifteen minutes later, I'm seated at a restaurant table outside, waiting for Hannah, throwing back a glass of white wine. The sun is warm against my face and arms, and I slip my sunglasses down to fight the glare. My hair blows over my shoulder, and I grumble in my head, wishing I didn't cancel that damn appointment this morning.

"Don't you look like a rock star," Hannah teases, coming to the table and giggling. She leans over and kisses my cheek, settling into the chair across from me. "What happened to your Expo session?"

I take a mouthful of wine and order another when the waitress comes over for Hannah's. "They decided not to work on the song he wanted me there for," I grumble before taking another sip. "So…." I shrug. "I was released to go do something else."

"Something else like what?"

I don't want to say the words because I know how it'll sound, especially to Hannah. Walking out the door, Jeff said, 'oh, hey! Now you can pick up the stuff at the dry cleaners.' I suddenly wanted to cry or slap him. I wasn't sure which, and I wasn't sure why. But it set me off, and I'm in a bad mood. It's not like I don't know that this happens during studio time. Best laid plans are never set in stone when someone gets struck with inspiration. I know that, but still….

"You did it again, didn't you?" she guesses.

"Did what again?" I bite the side of my tongue and shake my head before taking a breath, more pissed at myself than Jeff. We smile at the waitress when she brings our drinks. When she leaves, I drain the remainder of my first.

"Put the boy in front of yourself," she replies with a tight smile and a nod. Sometimes I hate that she knows me as well as she does.

"When he asked me to go in, he made it sound like he needed my help with what they were working on. If it was to just screw around, I wouldn't have canceled. God knows I need the haircut."

"Bet if you told him you had plans, he would have been okay with it."

I know she's right. But I dread that look when I have to disappoint someone. Ever since I was a kid, whenever I had to say 'no' for some reason, or cancel something, or God forbid, if I actually did something wrong, all I wanted to do was hide and figure out some way to make it up to them. Of course, I grew out of feeling bad for not going to a birthday party, but that look when I have to decline the invite still crushes me. I don't even think *they* care as much as I do about it.

I hate it, even more, when it's coming from my boyfriend. All I hear in the back of my head is my mother telling me how I'm never going to get married if I'm selfish and dress like a boy. Then I went and added a guitar! I could never explain to her how much the music meant to me, that sense of pride I felt when I figured out how to play something I heard in my head that no one else in the world ever heard before. To her, it was me thumbing my nose at her hopes and dreams. Talk about the look of disappointment! When she found out I was going to 'live in sin' with Leo, she couldn't decide if I was one step closer to marriage or ruining my life and reputation. No matter how hard I tried to explain to her that nobody cared about things like that anymore, she just gave me that sad, straight-mouthed look with her soft little sigh and muttered about how she 'doesn't understand my generation and our loose morals.'

Try as I might, I can't help but fluctuate between doing what I want and doing the things I was raised to do, never knowing if I'm doing anything right. It's part of why I love my music so much. Music makes sense to me. I can work on it and make it right for days if necessary. I can hear melodies and words and put them down on paper, and they're mine. They don't stare back at me with that blank face, lips pressed together, eyes holding mine for a fraction of a second longer than usual before blinking, nodding, and shrugging me off. They don't talk me out of joining a band so they can start their own. They don't ask me to support them while they try to get noticed, only to end up cheating on me. They don't ask me to do the laundry or pick up the dry cleaning, either.

I take another swallow of wine and watch the ends of my hair blow in the breeze for a moment. "I don't want it to look like I'm taking for granted everything he's done."

"Cass, one of these days, he's going to find out you do things besides wait for him to ask you for something."

"I just…" I exhale with a sharp breath. "… Want to pull my weight. He pays for everything, Hannah. Whatever money I bring in, he won't take."

"He shouldn't. He doesn't need it."

"That's not my point. I feel…"

"You don't owe him either, if that's what you're trying to say."

"I know," I mumble. "I just feel like I should do *something*. I want to show him that I appreciate all of this, and honestly? What can I give back to him? I don't have connections. I don't have any clout. What I have is the ability to make his life a little easier by taking care of the things he doesn't have time for."

"You make his life too easy. He just ends up asking you for more and he's going to start taking you for granted, if he hasn't already."

I sip my wine. "I heard about what his previous girlfriend used to do. They made it sound like she did everything. Like she was some kind of Mary Poppins or something and I don't do half of what she did."

"And what did his previous girlfriend do?"

"She was a model, of course." I roll my eyes behind my sunglasses. Just saying the words makes me feel inadequate some days. Today is one of them when I look at my jeans and brown and gold poncho. I tug at some of the gold fringe with my fingers and sigh.

"Right. And, going by the few models I've met, pretty sure her assignments were done in a day or a week or whatever. Then when she finished, she had a bunch of free time to be his full-time girlfriend, and run all his errands, then be at his beck and call without it interrupting her non-existent full-time day job." She takes a sip of her wine and arches an eyebrow. "And, when she did have a job or have to run to the various agencies for her go-sees, he somehow managed to function, I bet."

I take another mouthful of wine, turning my head away and watching other people enjoy their lunch. I just want to get drunk. "What's your point?"

"You're allowed to make personal plans and tell him no when things conflict. It's not a business deal. You're in a romantic relationship. Otherwise, he's your pimp."

I take another drink and slouch into my chair like some petulant child. I wish I could get this sense of obligation across to her the right way. He's not demanding I do anything. I'm sure he'd be okay if I said I had plans, but at the same time, I feel like I'd be disappointing him. Instead, I say, "he doesn't demand I do anything."

"Then why are you so afraid to tell him no?"

I put my glass down and sit up straighter. "I'm not afraid!"

She arches a doubtful eyebrow at me and drops her chin.

"I'm not. I just don't see why I can't help him out when he's got deadlines to meet and things he needs to finish."

"I don't...." Her chest rises with a deep breath before she tilts her head and drops her shoulders. "I only want you to realize that *you're* important, too. I don't want to fight about it with you."

If I'm honest with myself, I agree with her. It would be nice if he asked about me or my plans first, put whatever I was doing before his needs. I know he's said I need to learn how to fight for what I want, but does he want me to fight for his attention? Doesn't he have enough vying for his time? Isn't there enough in his life that he doesn't have time for? I don't want to be another thing that's draining. I want him to come to me and feel like I'm some kind of respite from all of that.

"I don't want to fight with you about it either." I sigh, turning my head to look at her and give her a partial smile as I shake my head.

Some nights, when I'm lying in bed waiting for him to come home, I can't help but want to be higher up in his priorities, too. It can be pretty lonely when you're dating someone whose time is spread so thin he doesn't have time to come home and shower. But, oh! When he does come home, and I am his focus, he does a marvelous job of making me feel like I'm all that matters. When we're together, and he's relaxed enough to talk... it feels like hours of being the most important thing in his world. When it's crazy like it has been, I hold on for the nights when he'll return to me. I don't see it as him taking me for granted. Somehow, Hannah does. "I just need to you understand he's not asking me to do anything I don't want to do."

I know she wants to say something more, but to her credit, she drops back into her chair and picks up her wine. "So, what's good here?" She glances at the menu in front of her on the table. I reach out and squeeze her wrist with a thankful smile.

"The wine... and the company."

Chapter 7

The hotel lobby is an absolute zoo. As I weave my way through the fans milling around wearing Expedition *Stripped Sunset* tour shirts, I notice some holding albums, programs, concert pictures, and can even see others with blurry photos of the boys coming in and out of limos, hotels, or possibly even airports. The starter fans, as Teddy calls them, young teenage girls in halter tops and tight jeans trying to act mature, seem the most curious. They're stuck in the corners and middle, where they're less likely to gain any access to anyone. They'll be passed over for the girls with more of their assets on display when the right handler happens along. Those are the ones that get invited upstairs to party with the band if they can be chill and more willing to bare the assets that got them noticed. They're closer to the elevators and entrances to get the first glance.

Guys in denim shirts and band concert tees pretend to hang back, mimicking the rock'n'roll cool. At best, they'll get invited to go upstairs and join the party. The worst, they might get lucky with a fan. Either way, their eyes light up, and they stretch their necks to see over the crowd, just as curious as the rest of them.

Excitement is palpable as everyone chatters and laughs with one another, keeping a keen eye out for any kind of movement of doors or elevators when they open. Are they all waiting for one of the band to wander through the lobby into this stampede waiting to happen? I get cursory 'are you someone important' glances when I come through the lobby doors, but they turn away when I don't meet their 'rock and roll vibe.'

There's piqued interest when I head directly to the third elevator bank as instructed and kiss Frank, one of the bodyguards, on the cheek with a smile and hello. That gets more attention. My stomach tightens as Frank stands behind me while I wait for the elevator doors to open. I hear curious murmuring grow louder with excitement and a few 'hey, look!' when I get in the elevator. I don't dare look up at this point for fear of catching someone's eye and becoming one of the people in their blurry photos. Folding my arms around my waist, I try to shrink and disappear. "Thanks, Frank," I mumble as the doors close.

A minute later, the doors open to a whole different kind of zoo, and I'm hit with the sweet earthy scent of weed the second I step into the hallway. There's less of a crowd but one hell of a party in the hallway. Music blasts from somewhere. Squealing, half-dressed girls run out of one room with roadies and managers grabbing at them. There's more laughter before they fall together against a wall to make out and grope at one another. Most of the hallway doors are open. People flow in and out, drinks, joints, or cigarettes in hand. Looking into the suite rooms as I pass, some have speakers set up, others have people gathered around a glass-top table doing lines or grabbing pills from the bowls on them, and another where people play guitars or bongos. Darryl is in the guitar room but nowhere near sober. I don't see Teddy or Gary anywhere. It's like Teddy's backyard party crammed into a hallway, and I am way too sober to appreciate it.

I manage to make my way down the hall to room 1608, with barely anyone paying attention to me. If they do, it's through glassy eyes and hazy smiles. The door is closed, and I knock, wondering if he'll even hear me. He does remember I'm coming tonight, I hope. After another minute, I knock again, louder, and glance down the hallway, watching the mayhem.

This time, the door opens. Jeff stands on the other side with a warm grin and half-lidded eyes, which means he's really stoned. He wraps his fingers around my wrist and tugs me inside before closing and locking the door. The room is dim, almost quiet compared to the noise from the hallway. I'm greeted with a kiss, long and hard, as he holds onto my wrist. His other hand buries into my hair and holds me against him. I'm surprised initially but warm into it, missing that kind of kiss from him. It's filled with such a need but also sweet recognition. "Hi," he whispers when he's finished, resting his forehead against mine and rubbing his fingers along the back of my neck.

"Hello," I whisper back with a smile.

He slips his hand from my wrist to intertwine our fingers and leads me over to one of the beds. It's a double room, and his luggage sprawls over the first bed nearest the door. The second bed has the pillows pulled out from a gold floral bedspread, leaning against the dark wooden headboard. There's a book splayed open, an ashtray with his pack of cigarettes, and a bag of weed lying beside it. A beer can rests on the nightstand holding a burnt incense stick. A faint smell of something sweet lingers in the air but doesn't do much against the smell of pot and cigarettes, though. On but without volume, the TV flickers dancing blue hues in the room as the only light. The curtains open to some darkened office buildings and the alley between the buildings, narrow and dark below. As I sit, he reaches over and lights a cigarette, sitting on the bed. "How was the flight?"

"Long, but fine." I toss my purse on the bed across from me. "How was the gig?"

He grins and arches an eyebrow. "Long, but fine."

"Not in the mood to party tonight?" I glance at the door.

"After the fifteenth night in a row, it gets a little old," he drawls, watching the pictures flickering on the TV. "Trying to rest my voice a little. It sounded kinda rough tonight."

I reach over and brush the curls back from his forehead with a gentle touch. "You look tired."

"I feel tired," he says, almost like he's not talking to me at all, still zoning out on the TV, "down to my bones." He shakes his head and blinks, taking another drag from his cigarette and a quick, deep breath coming back to me. Tapping the ashes in the ashtray, he lifts his gaze to me. "*Anyway*… welcome to New York."

"Exciting!" I smile and turn to face him.

"If you say so." He shrugs. "I've seen the hallway, this room, and a few building fronts. Every place we've been looks pretty much exactly the same as the other place, aside from maybe the bedspread being a different color. I've never actually seen any of the cities we've been to. Maybe someday…." His voice trails off as he slouches against the pillows, tapping his ashes again, bringing his knees up. "Sorry. I'm just…."

"You're really tired."

There's another knock on the door. He stubs his cigarette out and climbs off the bed to look through the peephole before opening it. My bag is rolled in on a luggage cart, and he hands the porter some cash, telling him to put it on the bed with his. The porter looks pale, and his eyes are wide, probably because of what's happening out there and who just handed him a tip. He's in his early twenties and, judging by his face, knows exactly who Expedition is. I'm pretty sure he's going to miss the rest of his shift and just linger at the party.

When the door closes, I'm already unclasping my bag, ready to get into a shower and wash off all this traveling. Jeff comes up behind me and wraps his arms around my waist, pulling me against him. I rest my head back on his shoulder with my hands over his in a sigh. "Glad you're here," he says in my ear with a quiet breath.

"Me, too." I turn in his arms to wrap mine around his shoulders. "I'm going to jump into the shower if you'd like to join me."

"I can do one better if you give me ten minutes." He kisses me once more before disappearing into the bathroom.

I collect my toiletries, realizing I probably won't be needing much, if any, clothing. Sitting on the bed with my stuff on my lap, I wait, watching the silent TV, hearing water in the bathroom and the party raging on outside the door. Some voices get loud as they pass, laughter and squeals. I hear thumping from the next room, and moments later, something shatters in the alley below with a burst of laughter. This is a dim, weird little cocoon I'm in with Jeff. I get the sense he's trying to hide, but there's nowhere for him to go.

A few minutes later, the bathroom door opens, and he steps naked into the doorway, stretching his hand out. I make my way over to him, and he takes my things, putting them on the bathroom counter as I stand dumbfounded, looking at everything. Thick candles are placed around the counters, toilet tank, and tub corners, with a bubble bath drawn. He unbuttons my blouse and continues to undress me without a word between us. My gaze rests on him, smiling as he steps into the water, holding my hand and bringing me with him.

"How did you...?" I begin as I settle into the bubbles, resting back against his chest as water sloshes over the side a bit, but he ignores it. Our knees stick out between fluffy white bubbles. God only knows how much bubble bath he used to get them this thick.

"I'm Jeff fucking Kingston, remember?" he chuckles, dripping water over my breasts and piling bubbles on my chest. "I ask, and people get me the shit I ask for."

"I like that you're Jeff fucking Kingston." I close my eyes as I rest my head back and sink a little lower into the warm water.

"It has its moments." He lifts a pile of bubbles on his fingers and blows to send them floating. "I wanted some quiet time with you before the whirlwind begins again tomorrow."

"I'll take whatever time we can get."

He drips more warm water over my shoulders, playing with the bubbles around us, layering them on my chest and our knees before shifting behind me. "We're running long this leg, babe. Interviews, sound checks, TV shows... it's nonstop."

"Well, then, I'm glad you're taking some quiet time now." I lift my hand to intertwine my fingers through his and rest them on his knee, squashing bubbles and causing them to slide down the underside of my forearm. "Getting a chance to relax. I can only imagine how insane it's been, going by what I saw out there."

He drops his head back to the tiled wall and sinks a little deeper with a sigh. "It's outta hand some nights, really. The shit they get into. Someone left the water running in a tub in the last place we were at. We're stuck paying for new flooring and carpeting for the room, plus wallpaper and paint for the room below, just because they thought it'd be funny. Now we're banned from going back. It's hard to believe we're professionals some nights. I mean, sure, some nights it's fun, but every night? Then, when it comes time to *do* the work, half of 'em are wrecked and doing a half-assed job. An' if I say somethin' about it, I'm bein' a poor sport an' need to lighten up. I just don't want us goin' out there makin' fools of ourselves." He's so tired even his drawl is thicker. "I dunno." He releases my hand and drips water over his knee. "Maybe I do need to lighten up. It's just...."

I turn onto my side, placing a gentle kiss on his chest. "It's been a long tour, babe. Everyone is trying to get through it the best way they know how, I think. You included."

He leans forward to kiss me, his hand in my hair. "Maybe you're right. I don't know anymore. I only know that I'm tired."

I stand up and grab one of the washcloths from the towel rack before sitting across from him. Soaking the cloth, I move forward a little and rest my legs over his. I wipe the washcloth over his clavicle and shoulder before dipping it back into the water and do the same to the other side. I continue, rubbing it over his chest, then take his hands to drip warm water over the blisters and callouses on his palm from his drumsticks. He's sealed the broken blisters with super glue to keep them from bleeding. His smile grows, and his eyes soften toward me as I watch his chest lift in a deep, calm breath. He places his hand over mine, taking the washcloth, and tosses it behind me with a small splash, using his hands instead to cup water to drip over my shoulders, breasts, and arms, inching closer to kiss me. "We're gonna have to take this elsewhere."

"I appreciated this." I stand up with him, water sloshing over the side again. He wraps a towel around my shoulders and pulls tight, bringing me in for a deeper kiss. We both blow out the candles and the burned wick smoke trails behind us to blend with all the other smoky scents in the bedroom. He takes my hand and leads me to the bed, each of us slow and gentle with our touch as we make love.

It's not long after we finish that he wraps his arm around my waist, pulling me back against his chest. Our bodies curl together and relax against one another. The TV still flickers, but I am so exhausted from being up so early and flying all day, I don't mind. I'm not even bothered by the noise in the hallway. I'm certain Jeff was out the moment his arm dropped over me. Listening to the party rage in the hallway and feeling Jeff tucked up behind me, I shake my head into the pillow and chuckle.

So, this is touring....

Later, we're sitting around in the radio station's lobby, listening to the feed over the speakers set up in the room. Everyone else seems wide awake, bored with the hurry up and wait, but awake. I don't know anyone outside of the boys. They've got some girls with them that I've never seen before. There's a blond with Gary with blue eyeshadow and glossy lips wearing a denim shirt tied at her midriff with a suede mini-skirt and boots. The brunette drapes over Darryl in a pale blue jumpsuit with brown clogs. Some girl, *not* his girlfriend because she's in L.A., sits with her legs over Teddy's lap in pink hip-huggers and a tight white sweater, her white boots scuffed along the toes and side of the heel. I sit with my head on Jeff's shoulder, struggling to keep my eyes open. I groan when he gets up to use the bathroom and stare straight ahead, zoning out and wondering why I'm here. I could have stayed at the hotel, couldn't I? He'd have understood, right?

But I wanted to see what they do, what it's like to be a successful musician, famous.

It sucks so far.

Teddy drops into the place left vacant by Jeff and chuckles, wrapping an arm around me with a nudge. "How're you holdin' up, buttercup?"

"How are any of you functioning after that party last night?" I whine with a shake of my head. "At least Jeff got some sleep."

Teddy releases one of his bright cackles as he drops his head back, making the rest of them glance over at us. They go back to their boredom, but he digs into the front pocket of his jeans and pulls out a little red and white capsule, dropping it into my palm. "This is how any of us, including Jeff, is functioning right now." He nods with a slight grin and winks. Everyone else is awake and functioning. It can't hurt. Why not? I drop the capsule onto the back of my tongue and finish my cold coffee.

"What the hell did you just do?" Jeff barks, leaning over and punching Teddy's arm.

Teddy looks a little surprised and scoffs, curling his lip. "Relax."

"What the hell did you give her?" he snaps again, his foot kicking into Teddy's.

Teddy motions to me with his open palm. "Why are you letting her drag like this?"

"It's *temporary*," Jeff argues. "She doesn't need to perform."

"She wants to know what life is like on the road, doesn't she?" Teddy stands up, nose to nose with Jeff. "What are you, suddenly a choirboy?"

Jeff pushes Teddy's shoulder and takes another step toward him. "Don't fucking give my girlfriend anything, understand?"

Teddy glances over his shoulder at me and arches an eyebrow before looking back at Jeff, shaking his chestnut hair off his face. "She looks like a big girl to me."

I look between the two of them and wonder what the hell I just took if Jeff is this angry. I didn't think he'd get upset if everyone else was doing it.

Teddy glances back at me. "They're diet pills, babe. You'll be fine."

"Know what? Don't even *look* at her right now, asshole." Jeff shoves him to the side.

Teddy pushes Jeff back even harder. Within seconds, people call 'whoa!' and grab elbows, pulling them apart as they try to throw punches and curse at each other. All hell is breaking loose until one of the radio secretaries comes in with a confused smile. Everyone freezes. Teddy shakes Gary off and smooths his shirt. Jeff shrugs his shoulders free from Darryl and glares in Teddy's direction. "We'll be ready for you in five, guys," she says, kind of stilted, looking around the room in confusion.

"Sounds good," Teddy says, his voice light and cheerful, glancing at Jeff.

"Great," Jeff says simultaneously, glancing at Teddy. Once she leaves the room, he steps closer to Teddy and pokes him in the chest. "Don't give her anything else ever again, got it?"

"Sure thing, boy scout," Teddy mutters, rolling his eyes. He steps across the room and plops himself down in a chair with a huff.

It all seems to have kicked in my adrenaline, anyway. My heart races, and I feel a little out of breath. Jeff sits and turns to look at me, his eyes watching mine for a second before he sighs. "You're fine, but you're going to be fucking wired."

"That's not a bad thing with today's schedule. They're just some diet pills, right?" I question, keeping my voice down.

His smile is soft as he looks at me and runs a finger along my jaw. "Yeah," he says with a breath. "Probably won't sleep at all tonight, but you'll keep up just fine." He rubs the side of his face with his hand and sighs. "Just tell someone if something feels too… something, okay?"

"I take it that'll make sense if it happens?"

His hand drops to his lap. "Yeah." He gives me a look, and I can't figure out why it's so sad. Eventually, he winks and offers a grin before leaning forward to kiss me. As he finishes, the secretary comes back to set the boys up in the booth. The interview begins, and you'd never know Jeff and Teddy were on the verge of fighting a few minutes earlier.

I wonder how many times they must have threatened to punch each other.

How many times did they do it?

I've never punched someone. I think it would really hurt your hand.

And they can't hurt their hands. It'd make it hard to play their instruments.

Hang on… what did they say?

Why're they laughing?

Us girls were left in the little lobby-waiting area while they do their interview. We all keep sizing each other up without a word, offering slight, awkward smiles. Maybe I could get my haircut so that I can have it feather back like Darryl's chick. Her hair is so much wavier than mine.

How much time does it take them to get ready in the morning? I always feel like other girls figure this fashion thing out so much easier than I do.

I wonder if I would look cute tying that little knot instead of buttoning the shirt down like Gary's chick is wearing.

Linda Ronstadt wears a shirt like that.

My belly button is not that cute, though.

Linda Ronstadt is so talented. How long did it take her to be taken seriously?

My finger picks at the hole in the vinyl chair I'm in.

I bounce my knee.

Then I catch myself to stop.

My mother told me it was rude ages ago but end up doing it again.

What did Teddy give me? I'm not as wired as coke.

But I'm wired.

I have to remind myself to take a deep breath.

Why would Jeff get so freaked out? He offered me my first hit of coke, after all.

Wait, it's over?

I stand up and feel a quick rush to my head, making me a little dizzy. Reaching down, I grab the back of the chair and giggle, blinking at Jeff. "How'd it go?" I try covering my dizziness with a perky smile.

"You were sitting right here, darlin'," he says with a chuckle. "How do you think it went?"

"I, um…" I blink at him, feeling my cheeks burn.

"Hard to focus, huh?"

I nod.

"It went fine," he says, slipping his hand into mine. "Feel okay?"

"Yeah, just got up too fast, I think."

"Yeah," he agrees, curling the corner of his lips like he knows I'm lying. As we wait for everyone to file out, each handed tee shirts and hats and key chains with the station call letters, he leans over and kisses the side of my head. "It's gonna be a long day, babe."

I glance at the clock on the wall. It's 8:12. How long does this awake feeling last?

"Oh my God, how long does this last?" I whine to Jeff, dropping onto the mattress. They've finished the interviews and we're back at the hotel. I'm still finding it hard to concentrate or keep any thoughts in my head. My heart is still in its own steady marathon. I'm jittery, shaky, and it's hard to sit and keep quiet. Again, Jeff gives me that sad little smile and drops to the mattress beside me. "I thought I'd be able to come back here and nap, so I could get through tonight. That's never going to happen. Maybe if I, I don't know, run around the block or something? But it's so cold out there. And I'm not a runner. I didn't bring running shoes."

"Cass," Jeff interrupts, turning my face to his, "*Cass*, it won't matter. You're in this for the long haul. That shit lasts hours. If you've never done it before? Don't expect to sleep until maybe tomorrow morning, darlin'."

"Oh." I blink at him. "*Oh!* That's good then. I'll be fine for the show. I'll be able to hang out after. This is good, right?"

"Sure, baby," he says, but I don't believe he's very happy about it.

"Why aren't you this wired? *Are* you this wired? Teddy said...."

He reaches out and puts a finger over my lips with a soft, "shhh." Catching my gaze, he attempts to hold it. I'm attempting to hold his and pay attention. "We've done them enough. They don't freak us out so much. Just helps us get through the long days. We can't afford to be sleepy and need to be able to focus on everything."

My eyes widen. "*How?* How can you focus? This is ridiculous."

"That's why I didn't want him giving you anything." He gets up off the mattress, kicks his shoes off, and turns to me. "Promise me you'll never take anything from anyone unless I'm there when they give it to you." I widen my eyes and nod. "Fuckhead really shouldn't have given you that. You didn't need this kind of...." He exhales and closes his eyes for a moment, sliding back onto the mattress and taking me into his arms like he's going to nap or something. What am I supposed to do? Count the threads in the carpeting?

"Kind of what?"

"Education," he says, and that sadness returns to his voice. His hand rests on my hair and he kisses my forehead. "You didn't need to know this much about how we do things."

Jeff napped for twenty minutes in the hotel. I managed to concentrate long enough to count forty-three flowers in the bedspread before I got distracted and had to start again.

Now that we're in the venue, I feel more settled. Their show last night was out on Long Island, so today they're setting the stage for the next two nights at Madison Square Garden. I've never been on this side of a set-up in a venue this size, but I'm comfortable around the instruments. Enough is happening that my wandering mind is occupied watching them do their sound check, and the light changes, plus the riggers, carpenters, and all the rest of the stage production taking place behind the scenes.

When they finish sound check, Jeff comes down from the stage and heads to the soundboard, going over more details, checking in with the lighting guys, stage manager, and the lead sound guy. I've seen him in the studio when he's focused on work, but this is much more intense. This goes beyond actual music, ensuring everything is perfect for the audience, not just "good enough"—*perfect*. I can't help but be impressed by his meticulousness and performance savvy. Watching him, I wonder how the heck long it took for him to understand how it all works together.

Teddy comes down for a few minutes and heads backstage, but Jeff stays another half hour. Finally, he turns to me and smiles, realizing I'm still hanging back, looking around, walking in circles, keeping myself occupied, and he reaches out to take my hand. "Hungry?"

"Uh, I guess." I'm not really. I don't know that I can sit still for a meal. He leads me back through the empty floor that will be filled with hundreds of people in just a few short hours. I stop mid-way between the soundboard and the stage, release his hand, and lift my head to the seats around us, grinning. The stage guys are still setting up the backdrops and lights, and the echoes of drills, cables, and equipment cases rolling ring through the space that will be filled with audience cheers and music soon. I turn and look up to the lighting being tweaked and back to the soundboard, trying to take it all in.

"What's up?" he asks.

"I've played gigs. I've watched friends' bands and hung out while things got set up, but none of it was *this*. If I ever felt like a musician before, I now feel like an amateur."

He looks around and laughs easily.

"It's not that I haven't paid attention at shows before, but seeing the details unfold like this gives me a whole other perspective." I'm swept up in the energy that's vibrating through my veins and in the air. I get a chill and shiver.

"It's pretty straightforward by now." He reaches back for my hand again with barely a glance.

"Don't you feel that anymore?" It's something I can sense, the waves of the energy trapped in here somehow, coming from outside, perhaps? "I want to absorb all of it. Remember this feeling," I whisper.

He scoffs, but there's a smile on his lips. "What feeling is that, darlin'?" He steps behind me and wraps his arms around my waist to drop his chin on my shoulder as we look at the stage.

"Anticipation vibrating so hard it makes your heartbeat," I whisper, my eyes still taking in all this preparation.

"That's the Black Beauty talkin', babe."

I pull away, but only enough so that I can look at him over my shoulder. "No, it's not. It's excitement waiting to erupt. You're gonna have one hell of a show tonight."

He grins and gives me a quick kiss. "That's our goal every night."

"No," I say, trying to make him see how serious I am. "It's going to be fantastic tonight."

"You some kind of witch now? Casting a spell? You seeing auras now, too?"

I turn to rest my back against him and take a deep breath with a knowing smile. "You have to be dead not to feel this."

"I know what you're saying," he murmurs in my ear. We stand together for another quick minute, letting it wash over us. "I catch it just before the lights come up when all that energy is focused on us."

The show explodes off the stage. They worked every note, and the audience returned an energy to them that was felt up into the rafters. From the friends and family section that's level with the stage in the audience, I could watch Jeff. At some point, he lost himself in it, too. I adore watching him work in the studio, but this was so much better. I thought he looked nervous, but after the third song, he let go and rode the energy.

Dinner was at some Italian place not too far from the hotel. The boys laughed with one another as if today's tensions never existed. Possibly, it was their nerves or anticipation for tonight playing with their emotions, and they knew all along it'd disappear like this. The party heads back to the hotel, and they make their way through the lobby to squeals and excited banter, scribbling on programs and ticket stubs as they're ushered through. Once or twice, they stop for snapshots with fans. Some girls are tapped on the shoulder by Frank or Jace and appear later upstairs, ready to join the party.

Up on the floor, it's like last night with people and music, only this time, Jeff and I are part of it. He doesn't open his room up, but we join everyone, grabbing drinks. Jeff's taken a few hits of some weed, so he's pretty mellow and laid back, laughing easily.

I'm still alert and scattered. The beers don't seem to do anything, so I drink water, hoping it'll help flush this stuff from my system. I'm beginning to think it's altered my mind. I am never coming down, forever unable to focus on anything, ever again. I've mingled and chatted with people but still feel disconnected and flighty.

As doors close and people pair off, Jeff finds me in the hallway talking with Teddy and his lady friend for the night. Jeff slips up behind me, sticking his hand into my back pocket. "Ready to turn in?" he asks, kissing the crook of my neck as I release a laugh.

Jeff unlocks his door and lets me in first. Before he closes the door, he sticks his head into the bathroom and closet — checking for groupies, I think. Then he closes and locks the door, pulling the little chain over to secure it. The TV is muted and the only light again. He crosses the room, tugging his shirt over his head, and drops it on the floor. He takes my hand, sitting on the edge of the bed, and pulls me in front of him. Lifting the hem of my shirt, he plants a kiss on my belly before his fingers unbutton my blouse and lets it drift to the floor. I move forward to straddle his lap, and we kiss deeply, hungrily. He tastes like beer and cigarettes. I smell a faint hint of soap from the shower he took at the venue mixing with the scent of weed and cigarettes.

I close my eyes, seeing his face behind the drum kit earlier, eyes closed, his body shifting and rocking, working up a sweat, and hitting every sweet note. Right now, his mouth, lips, fingertips, and hands play me. Our song comes out in moans and cries of pleasure until we lie spent on the mattress, the blue flickering light from the TV washing over our naked, sweaty skin. I shift beside him, resting my head in my hand, and trace my fingers over the stubble on his jaw and chin. He lies with his eyes closed, a hint of a smile on his lips. I brush back the damp hair from his forehead, and I wrap one of those loose curls around my finger.

How the hell am I still this wired?

Almost as if he can read my thoughts, he opens his eyes and reaches up to tap the tip of my nose with his fingertip. "How ya doin' over there?" His voice whispers in our quiet as we're tucked away back in his darkened, quiet cocoon as the party dies down outside our door.

I smile and blink back down at him. "Pretty sure I am never going to sleep ever again."

He chuckles and taps my nose. "Oh, you will." He sighs before sitting up, and heads to the bathroom, returning with a glass of water. I pulled the bedspread off and slipped between the sheets, waiting for him, watching the changing images on the TV. It's what my brain feels like—it keeps switching channels on me. "Here," he says, coming toward me with a closed fist, "put your hand out."

I open my palm, and he drops a small, pale yellow pill into it. I look from my palm up at him with an arched eyebrow.

"It'll help you crash." He hands me the glass of water.

As I swallow it, he climbs into the bed and opens his arm out for me to curl beside him. "I'm not going to overdose or anything, am I?"

He chuckles. "I'd never let that happen to you." His hand smooths my hair off my forehead. I try to lie still and calm my brain, attempting to focus on his fingers in my hair or the way his chest hair feels beneath my fingertips. After a while, whatever he gave me begins working. I can take an actual deep breath for the first time all day and relief washes over me. "How ya doin', darlin'?" he whispers.

"I'm starting to settle," I answer just as softly.

"Good. I'll make sure to get you before the show tomorrow."

I attempt to shift but am fading. "What? No. I wanted to…"

He chuckles. "You're not even going to feel me get out of bed, babe." His fingers still slide through my hair. "You're going to crash and crash hard. I'll make sure we get you before the show. Don't worry."

I feel like *Alice in Wonderland*. One pill makes me wired. Another makes me sink into my brain. All the while I'm chasing after Jeff with his watch as he rushes around, trying not to be late for his very important dates, and interviews, and radio shows, and gigs. My mind struggles with having to do all of this again tomorrow. At least, I know now… stay away from the red and white capsule.

I'm standing behind-the-scenes tonight instead of with the other girls in the designated section. From this vantage point, I watch Jeff lean over one of the amps behind him and do a few coke lines while the stage is dim between songs—a few times, too. I didn't notice that last night. I don't get the same vibe as I did last night. Maybe it *was* the speed; however, while the boys are on stage, I overhear the guitar techs backstage warning one of the newer guys that they're about to get their heads chopped off. I must have missed something. Even before the show, Teddy and Jeff had that tension between them. They weren't even looking at one another when they stepped on stage today, although I caught Jeff narrowing his eyes at Teddy and their unease spills over to the crew.

Jeff's the first one off stage, grabbing a towel from the stage handler. Before I get a chance to fall into step, he grabs my elbow and drags me with him. Not only do I feel his body heat, but it brings his anger, too. I try to pull my arm free, but he tugs me tighter and closer as we make our way to the waiting limo. Shoving me inside, he climbs in, dropping into the seat beside me.

"What the fuck do you think you were doing?" he explodes as the car takes off. I'm pressed against the door and blink at him, speechless. He's drenched from being on stage. His hair sticks to his forehead, his shirt is wet with sweat, and smells acrid and sharp. "Well?" he bellows.

"What do you mean?"

"What…." He grabs a vial from the console to do another bump of coke before pushing a breath out and wiping his forehead with the corner of the towel hanging around his neck. "Why the fuck were you handing Darryl his guitar?"

My mouth drops open. "He needed it."

"No. Why the hell were *you* handing him his guitar?"

"He asked me for it. The tech was helping Gary fix a string or something. He knew which one he wanted. I was standing right there."

"Don't you ever set foot on our stage during a show ever again unless you're a paid, fucking employee." He turns his face away from me, but I still feel his seething anger.

At the hotel, he grabs my forearm. It's loud and confusing, but Frank clears a path, and we are shuffled to the elevator as girls attempt to flirt and people shove papers and pens at him without either of us looking up. He doesn't even look over at me. I tug my arm free once the doors close.

When we get to the floor, the hallway is clear and quiet, but he puts his hand back at my elbow and drags me along. I stop, dig my heels into the carpet, and yank my arm from him.

"Get in the room," he barks. "I'm in no fucking mood." His eyes ice over, and his jaw clenches. Behind me, the elevator door opens, and he takes hold of my wrist and pulls me along as Darryl and his girl step off. No one's going to dinner after the show tonight.

Inside, after slamming the door, I turn around and slap him.

He barely turns his head, but he bites the inside of his cheek as though he's chewing on it. His fists grab onto the ends of his towel as he glares.

"Don't you ever lay your hands on me like that again," I warn. "I am not your property. I am not a child."

"Then stop acting like one!" He yanks the towel from around his neck and slaps it against his jeans.

"Because I handed a guitar to Darryl? Are you *kidding* me? It was thirty seconds."

"Thirty seconds that, if the union finds out, could cost us a million dollars in legal fees, Cassandra. Don't you get that?" He taps his forehead with his fingers. "You're not here as one of the fucking boys. You're here as my God damn girlfriend and that little stunt...."

"He *asked*..."

"What don't you get?" He tosses the towel to the bed and leans forward as he yells, those eyes boring into mine. "It wasn't your place."

"Who's going to complain? Who the hell saw?"

He slaps his hand against his thigh, and his shoulders drop. His voice is deep and low, but somehow more threatening. "Oh, I don't know, any number of the assholes backstage, the *thousands* of people in the audience, the guy we're going to *fire* for not doing his job." He unbuttons his shirt, yanking it from his jeans.

"Fire? For that? He was helping Gary!"

"Well, maybe if you let him do his job, he wouldn't be let go."

My mouth gapes, and I follow him with my gaze as he goes to the bathroom, slamming the door behind him. Seconds later, I hear the water for the shower.

I stand in the middle of the room, staring at the closed door, shaking with anger, confusion, and guilt. My heart races, and I'm almost out of breath. I cost a guy his job? That just doesn't seem fair. Darryl came back behind the drum riser. I was standing right there. He pointed to the one he wanted and said 'thanks' when I handed it to him. He didn't get pissed. He didn't look for the tech. He didn't glare. He just went back on stage. It didn't seem like it was that big of a deal to create this much of a rage.

When I hear the music out in the hallway, I open the door and peek out. We got back before anyone but, as usual, the party's starting. A few people wander between rooms holding drinks, laughter rising over the music. I glance over my shoulder at the bathroom door and am pretty sure he's going to be a while. Maybe he'll calm down. Maybe he'll be even angrier if I'm not here, but perhaps I can get some answers about why he's in such a foul mood. I take a deep breath and step out into the hall.

I check out a few of the rooms, looking for Darryl to ask him about all of this and grab a beer, finding him in the hallway with a bottle of vodka and a joint. "Everything okay?" he asks, lifting his eyebrows at me, reaching out to pat my shoulder.

"You mean aside from getting screamed at for handing you your guitar and getting your tech fired?" I drop next to the wall beside him with a groan and take a drink and don't hesitate to take the joint he hands me.

He pats my shoulder again and smiles. "He's my tech, and I'm not letting him go anywhere. Jeff's in a mood. It'll blow over."

"He's making it sound like I did something wrong."

He laughs and kisses my cheek. "Sweetheart, when he's in a mood, everyone does everything wrong. I can't tell you how many times he's fired half the people in this room, me included. Hell, he might just fire me again for asking you for the damn thing. We just know to stay out of his way."

"Great," I mumble and down half the beer in my hand, wondering how I'm supposed to stay out of his way. "Part of me keeps waiting for him to come drag me back into the room to scream at me some more." He tilts his head slightly and drops his shoulders in sympathy. "Did something happen?" I ask, handing the joint back to him.

"Not that I heard," he says with a shrug. "He woke up on the wrong side of the bed, that's all."

I sigh, offering him a smile, but don't believe it. I know coke puts him on edge. I know that look he gets when he's been on a blow binge, but something triggered it.

Teddy struts out of the elevator with his arms held out, boisterously announcing, "this is a raid! *This is a raid*! Gimme all your drugs and women, and no one gets hurt!" He busts into a loud cackling laugh as someone hands him a joint and a beer. He saunters over to me and Darryl, draping an arm around my shoulder. "So, where's Herr Grump Ass?"

"Showering," I answer, taking the joint from him, inhaling deeply.

"Good. Maybe he'll wash his cranky-ass mood off while he's at it," he says, taking the joint back.

I nod before exhaling smoke. "That'd be nice. Any idea why he's so pissed at me?"

"You breathed in the wrong direction. The moon is in Pisces? Spoke to someone with a dick within a five-mile radius of his existence? Take your pick." Jealousy? As if! "He's a moody son-of-a-bitch, Cass," he continues with a shrug and a half-hearted grin. "It doesn't take much to flip him out on a tour."

"Doesn't take much to flip him out in the studio anymore, either," Darryl adds before tossing his head back for another mouthful of vodka. When he lowers his chin, he belches. "Kingston's just being Kingston. I'm telling ya, I wouldn't worry about it."

But I am worried. I wait a little longer to give him more time to calm down and see if he's coming out, but when I go back to the room and try to use my key, he's put the chain lock on, and I can't get in. I glance down the hallway with tears in my eyes and exhale. "Jeff, it's me," I say through the crack. "Let me in." I wait a minute, but there's no movement. I can see through the crack the flickering blue light from the TV. There's no sound, of course. I know he can hear me. "Jeff, come on." I try to keep my voice down so I don't draw attention, but can feel my face and ears burning with embarrassment. Dropping my head against the door, I sigh. "Jeff, can we act like adults and talk, please?" I knock again, keeping my forehead against the door, closing my eyes, wondering what I'm supposed to do.

"He lock you out?" Teddy asks from down the hall. I close my eyes tighter with a silent 'fuck' as he makes his way down the hallway, stepping back as he draws closer.

Instead of the quiet knock I was doing, Teddy pounds his fist against the door. "Wake up, Jeff! You locked your girl out!" He grabs the doorknob and pushes against the chain, rattling the door. "Come on, asshole, open the door. Let Cass in!" I slump against the wall and slide into a crouch, wishing I could disappear as people watch from down the hallway. "Jeff! Hey! Jeff! Open up!" He looks down at me and winks. "He wants a scene so he can be indignant," he tells me, knowing Jeff'll hear that, too. Now, he kicks the door several times. The door slams shut, but then opens. Teddy smiles at me and sweeps his arm into the open doorway with a bow before heading back to the party.

I whisper, "thank you," with a sigh and close the door behind me.

"Happy now? Make enough of a scene for you?" He heads back to his side of the bed and picks up his book.

"Wait... *me*?" I press my fingers against my chest and drop my jaw. "*I* made a scene? You locked me out. What did you think was going to happen?"

He flips the page of his book. "Guess I figured you'd find some other guy to stay with."

I step back and arch my eyebrows at him, scoffing. "Excuse me?" His gaze dashes over to me before lowering back to his book, which I know he's not reading because there's not enough light. I lift my palms toward him and close my eyes.

Is this how we end? Am I going to be dumped half a world away from home? Is this what's happening?

"Okay, can you please just tell me what the fuck you're pissed about already? And don't give me handing a guitar to Darryl. What the fuck's your problem?"

"Are you stoned?" he asks, lowering his book to his lap. "Did I *give* you any weed?"

"No," I snap, folding my arms.

Before I can continue, he throws the book down the bed toward the TV. "Didn't I tell you not to take anything unless I gave it to you? God damn it, Cassandra, do you listen at *all*?"

"It's *weed*, Jeff," I argue. "We've gotten stoned a million times before now!"

"Who gave it to you?"

Resting my hands on my hips, I close my eyes tight, waiting for his bellow. When I don't hear anything, I open them to see him looking out the window with his arms crossed over his chest. "Jeff, what the hell is going on? I don't know what I did wrong!"

He turns to me, his expression bathed in the light from the TV. His eyes narrow, and his lips are tight, but he drops his shoulders and arms. "You're not one of the boys here," he tells me in a low, even tone. "And you keep acting like you're one of the guys, and people are talking."

I cock my head to the side and blink at him. "I'm doing what I always do. I always talk to the....."

"You're my *girlfriend*, damn it. Not a session player. Not a tech. You're not one of the God damned *boys*. You can't hang out with the crew when we're on stage! You're supposed to be with the rest of the girls in the designated section in the audience so we can keep an eye on you and keep you *safe*. All you seem to do is pretend like you don't know anything. You take pills from Teddy, you sleep through the morning, and hang out with the techs in the afternoon!"

I jerk a finger at him. "First of all, Teddy has never done anything to hurt me, so why the hell wouldn't I trust him?"

He works his jaw again, grinding away. I wonder if he did more coke while I was out there. Folding his arms, he cocks his head to the side, uninterested In hearing what I have to say since he tries to answer me.

I talk over him.

It's my turn to speak, even though my hands are shaking and my heart hammers against my chest. "And *you* gave me the pills that would make me sleep. *You* told me I wasn't going to hear you this morning, remember? Now, you're pissed that I did exactly what you said I would?" I narrow my eyes at him and shake my head. "For your information, I hung out with the crew all afternoon because being with them meant I could be closer to *you* backstage and not have to talk about fucking eye shadow and stupid shoes with the bimbos they're cheating on their girlfriends with!"

I motion with my arm toward the door. "Did you tell *them* not to treat me like one of the boys, like they *always* do? Because if you did, they're not listening. Are they getting fired now, too? Am I supposed to suddenly become someone different because we're in a hotel room and not at the studio? Is that it? Or are you pissed off because someone teased you about my hanging with the techs and not the sluts?"

He opens his mouth, but I continue, jabbing my finger in his direction again. "If you *ever* grab my arm again, I will walk right the-fuck-out of here, and you will *never* see me again. Don't *fucking* lay your hands on me. *Ever*. And lastly? Get the hell over yourself."

I storm to the bathroom, my turn to slam the door and lock it. I drop back against the wall and drop my head back, closing my eyes tight to keep from crying with anger. It's taking every ounce of my strength not to walk back out into the party and sleep in the damn lobby instead of that bed with him.

He wants to keep an eye on me when I know damn well that when I'm not here, he's doing exactly what I'm seeing Teddy, and Darryl, and Gary do. He's picking up some cute, willing groupie and having fun, but I can't talk about guitars with the tech five feet away from where he's playing drums? I strip down and turn on the shower, hoping it might calm me down.

I come out wrapped in a towel, crossing the room to my suitcase without glancing at him, grab my nightclothes, and go back to the bathroom to dress. He doesn't deserve to see me naked. I go to my side of the bed, climb under the blankets and hug the edge of the mattress with my back to him. He's lying on his side with his back to me, a chasm between us. I'd sleep in the other bed if it weren't so bogged down with bags and luggage.

I don't even know if he's awake or asleep at this point, and I'm too angry to care. I'm too angry to sleep, but I don't want to drag this on any further. I close my eyes but open them again with the flickering of the TV. Getting out of bed, I turn the damn thing off.

"Hey," he whispers when I climb back into bed.

"Go to sleep like a real person," I mumble, punching the pillow under my head to fluff it and resettle.

"No," he says, the mattress giving as he turns, "I mean, hey...."

I look over my shoulder. The window blinds are open, so it's not like it's dark in here with the way the city is lit. He's facing me, lifted on his elbow in shadow. I see the outline of his curls against the window and the roundness of his shoulder, the muscle of his upper arm. "Go to sleep." I turn and drop my head down with a huff.

"I had a bad night. I took it out on you."

"No shit," I mutter, still not moving, my hands in tight fists curled against my chest.

He rests a hand on my shoulder, and I immediately stiffen. "Cass, come on…."

"How about an apology, Jeff?" I turn to look at him over my shoulder. "Can you even say the words?"

"I'm sorry." I almost hear his eyes roll.

"Yeah," I grumble, rolling away from him, "because that was from the heart."

"I feel like…." He releases a heavy breath and shifts away from me, "like you have no idea what any of this is."

I scoff and drop onto my back to look at him. "I don't. But that doesn't mean you have to babysit me."

"Then why the hell am I worried every time I lose sight of you?" He turns his face from the ceiling toward me. "I never know what you're getting into or where you're running off to."

"I got into exactly the same shit you're into, and I didn't run anywhere. I was next to the stage or here in bed. It's not like you had to search far. It's like you want me to act like the other girls fawning over you. You know that's not who I am. I thought that's what you liked about me."

"No, that's not…." He exhales. "Never mind. I can't explain it."

"You seriously think I'm going to go off with one of the techs?"

"No."

"I'm going to take some random drug from some random stranger I never met?"

He hesitates but answers, "no."

"That I'm going *anywhere* without you? Without telling you?"

"You just did."

"Bullshit. You knew exactly where I was and you locked me out because of it." He's silent, which means he admits it. "I don't know what your problem is with me. I can't read your mind, but I seem to do something wrong at every turn. One minute it's not my fault, the next, you're pissed at me. I'm not allowed to fit in with the guitar techs. I don't fit in with the girls on the road…."

"You did," he says hastily. "When we first met, and that night at the Roxy."

Tears prick my eyes.

He sighs. "Like I said. I can't explain it. I don't want you to be like those girls out there, but...." There's a pause. "I need you to figure out time and place. You usually read situations better."

"And you're not usually this grouchy. You're so busy worrying about everything and what everyone is thinking you lost perspective."

"Cass," he sighs. This time he's sincere and rolls onto his side again to face me, reaching out to rest a hand over the blankets on my stomach. "I'm sorry."

"I've felt like I was out of my depth since I got here, but I didn't think you'd blame me for it. You knew I never did a big tour like this. I've *never* been a groupie. I didn't know what all this entailed and how you got by. Now I do, and maybe it's best if I go home so you can stop worrying about me, too."

"I don't... no, don't do that," he says with a quick panicked breath, his hand still flat against me but stiffening. "I don't want you to go." His voice is soft, almost inaudible. "Let's just get some sleep and start fresh tomorrow."

I sigh, feeling the tears sting my eyes as I blink up at the ceiling.

He shifts closer with a whisper, "please, stay."

I don't know if he's trying to hold on to me or on to some reality that's no longer familiar to him. Maybe he wants to hold on to someone who holds him accountable for his behavior. Maybe, just maybe, he is sorry he hurt me and does want me around, although I'm having a hard time believing it. Maybe he wants me to stay because he loves me. Maybe he doesn't even know why, but he moves to wrap his body around mine, holding me tight, whispering, "stay." I'd swear he's shaking.

I lie stiff and still for a moment, breathing into the shadows, trying to figure out how we got here, but my heart softens to this scared little boy, holding on for dear life right now. His vulnerability takes me by surprise after being so volatile. I release a quiet breath before placing my hand in his curls as he rests his head on my chest, clinging to me with his whole body.

"Please. Stay," he breathes.

Four hours later, the lobby has been cleared of groupies. Limos line the front of the hotel. Everyone acts like last night never happened, including Jeff. While we packed up, he chatted about today's schedule as I tried to stay out of his way. Now, he's laughing with the tour manager. He takes my hand as we head out to the limo and offers me a smile. "You okay? You're quiet this morning."

I don't know how to respond, so I attempt to smile and lift a shoulder.

He leans over and kisses my temple, stepping aside to let me in the limo first. "You can sleep on the plane. You'll feel better once we get to Boston."

"You're…" I begin, but afraid I'm going to set him off again.

He gives me a soft look and leans over to kiss me gently as the car slips into traffic.

"Never mind," I sigh.

He kisses me again before he rests a hand on my head, bringing it to his shoulder and kissing the top of my head. "I'm glad you stayed."

I lean against him with another silent breath, watching the buildings slip past us in the gray morning light, wondering, *'for how long?'*

Chapter 8

"Seriously? We have to do this?" Darryl whines as I come into the studio a few weeks later. Motionless, Jeff sits behind his kit with his chin lowered. All I see are the frizzed-out curls on the top of his head as he grips his drumsticks at his waist. Gary sits behind a keyboard today with his chin dropped into his palm. Teddy wanders in a small circle with his head lowered, too.

They're *still* working on that album, and I know it's driving each of them slowly insane. No one wants to think about doing it, much less work on it anymore. It's why Jace keeps adding short little tours trying to inspire something, thinking that if they play the old stuff long enough, new stuff will sprout out of sheer boredom. All it seems to do is make them hate one another and the music. I'm guessing Jace just announced another mini-tour by their reaction.

"When?" Jeff's voice lifts into the silence. He still isn't moving.

"About an hour from now," Jace answers, and all heads snap to him. He nods, lifting his palms, looking at each of them. "I know. You guys hate publicity and short notice, but *I* know that when I give you notice, you make a bunch of excuses and none of you show up. No excuses this time. You need to do this and be *nice*. People are starting to forget who the hell you are, you're taking so long. This will help remind them you're still around."

"How can they forget who the fuck we are when you have us out on tour every other damn week?" Teddy argues.

Jace turns to him and sweeps the room with his arm. "There's this whole swath of land between the big cities we book you in, gentlemen. They buy records, too."

"Reading an article in *Creem* magazine isn't going to make them buy a record we can't get made," Darryl grumbles.

"Okay, how about this?" Jace turns to Darryl first, but looks at them all in turn. "You have a contract. This is part of it. Smile and deal with it." His eyes land on me standing near the door. "And *you* need to go."

I press my fingers against my chest, unsure if he's talking to me.

"Yes. No Yoko's."

"*What?*" My stomach drops to my knees. I glance at Jeff, but he doesn't look at me. "He invited me in so I could use the piano in the studio for something I'm working on."

"No girlfriends," Jace says, eyes still on me. "Ruins their reputation."

"I was *invited*," I mutter under my breath before crossing the studio to hand Jeff a bag filled with a change of clothes and some papers he wanted me to bring. His eyes are so sad, almost apprehensive when he blinks at me without a word to stick up for me. "Do I need to move out, too, or am I allowed to live at the beach house?" I question Jace with a smirk.

"It's fine," Jace starts with a tilt of his head. "We'll just go to Teddy's if we need to take the reporter somewhere else."

"I was *joking*, you ass," I mutter without looking at anyone. So much for working on that song I wanted to finish today. I cross the room and slam the studio door behind me. My stomach churns with anger as I stomp down the hallway. I take umbrage with being called a 'Yoko' when I'm hardly ever in the studio with them anymore. Heck, I'm hardly ever in the studio period unless it's to drop something off for Jeff. Jace, as *my* manager, should know that I've been working on my songs and using a reel-to-reel A-3340S TEAC to record them at home. I can't break the band apart if I never see the damn band. Plus, Jeff invited me in to use the piano. I didn't even ask. He offered.

Yoko, my ass...

I hear the studio door open a second later, and Jeff calls my name. I stop and cross my arms.

"Don't take this personally, Cass." He steps in front of me, dipping his knees to try to get me to look at him. "It's publicity bullshit." Resting his hands on my upper arms, he then lifts my chin with his knuckle beneath it when I don't lift my eyes to him. "None of our girls are public. You know that."

"Oh, you mean I'm not the only *Yoko* in the band?" I lift my hand and shake my head, taking a step to the side to walk around him, but he doesn't release my arms. "Careful. Your reporter might show up early and see us together. Don't go ruining your mystique with some talentless, caterwauling, wanna-be."

"Come on. You know none of us think that. You know what it's like."

"Am I that much of a liability? I didn't realize we were hiding anything."

"It's tricky with the press. I want my privacy. I want it to be about the music and not people pokin' their noses into somethin' that isn't their business." He looks down the hallway in both directions before leaning in to kiss me. It *doesn't* help his case any. "I know you understand that." His voice is soft and tinged with his twang. I wonder if he adds his 'g's when he talks to reporters. I know he doesn't always sound as Texan when I listen to their radio interviews. Does he turn it up when he's trying to get away with something, or does he feel so comfortable with me he that doesn't try to hide it?

I take a deep breath, keeping my eyes on his. Right now, they're wide, a deep-sea blue in the dim hall light, almost pleading. He arches an eyebrow when I don't turn away or smile. I push my tongue against my teeth with a sharp exhale, remembering Jeff and his previous girlfriend when they were breaking up. Didn't she have the same expression I do now? Didn't he? I glance away at the ceiling and shake my head.

"Call me sometime when you have your life back."

He gives a weary half-smile. "I'm never gettin' my life back, darlin'." His voice sounds so disappointed and tired.

"You know what I mean." I sigh, keeping myself from rolling my eyes. I should be more sympathetic, shouldn't I?

"I'll be home later." He takes a step closer to kiss my forehead before giving me a gentle kiss on the lips. "I'm sorry. You can use the piano tomorrow, okay?"

"Just tell Jace that the next time he calls me a Yoko, I'm castrating him."

I stopped to grab breakfast with Hannah a few days later before heading into the studio with Jeff's change of clothes and miscellaneous papers. He's been checking in a little more, kind of like a kid trying to do chores so they can get out of trouble and go to the school dance. I've been trying to keep myself busy. Thankfully, it's not hard to do because Jace lined up a few more bands to potentially use my songs.

When I head into the sound booth, Steve is behind the board with his head in his hands. I hear Teddy and Jeff snapping at one another, Jeff behind his kit, and Teddy behind the keyboards, on opposite sides of the room. In frustration, Jeff slams his drumstick on his snare three times with enough force to snap it, then tosses the pieces into the air and stands up. His gaze lands on me. "I'm taking a break," he announces, not looking at anyone, and heads across the room. Everyone else seems relieved.

He comes into the booth and grins at me before giving me a quick kiss. "Hey," he sighs. "You got any plans?"

"Me? Now?" I hand him a brown paper bag with his stuff and a folder. He drops it on the couch behind him and slips his hand into mine, motioning with his head for me to follow. Stepping into the hallway, he waits for the door to close and leans against the wall, still holding my hand.

"What's that all about?" I ask, looking at the closed door.

"Same ol' bullshit." He rolls his eyes. "Seriously, you got plans today?" I start to say something, and he closes his eyes. "Let me put it…." He exhales. "Can you cancel what you were gonna do?"

"Why?" I ask, drawing the word out, cocking my head to the side. Does he want me to help them in the studio? Have another errand for me?

He glances at the closed door with a slight wave of our hands between us. "I really wanna play hooky. I wanna get out of here." The corner of his lip turns up with a devilish grin. "Wanna play hooky with me?"

"What'll *they* think?" I motion to the door.

"They'll be here when we get back. Nobody ever leaves." He leans forward and kisses me, letting it linger. "What do you say?"

"I…" don't want to be a Yoko, hearing Jace's comment in my head from earlier this week. I need to work on some things and get the dry cleaning, but I don't have to do it all right now. He arches an eyebrow and keeps his eyes on mine. They're bright sky blue today, and I can't remember the last time we spent any real time together. "I'm in," I confirm with a nod and a smile. A few hours with my boyfriend does not make me a Yoko. Besides, Lennon asked Yoko to hang around. Whatever happened with the Beatles wasn't entirely Yoko's fault.

"Far out." He leans over and kisses me again before tugging at my hand. "Let's go."

"Where do you want to go?" I ask, following him down the hall, glancing over my shoulder as though the school principal is going to come chasing after us.

We slip out the side door to the parking lot. He shakes his keys free, patting his back pocket for his wallet as we head to his car. Coming to my side, he opens the door for me like that first time we went to dinner. He slips on his sunglasses in the car and revs the motor, sliding into traffic with confident ease.

"Let's just see where we end up," he answers, resting his hand on my thigh. Already, he's left some of the tension behind. He smiles easier. Even his shoulders seem to relax. He grins at me and opens the window, taking the turn for the Pacific Coast Highway. I slouch into the seat, kick my shoes off and rest my feet on the dashboard. When he gives me a look for that, I stick my tongue out at him, making him laugh. He reaches over to brush his fingers through my hair, blowing with the open windows. "When you see something interesting, let me know. We'll stop."

We don't talk a whole lot, but there's an ease between us, at least. Stopping to have lunch at some little roadside place on the water, we then wander a flea market. Outside of the studio and his usual haunts, no one bothers him. A few people might recognize him. A few girls giggle in his direction, and some guys' mouths drop open, but no one approaches. He's almost an Average Joe out here in the wilds of California. We take our time walking through the stalls, holding hands. Sometimes, he wraps his arm around my shoulder as we walk.

I miss him. This. Being with him and not talking about the album, not about songs, not thinking of the next tour, TV show, or radio interview. Out here, he's not a rock star or a musician. Even he doesn't have that distracted, distant look like when he's plotting, planning, and scheduling and lets himself relax. I'm his girlfriend—*just* his girlfriend—not his gopher and personal assistant *and* girlfriend; and I like how it feels. I like the way he looks at me when we sit to have a drink, reaching across the table to take my hand and run his thumb over the back of it. I like watching him watch the world around him without being in a weed haze or on a coke binge, and I don't even know how long it's been since I've even seen it.

We wander down the other side of the flea market. I buy a macramé purse. He buys some tee shirts and a lamp that will look great in the living room. I turn to him as he pays for it, running my hand down his arm. "Is this the first piece of furniture you've bought for a house?" Everything we have now is rented.

He lifts it and cocks his head to the side with a chuckle. "You know, it might be."

I reach over and brush his curls back, leaning in to give him a warm kiss. "Congratulations."

He seems to straighten, and his eyes crinkle with his smile. "I bought a lamp." He chuckles, his arm out straight, holding it in front of him, so proud of himself. We head back, picking up dinner to take home with us. I grab the food. He takes the lamp and shopping bags from the backseat and follows me inside. Teddy's voice barks when I open the door and I glance over at the phone. The machine's picking up his message. It's just a stream of angry curses before he screams,

'Get your ass back here now!' and hangs up.

Jeff puts the lamp and bags on the dining room table and looks over to the sideboard where the answering machine blinks with unheard messages. His shoulders drop, along with his face. Neither of us wants to listen to those messages, but aside from Teddy's ranting, there may be messages for me about my work, but I can't bring myself to hit play.

"Let me shower and change, and we'll head back so you can get your car, and I can get mauled by Teddy," he says, all energy drained from him, like this afternoon never even happened.

"What about dinner?" I ask, keeping my voice tender. "You're gonna need to eat."

He's already starting down the hallway, running his hands through his hair. "I'm not hungry. Just… stick it in the fridge for now." As he disappears into the bedroom, I hear his sigh.

"Rock star reporting for duty," I whisper.

A week later, the *Creem* article comes out with a headline *'It's Good to Be Kings.'* I don't get past the picture they used on the cover. The guys sit together on a couch in Teddy's house, each of them shirtless with their instruments. Jeff sits with drumsticks in his hands like he's tapping them on the girl's ass that's draped across his lap. The band stares directly at the camera without smiling in that 'sexy brooding' look. By the glassy redness of their eyes, none of them are sober. More half-dressed girls drape themselves over the others, paying no attention to the camera.

When Jeff comes into the kitchen, I drop the magazine on the table in front of him. "Sure gonna sell a whole lot of records with that. Nothing says musical credibility more than half-dressed groupies on your lap."

"We have no say over this crap. You know that."

I arch my eyebrows. "Right. I was a threat, and this," I point to the cover, "is all about the music and screams integrity?"

"I'll say it again. We don't have any say over it. They call to fact-check. They don't call for an integrity check."

I roll my eyes, knowing they don't, but it still irks me. I can't be in a twenty-mile radius fully clothed and working at the piano, but this… this is somehow acceptable and is a comment on their credibility as musicians? "Obviously," I mumble.

"Obviously." He sips his coffee and turns to the article. At least the next image is a stage shot from one of their tours. "D'you approve

of this…." His voice trails off, and he pushes himself up in the chair, folding over the article. His head lifts and he glares at me.

I lean back a bit and widen my eyes. "What?"

"Who the hell did you talk to?" His eyes narrow.

My eyes widen further as my mouth drops open. "No one! Why?"

He turns the magazine to face me and pushes it closer, his finger stabbing at a paragraph.

While Expedition is an expert in writing their own material, this time around, they've enlisted the help of Kingston's sometime girlfriend, Cassandra Taylor, a former session player (Curt Parents, Jackson Browne, Bell Telephone jingles). It's rare that Expedition invites girls into their inner circle for anything other than decoration. While Expedition has been busy writing this album, Kingston's been seen with Taylor on a more personal level. She has co-writing credit on at least one of the new songs and is one of the few session players to break out of the session player pigeonhole. No one is certain if the song led to a date, or a date led to the song. Hearing the track, although not penned exclusively by Expedition, it has all the hallmarks of sounding exquisitely like them, with their usual outlook on life and love in Southern California. It's possible Expedition may have birthed a songwriter while trying to birth their long-awaited album.

I push the magazine back at him. "I didn't talk to anyone."

"Well, *someone* did!"

"Well, it wasn't *me*! I had to hide, remember?"

"You didn't have to hide," he grumbles, scanning the rest of the article.

"Just not be seen. Either way… I wasn't. When would he have talked to me if he was with you guys draping groupies over your lap?" I flip to the cover photo and motion to it. "Maybe he saw the song credit and asked some questions. It's on the songs list. He could have done some digging on his own like, oh, I don't know, a *reporter* does. Was no one supposed to know I helped with a song? Is that why you were so proud of me that you gave me a guitar so I could pretend I never wrote something on the album?"

"I don't need the speculation about my relationships in some stupid magazine."

"It's buried in the middle of the article. Who the hell is going to care?"

He curls the corner of his mouth and tilts his head at me. "You'd be surprised."

"You got another beach house where you're keeping some other girl? Is she mentioned in a different paragraph?"

"You're not funny. They had no right putting it out there."

"Who did the fact-checking? Go bitch at them. I'll keep a low profile, so you don't have to acknowledge me in public, okay?"

He exhales heavily, pushes his chair back, and picks up the phone. Glancing at me over his shoulder, he stomps out of the kitchen, the telephone cord following him down the hallway. "Jace? Who the fuck approved this shit in *Creem*?"

I slip out of the chair and pad toward the hallway, almost ashamed to eavesdrop on his conversation, but I tell myself it concerns me, too. My name is in that paragraph.

"I don't give a shit if people know about her. Why is he *writing* about her? We have five other tracks finished he could be talking about." I pull back slightly and bite my lips. "It tells me we have more fucking work to do." He's silent a moment. "Her song *is* good. That's not my point. My point is that ours need to be better."

My boyfriend is freaking out because an international rock critic wrote a paragraph about me? It's his insecurity speaking, right? I am one hundred percent certain their songs are far more polished and Expedition sounding. He's too panicked about finishing and how long it's taking them to do it. I slink back to the kitchen table to read the rest of the article, hoping to find something that highlights the other songs, but honestly? They're featured on the cover of *Creem* magazine. How can he be worried about one stupid paragraph in a three-page spread? A tiny voice in the back of my head questions why he isn't excited for me about my talent getting recognized. Still, I shove that question back into the darkness of my brain. He's tired and worried about his band, that's why. This isn't about me.

He comes back half an hour later and drops the receiver into the cradle. "Jace approved it. The guy saw your song credit and did some digging. Jace wanted to let them know you had real credentials as a musician, but didn't think they'd mention the dating. Typical Jace getting his money's worth out of publicity."

"Oh." I lift my shoulder and look out to the beach with an ache in my stomach. "Would it be that awful to have to acknowledge..." my song is good? "... your relationship with me? We live together. It's not like people don't know I exist. Groupies have all sorts of random pictures. You never know...."

He heads out of the kitchen without even acknowledging what I'm saying.

"They talk about Lana, too, you know." I turn the magazine and point to a section, but all he does is glance over his shoulder.

"That's Teddy's problem."

Problem? Interesting word choice.

Jeff comes into the living room a few hours later to find me on the couch with my guitar and notebook. He's in a pair of jeans and one of his band tour shirts. I don't acknowledge him, trying to finish this verse. Out of the corner of my eye, I see him fold his arms and lean a shoulder on the wall in the hallway, but still keep my head down to my notebook, scribbling the last few ideas down before looking up. "You need to head out?"

"Is that what you wanted the piano for the other day?" He takes a step closer, arms still folded.

I strum a chord and lift a shoulder. "I reworked it. I'm better on guitar, anyway." I don't tell him it took me all day to rewrite it, and now it's turned into something else in my head. With a glance at my notebook, I strum another chord.

"I just realized I never actually watched you work." He shakes his head. "I mean, on your own stuff."

I glance around me. There's a notebook on the couch cushion beside me, a mug of tea on the coffee table in front of me, the reel-to-reel pushed back further on it, and my guitar on my lap. I'm wearing white shorts and a plain blue tee shirt with my hair pulled back in a ponytail. There's not much excitement in watching what I'm doing. I shrug and give a quick grin. "Tah-dah?"

He strolls in, steps down into the living room, and rests his hands on the back of the easy chair across from me. "What're you working on?"

"Not sure yet. I think it wants to be more rock than I'm letting it be right now, but...." I crinkle my nose. "I don't know, still trying to figure it out."

He looks at my little setup, his eyes darting to the notebook and pencil, the reel-to-reel, and back to my face. When he does, his expression changes. His eyes aren't as bright, and his smile dims. "I miss that." He motions to me with his chin, a soft twang nestled in his 'that.'

"What?" I glance back down. "Tea?"

"How simple it used to be writing a song." His voice fades, and his chest lifts with a breath. "Lack of pressure…. Your own thoughts without fighting…." He turns his head to the beach for a moment. Clearing his throat, he straightens with a sharp breath. "Anyway, um… I'll leave you to it."

"Thanks, I just… I'm supposed to meet with someone tomorrow, and I'd love to have this finished." He nods, barely smiling. "Do you have time? I should be done in, like, an hour? We can go for a walk? Early dinner?"

He points a thumb at the door. "Nah, I should head into the studio. God knows that album isn't makin' itself."

"Oh." I don't know why, but I suddenly feel guilty. He's been home most of the afternoon, and I've been here writing instead of with him. "You sure? Half an hour? I just want to get this down."

He shakes his head, but his eyes are soft when he looks at me, and his smile warms. "You write." He steps closer, leaning down to kiss me, but draws it out a bit longer than I expected. As he pulls back, he motions again with his chin to the notebook and a quick wink. "Get back to it, now."

"You'll be home tonight?" I pick up my pencil, watching him grab his wallet and keys from the sideboard.

He puckers his lips and tilts his head. "We'll see. I'll call." He heads to the door, glancing at me over his shoulder with another grin. "Get to work."

I smile and tap the pencil's eraser against my forehead in a salute. Once he's out, though, I drop back into the couch, watching the empty door with a sigh, feeling as if I missed something, but I'm not sure what. More and more lately, I keep catching that sad look in his eyes, almost a longing. Today, it almost felt like a longing for me, although I've been here.

Since I got back from their tour, I've been on a creative streak, and while Jace may call me Yoko, he's still managing to line up some artists to showcase some of my songs. Yesterday, John Boylan called me… *the* John Boylan, record producer and sometimes manager John Boylan… to see if I had something for Linda Ronstadt. That's what I'm working on. That's why I didn't blow this off to hang with Jeff. But after his reaction to my name being mentioned in his article? I don't know that he'd be excited for me. Then, there's that look in his eyes just now. Deep down, I know he'd understand needing to finish this just as much as I understand when he needs to work. But still, when I hung up with Boylan, I called Hannah to squeal with excitement. My stomach tightens with guilt because I haven't told Jeff.

I sit up and sip my tea before settling the guitar back on my lap.

I'll tell him tonight when he comes home… *if* he comes home tonight. Whenever he comes home, I'll let him know. I look back to my notebook, scribbling another line, but sigh, looking back at the empty doorway. I have a distinct feeling he was trying to reach out to me.

My stomach tightens again a few hours later when I call to talk to him at four o'clock, but the sound tech tells me he's not scheduled to come into the studio until eight tonight.

Cars pull up to the house, and moments later, Jeff's voice comes up the driveway, among others. The front door opens with sounds of more laughter and chatter, a few girls' voices, along with Jeff, Teddy, and Darryl's. The light flicks on, and the stereo suddenly blares. Before I take the guitar off my lap and stand up, Jeff sticks his head in. "Hey, babe. We got company. Come on out." I take a breath, and he steps in. "What's your problem?"

"What?" I climb off the bed.

"You gave me a look," he says, keeping his voice low. "It's my house, too, you know."

I widen my eyes at him. "I didn't say anything." He presses his lips together and curls up one end. "Jeff, I'm in bed wearing shorts and a tee shirt, working. I wasn't prepared for company, okay? You realize it's 1:30 in the morning, right?"

He glances at the alarm clock on the bedside table. "I didn't, no," he says, but now he gets playful and gives me an impish grin. "But you're awake."

Yeah, I'm awake—working on a song and wondering where the hell you've been for the last twelve hours. I'd love to see how he'd react if I tried something like that.

"Come on, come hang out with us." He stretches his hand out to me, keeping his other on the doorknob.

"Can you give me five minutes to put some clothes on and brush my hair, at least?" I step out of the shorts and grab a pair of jeans from the floor as I watch the door for someone to come barging in.

"Only if I can get you out of your clothes later." He giggles. He only giggles like that when he's wasted. Stepping further into the room, he pulls me into his arms and kisses me hard. I can taste whiskey and the bitterness of the cocaine. "Damn, you're sexy."

"And you are wasted." He rubs his nose against mine with another chuckle. "Give me five minutes, okay?"

He steps back but leans in for another quick kiss. "We have beer and stuff, right?"

"Beer in the fridge, stuff in the sideboard." I pull a tube top on under the tee shirt before lifting it over my head.

He stops at the door again and blinks at me. "Where'd you get that?"

"Get what?"

"That top?"

"In New York. Why?"

He shakes his head. "Just never saw you in something like that." I'm not sure if he means he likes it or doesn't. "I'll meet you out there."

"In a few, yeah." I head to the bathroom, putting a dab of mascara on at the last minute. It'll have to do, considering they're probably all completely wasted and won't care what I look like, anyway.

When I cross the dining room to the living room, the boys are on the couch, and there are three girls I've never seen before with them. There's a brunette who's a bit heavier with wavy hair hanging in her face. Her blue eyes, although glassy and red, peer out between strands of her hair, and she smooths her hands over Darryl's thigh as if claiming him.

Then, there's the petite brunette next to Jeff in a red halter top with exposed shoulders and cut-off jeans. Her hair hangs long and straight down her back in a low ponytail. She's got the heel of her bare foot digging into the cushion and gives me a long once over with an arched eyebrow. I return the look, wondering if she's where he went this afternoon while I was working.

Teddy realizes I'm here and calls my name with a drunken laugh. A slender blonde in a pink miniskirt and halter top has her legs draped over his lap, her hand resting on his crotch. She's not Lana, his girlfriend. I wonder how many times Lana has watched Jeff cheat on me and never said anything either.

Jeff lifts his head from the line he's doing on the coffee table and smiles at me, opening his arm out for me to join him. I'm happy I tucked my work away on the dining room table. Little Petite on the other side of him doesn't look particularly pleased, but he doesn't seem to care. I drop onto the couch beside him and kiss him, long and hard, claiming my property. He returns it just as fiercely, thanks to the coke, and hands me the straw to do a line. At this point, I may as well. It'll help me catch up to them.

As usual, the powder floods into my bloodstream, and I turn to kiss Jeff again. I still love how turned on it makes me, the way his fingertips feel on my skin when he presses me back into the cushions.

We separate, and he's looking right at me, his gaze darting across my face. "God, you're sexy," he mutters before kissing me again.

I watch his jaw tighten and clench between sips of his whiskey and laughter as he turns to the party guests. Between the coke, there are cigarettes and potato chips and a whole lot more alcohol. The girls are backup singers for the band Breezy and were hanging out until their lead singer passed out on the couch in the studio. That's when they came back here.

I'm not sure the girls knew Jeff had a girlfriend waiting for him, and some of them might have had different ideas about what was going to happen. If I weren't here, it probably would have. Jeff's roaming around barefoot already, his shirt undone completely. He's flirting with each of them but keeps touching me, his hand on my knee or thigh, the small of my back, holding my hand. I don't know if that's to reassure me or let the girls know he's got his girl or if it's plain old guilt because he's already screwed around with one, or all, of them at the studio.

The girls reshuffle within the hour and flank Darryl and Teddy instead. They also decide to go play in the water, which I think is a terrible idea considering how wasted everyone is. My dissent is dismissed, so we all head down the deck. A floodlight points on the sand by the surf, and the girls decide it's the perfect spot to strip down and play naked in the surf. Teddy strips to his boxers. Darryl strips completely. I stay on the sand, laughing as they splash and run around.

Jeff comes up behind me. "Wouldn't be hard for you to join in." His fingers reach to the front of my tube top and he pulls at the elastic fabric, snapping it back into place.

I squeal and press my hands against my chest, pulling back from him, not quite amused, although he's laughing. "I'm fine where I am, thanks." This whole thing feels wrong and I try to laugh it off.

"Always gonna be on the sidelines, aren't you?" he says in a dull, low tone with a shake of his head. He slips his shirt off his shoulders and jogs down to the surf. He's not quite participating either, wearing jeans. He wants to believe he's playing along, but he's playing by his own rules, too. The rest of them splash and squeal in the water, but I step out of the spotlight and head further up the sand toward the house, still watching.

Waiting.

One of those girls will go for him if they see I'm not there. I'm pretty confident about which one, too. From the shadows, I hear the girls squeal as they're splashed. Initially, Jeff stays in the perimeter, occasionally reaching down to slap the water when one of the girls comes close.

Darryl is so drunk that when he tries to kick the water, he loses his balance and lands on his ass in the surf as a wave crashes and soaks him. Everyone laughs at that. Wavy brunette keeps splashing Darryl and seems to have set her sights on Jeff off to the side. She takes several steps toward him, kicking water at first, and then bends down to splash with her hands in his direction, her boobs seemingly getting in the way. She stands up, gripping them with her palms, her eyes on Jeff. He has a wicked grin on his face watching her, the corner of his mouth curled up. He opens his hand and leans over to the water, but Darryl is right beside her and grabs her ankle. She loses her balance and drops beside him into another wave.

Blondie and Teddy seem to have paired off already and focus on getting one another wet with intense splashing. I'm not surprised. Teddy always goes for the blondes. After Wavy ends up in the surf, Blondie pretends to lose her balance and falls against Teddy. The only time she's not squealing is when she's shoving her tongue down Teddy's throat.

Jeff takes a few steps forward now, kicking at the surf more and laughing, soaking Wavy and Darryl as they try to crawl out of the water. Little Petite takes it upon herself to defend her friend and steps in front of Wavy, splashing Jeff. "Be nice! Be nice," she squeals with her high-pitched laugh.

Jeff laughs and turns his attention to splashing her, now. Wavy attempts to splash around Little Petite to get Jeff. He steps forward and sprays Wavy in return, but Petite doesn't back away. Instead, she steps forward as he stands up from the surf, wraps her arm around his waist, and they kiss. Moments later, they part when Teddy splashes them, but I don't need to hang around and watch anymore.

It's not like I didn't have an idea he'd cheat on me, especially after seeing what I saw on the road. But it's a whole other thing watching it happen in front of me. It's something else entirely when he brings it home to you. I wipe tears from my eyes as I head back to the house, trying to keep my breath steady, trying to figure out what the hell is happening, denying the truth splayed out right in front of me.

Then I realize I was Little Petite. Jeff had a girlfriend when we hooked up, and I didn't give a second thought to her. He brought me home to the bed they shared, to the house they lived in. My stomach drops with a good idea of how she felt when she came home to find the bed a mess. Did he leave the bed unmade on purpose, so he *would* get caught? I wonder how long she managed to stay? Was that some kind of message? Is that why he brought *this* girl home? Does he *want* me to see this and break up with him?

I stand with my back to the beach on the deck, listening to the squeals and laughter. Each one is a sucker punch in my gut.

What lies did *she* tell herself to make it okay? How many more am I going to tell myself as red sirens wail in my head, whirling in panic. *I don't want to lose him… I don't want to lose him. I'm not okay sharing him.*

About five minutes later, Jeff comes into the house soaking wet, leaving wet footprints on the tile floor. I'm in the kitchen pouring myself a scotch, trying to get my head around what is going on. He turns me around from the counter and takes me by surprise when he kisses me, his lips salty from the ocean. I feel the fine grains of sand beneath my hands when I place them on his chest, returning the kiss with the same desperate passion.

I pull back. "You kissed her." My tone is accusatory but breathless.

He takes my hand and leads me down the hallway to our bedroom, closing the door behind us.

"Why did you *kiss* her?" I try again, my heart racing, but I don't know if it's anger or want.

He kisses me again with a desire I wasn't expecting. Peeling his jeans off, he steps toward me. He wasn't wearing anything beneath them. That's why he kept his jeans on. After living with him, I realized he's self-conscious about his physique. It's why he keeps a shirt on. Even though it's open, it hides his shoulders. He didn't want to get naked in front of everyone, either.

"I don't have anything to prove…." I try again as he reaches for my tube top and slips it down to my waist. His eyes bore into mine, taking my thoughts from me. I'm confused and angry, but I still want to grab him and kiss him until my chin is raw and my lips are numb. I *want* to be ravaged by him when he looks at me like that, and he kisses me as if he's trying to prove a point, but I don't know to who.

My jeans get unbuttoned and unzipped, and we step toward our bed. Without another word, I lose the rest of my clothes by the time we hit the mattress and cling to each other, kissing long and hard, grabbing onto the other, pulling us closer.

The stereo turns up when the party comes back inside. Loud voices and laughter ring out in the living room, but no one bothers to look for us. Maybe we're making more noise than I think, and they don't have to search for us. He's done way too much coke for this, but we fumble and grope, anyway. It's not the best sex I've ever had, but I feel claimed and he…. I'm not sure what he was trying to prove.

Our sheets have sand in them. Jeff's passing out. The sun's coming up. The noise from the living room quiets to murmurs, moans, and mumblings. Jeff's arm flops over my back as he sleeps on his stomach, breathing deep and loud. I close my eyes, trying to focus on the sound of the ocean to drown everything else out, everything this night was, the sight of Jeff kissing that girl in the surf, the nagging voice in my head that regrets letting him touch me just now. Tears slip onto my pillow silently, but I'm not sure if they're sad or angry, maybe both. I don't like anything that's happened tonight. Myself included. I feel cheap. I feel used. I feel confused.

Not much later, I wake to Jeff attempting to pull me closer, nuzzling my neck, but I reach back and push his shoulder away, grumbling, "no." He doesn't want to hear it and moans against my shoulder, his hand coming to rest on my breast. I pull away more and snap, "stop."

With that, he groans and drops heavily onto his back. "What's your problem?"

I blink at the window in front of me, trying to figure out something to say, clutching the sheets in my fists. "I'm sleeping."

"No, you're not."

"I was. I feel like shit. I'm tired, and I don't even know what the fuck is going on, so no."

"What do you mean 'what the fuck is going on?'" I feel him roll onto his side to face my back.

I close my eyes for a moment and take a quick breath. "You were kissing some naked chick last night."

"She kissed me. It happens."

"You kissed her back. I watched you do it." I blink, watching the leaves of a bush sway outside the window as those words eat away at my insides.

He sighs, and it turns into an annoyed groan. "You didn't care last night."

It feels like my lungs are over-inflated and my heart pumps anger into my veins. "I did care last night. I walked away, remember?"

"And I came to find you," he snaps. "*Remember*?"

"What'd you mean by 'I'd always be on the sidelines,' Jeff?" Tears sting my eyes. I'm surprised by them, try to hide them, and clear my throat.

He groans again. "I don't fucking know. Nothing. I just said it."

I don't believe him and lie still, biting my lips together.

"Why do you constantly refuse to just let go and have some

fucking *fun* every now and then, Cassandra? You always overthink everything."

"How is me being embarrassed fun? I didn't see you dropping trou and running wild in the buff. Were *you* having fun?" I sit up and turn to face him, sheets tangling around my legs.

"I joined in." His eyes slant at me. "You walked away."

"When you started kissing her!"

"She kissed me!"

"You didn't push her away. I wasn't going to stand there and watch."

He sits up and shakes his head, his hair matted and sticking up. "Ever think that maybe she wouldn't have if you were part of it? You didn't use to walk away. When I first met you," he jabs a finger toward me, "you wouldn't have."

"I'm not going to fight for you, Jeff." I raise my hands and let them drop to the mattress, shaking my head. "You have to want to be here. I'm not going to beg."

"Where the fuck am I, Cass?" He slaps his hands against the mattress on either side of him. "How the fuck am I cheating on you when I came to the house to find *you*? An' she probably felt like she *could* kiss me because I was out there on my own. My girlfriend was standing around hemmin' an' hawin' an' worried about what other people might think of her when she's barely dressed in the first place, I might add, instead of just joining in the God damn fun like the rest of us."

"I wasn't as wasted as the rest of you. God knows when the hell you all started. I called the studio, you know. You weren't scheduled to be there until eight o'clock, but you left here at three. Then, you come back home from where ever the hell you were, wasted and high, with a bunch of strange girls, and say we're having a party?" I poke a finger into my chest with each statement, making a point. "I wasn't drunk. I wasn't stoned. I was working half an hour before you showed up. But, as usual, what *I* was doing doesn't mean shit to you." I wave my hand forward and tilt my head side to side. "You show up, and the entire world has to stop on its axis, and I'm supposed to drop everything.

"A bunch of girls I've never seen before, strip naked, and somehow, I'm wrong because I don't want to run around with boobs flopping in front of people I'm going to have to work with. Jesus, Jeff, *you* didn't even get naked in front of them, but *I* was supposed to?" I drop my hand to the mattress with a thump between us before crossing my arms over my chest. "I walked back to the house. I didn't ask you to come with me. I didn't make a scene. Why are you pissed at me? For letting you do what you wanted? If you don't like how I act, why the hell don't you just break up with me?"

His head draws back, and he blinks at my outburst as though he were surprised. "Why don't *you* break up with *me*?"

I feel breathless, and my gaze scans him for something, only I don't know what. But my heart answers, "because I love you, damn it!"

"Well, I love *you*! This shouldn't be this God damn hard, Cass!" He runs his hands through his hair and shakes his head up at the ceiling. *"Damn it."* He takes a deep breath and pushes the sheets aside before stomping to the bathroom and slamming the door.

I sit for a moment, looking at the door before I untangle from the sheets and get dressed. Wiping the few tears that spill over, I pick up the tube top and hold it a moment before dropping it in the trash. *So much for trying to fit in*. I put on a pair of shorts and a dark blue tee-shirt, nothing provocative or exciting about any of it. Nothing that will raise an eyebrow or draw attention, as usual. As I head out of the room, Jeff comes out, looking for me in the bed and around until his gaze lands on me. "Where're you going?"

I reach for the doorknob but turn to face him. "I want coffee. We have a house full of people who will most likely want coffee, too." Although I'd like to poison it and make little Miss Naked Surf Kisser chug it.

"They're gonna be passed out for hours still," he says with a wave of his hand, heading over to his chest of drawers. "Let's go for a walk on the beach."

I drop my hand and blink at him. "Why?"

He pulls a tee shirt over his head, turning to me. "Because I want a do-over," he says, curling the corner of his lips. "This morning sucks, and I'm not in the mood to keep fighting with you. Let's just take a walk and clear our heads."

"Can I make coffee first?" My voice is flat, not feeling all that 'over it.'

"Make enough for both of us," he says, stepping into a pair of clean jeans as I open the door.

Am I crazy? What the hell is going on? He kissed another girl in front of me. I have a right to be pissed off. He insulted me… didn't he? When he said I was standing on the sidelines? He meant that to be an insult… right? He's also much too awake and cheerful, so I wonder if he swallowed a black beauty in the bathroom or did a line or two somehow? Maybe both for all I know. God knows where he's got shit stashed anymore.

No one flinches when I rummage around the kitchen. Teddy and blonde bimbo won the spare room. Darryl and the other two share the couch, all still naked and snoring. I am not looking forward to cleaning those cushions later on. By the time Jeff comes out, coffee has finished brewing. I pour mine, leaving him to do his own, which he does without a word. He stretches his hand out to me, ignoring the fact that there are naked people passed out on our couch. I don't take his hand, but I walk out the sliding glass doors and down the steps to the beach.

Why am I doing this? Why am I going along with this?

Because he's not always like this, that's why. He comes home after a studio session and climbs into bed with me, and wraps his arms around me to tell me about his day in a soft whisper. He drives past a patch of daisies in the neighbor's yard and stops to pick a few because he knows they're my favorite. There *are* moments of clarity between this mayhem and confusion when he acknowledges me for who I am. They're just not as frequent anymore, and I miss *him*. I'm tired of waking up to the rock star. I want to wake up with Jeff.

"Please don't be like this," he says, following.

The sun already feels warm on my face. The wind blows my hair back, and I take a deep breath of the salty air, closing my eyes for a moment as I step through the sand toward the loud, angry surf. Part of me wants to avoid it as though it's contaminated after last night. He comes up alongside me and drapes an arm around my shoulder, sipping his coffee and looking out over the water. It's another perfect California day. I blink back tears and sip my coffee, taking another breath. "Can you...." I begin, but I swallow the words, unsure how to finish.

"What?"

I sigh. "Nothing."

He came to me. He woke up with me. He's here with me now. It has to be enough. I have to accept the half-truths he tells me, or I'll drive myself insane. He's a rock star. Women kiss him. They throw themselves at him. He's going to kiss the pretty girls and hang out with his friends, go to parties and bring parties home. It's part of the package, along with the drugs, alcohol, long hours, and months away on tour. This is the baggage he comes with, and I have to learn to live with it or walk away.

But when he stops in the sand, and I turn to him, despite everything in my head screaming, *run away*, I don't. I let him draw me closer and kiss me, feeling the solidness of his chest beneath my palm, breathing the air he breathes, and feel like I'm drowning.

Coming out from my shower an hour later, I hear Jeff and Teddy's raised voices, but when I come down the hallway, the rest of the house is empty. The bimbos and Darryl aren't on the couch anymore. Darryl's car isn't in the driveway when I glance out the front door. The sliding glass doors are mostly closed over, but not all the way. Teddy's wearing jeans, and his Hawaiian shirt hangs open. His lips press together as he shakes his head at Jeff, his eyes narrowed. "You're a fucking moron," he grouses.

"Fuck you," Jeff returns, waving a dismissive hand as the corner of his mouth curls. "I didn't hear you complainin' last night when we came back here."

"I don't remember coming here *to* complain." Teddy thrusts his chin forward and widens his eyes. He shakes his hair out of his face from the wind. "You keep saying how much you're in love, dude. *You* keep telling me how awesome she is, that you'd be lost without her, but turn around, do this shit and wonder why she's pissed off? *Of course*, she's pissed at you, asshole. One of these days, she's not going to take your bullshit. One of these days, she's going to figure out she doesn't *need* you and leave your fucking ass. Then what're you gonna do? Write a fucking song about it?"

Jeff turns to look at the ocean, resting his hands on his hips. I watch him shake his head as the wind blows his curls, but can't make out what his response is.

"Yeah, well, I love you, you're like a brother to me, but maybe if she does, I *would* make a play for her," Teddy says, resting his weight on one foot and crossing his arms. Jeff snaps his head to look at him. "But she's too much in love with you for me to even have a chance, so get your shit together, Jeff. She's not some dumb groupie hanging on your every move. This one has a brain, and she's going to use it. She ain't dazzled by your money. She ain't gonna be dazzled by your talent the more she starts working with other artists, and your charm and wit only go so far when you're a dick, so knock it off."

I watch Jeff's shoulders drop, but he keeps watching the water with his back to me. Teddy rests a hand on Jeff's shoulder and shakes his head, also turning to look at the ocean. I can hear the rumbling of their voices, but it's too hard to hear actual words now that the wind takes them. But I stand for a moment, looking at their backs. I don't know how long they've been friends, but when I watch, I can see the bond between them. Teddy keeps his hand on Jeff's shoulder. The wind keeps blowing their hair, and Teddy's shirttails back. Jeff nods a few times, and a moment later, they both crack up into a laugh.

I go back to the bedroom and curl up in the bed, closing my eyes tight. I can't think straight. I don't know what I'm supposed to do, who I'm supposed to believe, what I heard. I guess I'm surprised Jeff would say anything about me, much less tell Teddy he loves me. Why would I think Jeff wouldn't talk about me? What does that say about me? I never considered Teddy could be interested in me, either. That he'd see me beyond Jeff's chick or that chick who plays guitar. I know one thing for sure… thank God I didn't strip naked and dance in the surf last night. I wonder if Teddy would tell me where Jeff was yesterday afternoon. But do I want to put him in that position? Put him in the middle? Would that make me a Yoko after all? And really, don't I know where Jeff was? With that chick kissing him in the surf, right? Or maybe someone else, for all I know.

"Hey, babe?" The bedroom door opens. I roll over as he says, "oh, sorry. I didn't know you were sleeping. Just wanted to let you know we were taking off."

"Alright." I roll back again and tears sting my eyes.

He comes to his side of the bed and sits, resting his hand on my shoulder for me to face him. I do and watch his shoulders drop and his eyes soften. "I'm sorry, babe," he says, his fingers combing through my hair with a soft touch. "I know last night was a drag for you. I'll make it up to you." He leans over and kisses my forehead, then the tip of my nose, and then my lips in quick, tender pecks. He drags a finger over my jaw and smiles down at me. "I do love you, you know." I can only nod at him and take a silent breath. "I'll check in later. You'll be around?" He's already pushing himself off the bed and crossing the room.

I doubt it matters if I answer him, but I take a breath and whisper, "no. I'm going to meet Linda Ronstadt with some of my songs. Aren't you excited?" I glance over my shoulder to the empty doorway. "Thought so," I sigh, turning back to the window, hearing his and Teddy's laughter in the driveway. "I'm excited," I whisper to myself, wiping the tears from my eyes. No matter how much I want to, I can't cry. I can't meet a potential client with red, puffy eyes. I can't worry about whether or not my boyfriend is proud of me. He told me I'd have to fight for my career. Today, I have to fight how sick and exhausted I feel to make this happen. I'm a professional, damn it. I have to fight my emotions and act like one.

I walk into the sound booth a few days later after running Jeff's morning errands. I'm late because, of course, they didn't have whatever it was he wanted ready yet. Jeff leans over his kit, sits back, pinching then wiping his nose with a finger, and continues sniffling. His gaze darts around the room, not resting on one thing for long, almost as though he's checking to see who might have been watching him. He's already grinding his jaw and narrowing his eyes at everyone. He gets suspicious and jumpy when he's done too much coke. I hate when he's like this. Thankfully, I can't linger to watch his bad mood erupt. I drop into the studio to hand off his things and am halfway across the room when he calls after me. "Hey, Cass? Where're the contracts?" Jeff lifts his eyes from shuffling the papers in his hand and stomps around his kit.

"I don't know," I say with a dismissive shake of my hand and head back out.

"What do you mean, you don't know? I asked you to pick up contracts." He drops his hand, slapping the papers against his thigh. Darryl and Gary turn their backs to us and drop their chins, pretending to pay attention to their instruments. Teddy bites his lips together and glances between the two of us.

I'm not in the mood for his coke-infused rant today. "You asked me to pick up some papers from Jace." I motion to the papers in his hand. "That's what they gave me. I didn't ask what they were. I figured they'd know what they were supposed to give me."

"Why didn't you ask if they were contracts?" His eyes narrow at me. "Jesus, Cass, I asked you to do one fucking thing for me...."

I glance around the room, feeling my cheeks flush, but anger soon follows. "No, Jeff," I rest my hands on my hips, "you asked me to do about *twenty* fucking things for you without once bothering to ask if I had anything going on. I'd love to stand here and be told how much I suck and what I've done wrong today, but I'm late for an appointment."

"Yeah, an appointment with a career I started for you," he mutters, flipping through the papers again, shaking his head.

"All right, fine." I lift my hand and roll my eyes. "You can tell me about my career, too, later on tonight when you wake me up at two a.m. to dictate to me what I need to do for you tomorrow without so much as a please or a thank you." I shake my head at him and stomp away again with my heart racing and a heavy breath.

"Thank you for not doing what I *asked* you to do," he calls after me.

"You're welcome." I raise my hand with my middle finger sticking straight up without even looking back at him.

"Wait a second!" I hear the papers snap to the floor and the quick footsteps of his boot heels as he storms after me. "You think you're the only one that had shit to do today? I'm sorry, did I *inconvenience* you?" He's a step behind me and takes hold of my elbow with a quick tug.

I whirl around and slap him, taking a step toward him with my finger in his face. "I told you *never* to grab me again. I am *not* your possession."

He lifts his hand to return my slap, but as I narrow my eyes at him, almost in a dare, Teddy, Darryl, and Gary all cry out with "whoa!" or "hey!" and "stop!" Jeff takes a step back, his open palm turning into a tight fist. His lips press into a thin, angry line. His eyes are such a dark blue, they're almost black. Clenching his fist, he takes a few steps back with a slow shake of his head. His teeth grind, and I watch his jaw tighten over and over. He gives me a once over, looking me up and down, before curling his lips and dismissing me with a wave of his hand. "Get the fuck out," he snarls.

"Yes, your *fucking* majesty." I dip my knees and cock my head to the side. I don't know why I continue to taunt him aside from just being fed up and pissed off. It's like I can't keep myself from poking the bee's nest.

He pivots and storms toward me again. "What the fuck is your problem? Huh? You on the rag or something?"

"Right, because I can't *possibly* have an opinion or be fed up with your bullshit without it being blamed on my period." I take a step forward and narrow my eyes at him, leaning closer—my heart slams into my chest. My entire body shakes as I grip my waist with white knuckles. "Ever think the problem might be that I'm *not* on the rag?" Every eye in the room is on me in the sudden, frozen silence, but I only keep mine on Jeff. It stops him dead in his tracks. His chin drops, hands on his waist, and he rests his weight on one foot.

"Yeah, that's how I thought you'd react." I cock my head to the side and smirk. "Relax. You're not gonna be a father."

He lifts his head, the corner of his mouth curls, and he snorts. He arches an eyebrow and those dark eyes narrow into mine. "It'd only be another thing I'd have to take care of for you, anyway."

I lift my palm to him and shove the air between us. "Go to hell, Jeff." I stalk out of the studio in the abject silence around me.

Once the door closes, I lean against the wall, covering my mouth with shaking hands to try and keep the sob silent, but it's pointless.

My shoulders shake as I keep trying to swallow the tears, playing what happened over in my head, seeing that disgust and anger in his eyes. I stride farther down the hallway, praying no one hears or strolls out of their studio. My heart does triple time, and cold sweat drips down my lower back and under my arms. I keep swiping at my tears, but they're coming too fast. I have to calm myself but don't know how.

When I hear the door open, I step faster, needing to get out of here. I can't listen to him or be screamed at about this right now, but the footsteps quickly catch up with me.

"Cassandra…"

It's not Jeff. Spinning around, I see Teddy reaching his hand out to me with soft, sympathetic brown eyes. I fall against him, sobbing.

He wraps his arms around my shoulders, and his chest rises with a deep breath. "Shhh," he whispers, smoothing my hair. "It's okay. It's gonna be okay."

Teddy drives me to his place, never once asking me anything or probing for information. He's been quiet and patient, waiting for me to talk. Putting a mug of tea on the table, he sits across from me, clasping his hands together, and keeps quiet, watching.

I grip the mug, feeling the scalding heat of the ceramic on my palms. "I can't do this anymore." My voice is soft and tired. "I won't keep doing this with him." Tears come again, but now they're silent and simply slip down my cheeks unchecked. I don't think Teddy is going to judge me for them.

"What're you going to do?" His voice is as hushed as mine.

I lift my eyes to him but don't answer.

"He's an asshole sometimes." He lifts his palms. "I know I can't make excuses. But you know him as well as I do. We've been in the studio for four days straight. We're wrecked. Our brains are fried. We keep doing shit to keep us moving and awake—anything to help us find something to get this album done. He's under a lot of pressure, not just from himself, but also me." He nods his head side to side in admission. "The label… You *know* him, Cass. He's wrecked on coke. He didn't mean what he was saying."

I barely nod, but it's not in agreement. Pressing my lips together, I take another shallow, short breath. "But I did." More tears come. "I meant every word." I release the mug and sit back into the stiff, wooden chair. Everything seems to be measured and slow, like the faint tick of the clock over the sink. "And I can't keep pretending he's going to wake up one morning and put what's important to me first. He's always going to put himself first. It's time I do that before it's too late and I lose myself completely."

His chest rises in a sigh, and his gaze watches me. "You can't give him...."

I shake my head, knowing what he's asking. "I've done nothing *but* give him chances, Teddy. I can't do it anymore." It's hard to take a breath after I say that. My insides twist and jerk even though no one can see it.

"Cass," Teddy murmurs, his entire body seeming to slump as he takes a breath, bringing me out of my thoughts. "What do you need? Anything?"

"I need you to keep him busy, so I can go back to the house and get my things."

He sits up a bit and blinks at me. "You're not even going to tell him?"

"I will." I wrap my hands around the mug again, lowering my eyes to the coppery liquid, watching it blur. "After I'm out." I lift my eyes back up to him, tears blurring his image, too. "I don't trust myself, Teddy. Please. Help me walk away from this."

Jeff sighs on the other end of the phone the following day when I call him, but I don't get the sense it's in anger or annoyance, more worry. "Where are you, Cass?"

Curled up on Hannah's couch, cradling the phone in two shaking hands. But I don't want him to know.

It didn't take me long to get my things. I lingered, knowing he wasn't leaving the studio thanks to Teddy distracting him for me. When I looked around, I realized I could leave almost everything. My clothes and my guitars were all I wanted. I couldn't take the sound of the ocean to lull me to sleep, or the warmth of his arms around my waist when he climbs into bed after a long session, or the sound of his laugh—the way it crinkles the corners of his eyes. It's been too long since I've seen that anyway, and has been replaced by those darkened, narrow slits glaring at me.

I headed out to the deck to sit on a lounge chair, curled my legs up in the moonlight, and watched the ocean take away whatever illusions I had. By the time the sun came up, my suitcases and guitars were in my car. From there, I sat on some side street, trying to figure out what I was supposed to do as my stomach clenched and my brain scrambled. I refused to let myself think of missing him. Thinking about him paralyzes my insides, and I can't catch my breath.

"I'm sorry, baby," he says when I don't answer him. "I was so far out of line. I know I was. I'm havin' a really crappy week, an' I was taking it out on you. I didn't mean to." His twang is back. It's how I know he's sincere.

I still can't speak.

"Cass? You there, baby?"

I shift on the couch and close my eyes. "I'm here," I whisper.

"Where are you? Let me come get you. We'll talk. We need to talk all this out."

"No," I breathe, closing my eyes in resolve. Too much has happened. Too much has been said.

"Please, let's talk." His voice is sad and gentle. "I know I screwed up. I want to fix this. I do love you."

I hold my breath even though a sob is aching to break out of my chest. "You too," I manage, dropping my head back to blink at the plain white ceiling. "But I won't...." It takes every ounce of strength I have to continue. I close my eyes tight and feel like I'm free-falling into a dark abyss. "Take care of yourself, Jeff."

This whole thing isn't happening. At the last minute, fairy magic is going to swirl in the room and catch me, fix it, only this is too raw and real to believe in glittery stardust fixes.

I do things out of habit. Things I've done a million times before that I don't think about—because I can't think. I can't let myself think. I do things like putting the receiver down in the phone cradle because that's where it belongs—even though I still hear him talking on the other end.

In the silence that follows, I take a deep breath, wondering what I'm supposed to do next.

1983

Chapter 9

As I wait in the studio for my 9:30 appointment, there's a quick tap on the door as it opens. Mike, the studio director, peeks his head in and grins before opening it even further. "Hey, Cass, can I barge in here a second? You don't mind, do you? Just giving a quick tour of the place." It's strange for Mike to be showing someone around as the owner, but then he steps aside, and my heart stops. "Do you know Jeff Kingston? You guys ever cross paths?"

Jeff smiles, and it crinkles the edges of his eyes like it used to. My heart and stomach somersault together, trying to hide the catch of my breath all at once. "Oh, we've met," Jeff says, his voice light and cheerful. "How're doin'?" He leans over to kiss my cheek, his eyes searching mine, looking just as shocked by my presence as I am by his.

I put my arms around him in a quick, awkward embrace and inhale the spiced earthy scent of him. Gone are those pretty, wild curls I used to loop around my finger lying in bed. They're cut short into rumpled waves and brush back off his forehead. He's clean-shaven, filled out, broader chest. My mind wanders to how it would look bare now, more solid beneath my fingertips somehow? But his eyes… his eyes are still the same faded denim-blue with that hint of a darker rim that seems to hold the color in place, soft and gentle as he looks at me.

"How're *you*?" I ask, flustered and blushing for no reason aside from the fact that I've managed to avoid speaking to him for seven years. The first few by choice—the last because our paths didn't cross anymore.

He sticks his hands into the front pockets of his jeans, and he lifts his shoulders around his ears quick. Classic Jeff Kingston. Classic nervous habit. "You know, same old grind. Checking out new places to record." He reaches out and brushes a hand over my arm. I take a breath as he does, ambushed by memories of sweaty nights with ocean breezes and spilled champagne. "What about you? What're you up to?"

Mike starts speaking again. I wish he'd disappear. I wish time would stand still for a second so I could stare at Jeff and soak him in without being watched. He hasn't lost his smile, and he keeps looking at me with those eyes. *God, what does he remember? What's he thinking?*

"So, you're thinking of recording here?" I ask Jeff, trying not to sound too curious, as though I'm making conversation. It'd be smoother if I didn't interrupt Mike in the middle of a sentence to ask him.

"Yeah." Again, he lifts his shoulders. What's *he* nervous about? "I've got some things I'm looking to do and thought Cornerstone would be off the beaten path."

"I don't know about that." I chuckle. "It's pretty beaten from where I'm standing."

"Right?" Mike agrees, picking up his sales pitch. "Maybe not as slick as Record Plant or Sound Factory, but it's 1983 and we can compete with the best of them. We got the best songwriters, anyway." He wraps an arm around my shoulder with a bright smile before looking at Jeff. "Why don't I show you Studio B? I think that's more of what you might be looking for."

They turn to leave and I'm close to taking a breath, but Jeff turns around. "You in town long?"

"I live here." I smile.

He pauses a second and glances out the door before turning his gaze on me again. "Oh, I thought you..." He shakes his head and I can see those curls wiggle in their halo in my mind's eye. "Can we... I'd like to have dinner with you... sometime, maybe soon?"

"How long are you around?"

He grins at me. "I live here, too."

"Tonight?" I ask before the rest of my brain catches up. Get it over with. If I have to wait, I'll make up some excuse and not go through with it. I'll have too much time to think about what happened, and I've worked very hard not to think about it. "My place?"

"Um, tonight's good. I can do that." He nods with that little boy grin. *Oh, that little boy grin....*

I turn to the desk and scribble on my pad, tear the page off, and hand it to him. "That's my address." I don't know what to expect and don't want a restaurant full of people gawking at us while we eat. If I can eat. I'm already flustered. "7:30?"

"7:30." He leans over to kiss my cheek again. "You look great, Cass," he murmurs as he pulls away. Just hearing him say my name again sends shivers dancing down my spine with a flood of memories long buried. I am totally unprepared for him again and sit back down at the soundboard, looking at the empty doorway.

How is it seven years already? I've seen him at a few events we both attended but managed to maintain our distance: a quick glance, a simple nod of recognition, nothing more. I haven't *spoken* to him since that last time over the phone.

Now I remember why—I didn't trust myself.

I'm still not sure I do.

Is it coincidence or occupational hazard that Jeff Kingston enters my life in recording studios? I wonder this for the umpteenth time as I chop onions and peel potatoes for the roast chicken I'm making. Questions follow with each slice of the knife. What am I doing? Why am I doing this? What was I *thinking*? What good could *come* from this? Why does he want to have dinner with me? After all this time? What do we have to say to one another?

Even so, I'm not prepared for Jeff walking back into my life. I've never seen him coming and once he shows up, I feel like I've been sleepwalking. Just his smile makes my entire being take a deep, calming breath. *Why*? What spell does he have over me, even after all this time?

There aren't many answers. I keep reminding myself that it was so long ago. I'm not the same insecure girl. I've built a life I'm proud of, that I love. He shouldn't be able to rock my foundation like he did the first time we met.

I do a once-over of my little bungalow, making sure it's in order. It's not swanky, but it's comfortable and mine. There are two bedrooms, and I added on a music room so I could have clients come to me once we've established a working relationship. It's not on the beach, but I'm within walking distance, and that suits me. Open windows let the warm breeze in, and I listen to every car that comes down the street wondering if it's him. My heart quickens as it approaches and slows as it passes.

Why am I so nervous? It's just dinner.

Then again, it was supposed to be just dinner that first time, too, wasn't it?

No, today, I mean it. It's *just* dinner.

If he shows. He wouldn't *dream* of standing me up, right? Mind, he's not late yet. I'm just nervous. Another car comes down the street and stops. I glance out the front window when I hear a car door slam and force myself to stay sitting on the couch until he knocks. I don't want to look too eager, after all. I want to look like none of this matters. I have a life. I want him to see that I don't need him in it, that I've managed just fine without his approval and guidance. Although, I still hear his words each time I start a new contract with someone: *Fight for this, Cassandra. Don't let anyone tell you you're not good. Prove 'em all wrong.*

If only he knew that in the end it would be *him* I would fight to show what I could do. Again, my world runs in circles.

When he knocks, I glance once more at my reflection in the mirror by the door before opening it with a smile. One thing that hasn't changed in all this time is my make-up. I still don't pile it on, wearing only a touch of blush and a bit of mascara. My hair is shorter, though, just below my shoulders, and held off my face with a colorful rolled-up scarf.

"Am I late?" he asks as I step aside to let him in.

"Right on time."

He kisses me on the cheek and offers me a bouquet of daisies and a bottle of wine. "It was daisies, right?"

I grin and nod. "My favorite," I confirm. "Thank you."

"Worth it for that smile."

My cheeks burn with a blush, and I grin, looking down at the happy flowers. "Come in. Dinner should be ready in about half an hour. Should we open the wine?"

"Sure. Why not?" He glances around the living room. There are comfortable overstuffed chairs and a sofa arranged around a glass coffee table. Colorful beach prints decorate the otherwise plain white walls. The floors are polished bare wood with a white throw rug in the center. He hesitates, unsure where he's supposed to go.

"Kitchen's this way." I feel like I'm a hostess at a restaurant, not my home, and start down the short hallway to the kitchen. I turn my head a bit to glance at him, but his eyes are taking in everything. How can seven years make so much of a difference and yet not change him at all—aside from the curls? He seems calm, anyway. My palms are sweating with nerves. "Hungry?"

Coming into the kitchen a few steps behind me, he grins. "I like that hallway."

I furrow my eyebrows and glance behind him, resting the flowers on the counter before taking a vase down from a cabinet to place them in.

"Eight gold records, Cass? That's fantastic."

"One of them is yours," I chuckle. "Started the whole thing rolling for me."

He pushes his lower lip and tilts his head to the side. "I just got there first. Someone would have figured out your talent, eventually."

"Thank you." My cheeks burn again, and I turn to get wine glasses down to distract myself from the blueness of his eyes. My kitchen walls are the same blue. *Damn it.* I'm never going to forget that now. "What are you doing in Los Angeles? I thought you moved back to Texas?"

"I was going to ask the same thing." He laughs. "I heard you moved to New York. What happened?"

"I spent more time flying to LA than being in New York and, well, my best friend is still here."

He furrows his eyebrows and squints in thought. "Heidi?"

"Hannah," I correct him with a grin. He's trying so hard. At least, making an effort. "What about you? What brought you back?"

"Same thing," he says, peeling the covering from the cork as I slide a corkscrew over the counter toward him. I fill the vase and arrange the daisies. "I kept coming back. All my work is here. It was only meant to be a temporary thing, anyway."

"What was in Texas?"

He concentrates on opening the wine a moment and I get a second to look at him again. His jaw is still strong and those crinkles around his eyes make his smile come to life. He pours the wine and hands a glass to me. "My sanity was in Texas," he answers in a low, quiet tone, making me even more curious. "Apparently, I lost it somewhere, and it showed up there."

I'd love to probe *that* comment deeper but don't feel like I have the right. He obviously doesn't want to talk about it, looking as sheepish as he does, avoiding my eyes when he glances up. Instead, I take a sip of wine and turn to check on the simmering potatoes, saying, "slippery little sucker, isn't it?"

"You could say that." One of the stools creaks as he settles at the counter across from me. "When'd you come back?"

"About three years ago. You?" I glance over at him, trying to keep myself busy to keep from gawking at him. It's surreal to have him here, to speak to him. Here we are, pretending like we're old friends catching up instead of a couple that crashed and burned.

"Two. It was time to get to work on another album, and I was tired of trying to do it long distance, FedEx'ing tapes to my producer, and all that bullshit."

I open the oven and take the chicken out. "I didn't know you released a new album."

He chuckles. "I didn't yet. That's why I'm looking at studios. I've got most of it done aside from about three songs, now. It's time to start laying down the tracks, and I was looking for some new places. I feel like walking into the Record Plant is just gonna give me the same old record, you know? I needed a change of scenery. What do you think of Cornerstone?"

Resting the chicken on a plate, I continue busying myself with prepping dinner. "I love it there. Mike's great to work with and, well, you heard his sales pitch. He talks me up to everyone that comes in the door."

Jeff motions with his chin toward the hallway. "Doesn't look like you need much help."

I grin. "Well… just in case the work dries up, it's nice to have something waiting in the wings."

"Can I do anything?" he asks, standing up and rubbing his palms together. He's rolled up the sleeves of his white Oxford and his arms even have a slight tan. As always, he's in faded comfortable blue jeans sans bell bottoms, of course. "What can I do?"

"You can carve." I pull open a drawer and rest a knife and fork next to the chicken as he comes around the counter.

Even with the scent of chicken filling the room, I can make out the soft spice of his cologne with him standing so close. I think he's happy to have a task to keep him busy, too. Who the hell *are* we? Where's that rock'n'roll confidence? "Do you still play?" he questions.

"Occasionally. I'm doing more collaborating and writing than anything, really. Darryl's had me on his last album, though."

"Yeah, I heard. Your playing always impresses me."

"Any plans for Expo? You only released that one… what was it? Three years ago now?"

"Mmm," he hesitates, "not much right now. We're all kind of doin' our thing for the time being. I'm working on this solo album. Teddy's trying to get another one out so we can compete for the sales again." He chuckles. "I'm not sure Gary wants to leave his cows. You know he's got a dairy farm in Kansas, right? He got a little burned out on the industry."

I glance at him. "Didn't we all?" I tease as he laughs and nods, looking down at the chicken. "So, is that it? Is Expedition over?"

"Nah." He lifts a dismissive shoulder, concentrating on carving the chicken. "If we were able to get that Godforsaken album out in

'77 and managed to tour it without shooting each other, we'll never break up."

I wonder if he remembers I was around for that album. Six months of it, anyway. It took them *another* six after I left to release it. I secretly watched the charts, waiting to see when it came out. I couldn't bring myself to go to a show when they toured it for a year.

"We just give ourselves time to do the shit we want we to do first, now." He smiles at me. "I think we're trying to make up for lost time, I guess. I mean, I'm not particularly champing at the bit to do another solo album, but I gotta keep myself busy, right?"

"I think that's how I ended up on Darryl's album." I laugh.

He cocks his head to the side. "You had to fill time?"

I smile at him. "Ebb and flow, like always. Besides, I would never turn Darryl down if he asked me to play on his album. I'm thrilled he even wants me on it. I wish he'd do more instead of just producing like he's been. Not that he's not a good producer, I just love hearing him play."

"Yeah, he still blows me away, and I got to watch him do it every night for a millennium or twelve." He shifts at the counter, turning his head to the side with his sarcasm. "At least he's still playing guitar and hasn't gone over to the electronics and synthesizers."

I groan. "And just when you thought it couldn't get any worse…? They add *keytars*!" I grouse. He cracks up, and the sound makes my heart skip a beat as I drain and prep the mashed potatoes.

Laying in shadows on our king-sized bed, windows open to the sound of the ocean, and that laugh in my ear….

"What the hell are keytars?" I manage to choke out. "I mean, how do you rock out on a keytar solo and look cool? You don't. It's impossible. You're playing a portable keyboard. You press it. It makes a sound. It's what they're designed to do."

He's still laughing. "You have some opinions about this."

"They're about as cool as the kazoo. Hate the stupid things." I chuckle. "Come to think of it, a kazoo is more interesting. I went to dinner with a guy once who played one, keytar, not kazoo. He spent a good hour trying to tell me that it took skill to play it. We were at a restaurant that had a piano and I went over and started playing it. You know, a real live, baby grand, all 88 keys? He still wanted to tell me that keyboard was harder because it had more dials." I turn and put my hands on my hips, facing him. "I've been working in a recording studio for years. I know my way around a soundboard and he wanted to argue dials?" I exhale sharply and wave a dismissive hand. "He was an idiot."

"Did he know what you do for a living?" He stands back, the chicken carved neatly and arranged on the plate.

"Some people still think it's cute that I'm a *girl* in the music industry." I sigh. "I don't waste my time trying to change their minds anymore. I just prove them wrong."

"Atta girl." He chuckles.

"Yeah." I laugh lightly, too. "Took me long enough, eh? Why don't you put that on the table and take a seat? Everything is ready."

We sit at the kitchen table and busy ourselves with plating our food without really saying much aside from, "here you go," when I put some peas on his plate.

He says, "thanks."

My hands are sweaty and I wonder if my cheeks are flushed. I suppose I could blame it on the heat of the stove. My heart skips a beat when he smiles over at me and looks away. He's been busy biting his bottom lip. I don't know if he realizes he's doing it.

Once we fill our plates, we try to have a conversation again. He compliments me on the chicken. I thank him. In between, we keep glancing at one another like we're kids in study hall and look away when the other looks in our direction and we blush. The meal is only so engaging. There's only so much you can say about a roast chicken.

After another five minutes of glances back and forth, he puts his knife and fork down and sits back in his chair. "Thanks for doing all this."

"Sure." I smile at him.

"And thanks for agreeing to see me," he continues, his voice softening. "I know this is uncomfortable for you. I just wanted a chance to tell you how sorry I am for… well, everything."

"Oh, Jeff. It was so long ago." I attempt to blow it off. Be the bigger person, right? Play it all down. It's been *seven* years.

"Doesn't matter." He shakes his head and curls the corner of his mouth. "I was an asshole to you, and you deserve an apology for that and more. He takes a breath as he turns his head toward the window. "I want to say it was the coke talking and put all the blame on that, but it wouldn't be fair. I'm taking full responsibility." He rubs his palms over his thighs as he talks, his shoulders tense and his gaze locks onto mine. "And I'm sorry. It was a shitty thing to do to you and believe it or not, I still think about that day." He works his bottom lip again for a moment. "I… I play it over in my head and think about what I wish I'd said differently or done. An' I know I can't take any of it back, but I wanted you to know. The second I saw you today, I had to take the chance."

I take a quiet breath and swallow, trying to keep the tears from my eyes, not realizing how much I wanted to hear him apologize. "Thanks," I reply, barely above a whisper, looking down at the grain of the wood in the table.

"Did Teddy ever tell you he punched me?" I glance at him, crinkling my forehead, and making him chuckle as he continues to run his palms over his thighs. "Yeah. After you stormed out that day. I turned around to say something but got a right hook. Dar and Gary didn't even try to stop him." He laughs, albeit a little stilted. "He had a crush on you, you know. Teddy did."

"I'd heard that." I nod, pushing peas around my plate.

"He never asked you out?"

My fingers fiddle with the edge of my napkin. "I politely hinted that I didn't want him to. He was always going to be in Expedition and…" I shake my head. "I don't know. It was too hard. He's been a friend, though."

"Good." He picks up his fork and starts sticking his peas with the tongs and scooping mashed potatoes. "I'm glad. He never talked about you, even when I asked."

"I asked him not to."

He blinks over to me.

"I didn't think you deserved to know. I mean, I figured you'd know anyway because LA can be a very small town sometimes, but I asked him not to share details."

"He didn't share squat." He chuckles.

"He didn't say anything about you, either."

He lifts his eyes to mine. "Did you ask?"

I hesitate. Of course, I wanted to know what he was doing, the truth behind who he was seeing, how he was getting along. Was he happy? Did he miss me? Did he talk about me? But, no. I didn't ask. "I wanted to."

His gaze scoots from mine and he looks down at his plate. "But didn't."

I shake my head. "Do you have any idea how hard a break-up is when you see your ex in newspapers, on TV, and magazine covers? And then, you're wandering through a mall somewhere halfway across the world, minding your own business, and hear him singing over the sound system? I'd go to work, and someone would bring up the new single, a new album, solo careers starting… You were impossible to get away from, Jeff. I had a good idea what you were up to for a long time."

"Hmmm." He nods with consideration. "That sucks. I'm sorry."

I offer him a smile. "Something I kept in mind the next time a rock star came knocking on my door."

"Bet there's a path."

I stick some chicken in my mouth and chuckle. "You didn't see them taking numbers around the corner?"

"I paid 'em all off so I could be first in line." He smiles and his eye crinkles deepen.

My heart melts just a little more, damn it. I'm torn from them when the phone rings and we both turn to the sound.

Ring.

I check the clock over the doorway.

Ring.

Jeff looks at me as I sit, stuck in my chair.

Ring.

"Do you need to get that?"

Ring.

"So, what're you doing now?" I question, keeping my eyes on Jeff, doing my best to ignore the click of the machine as it picks up, hoping I turned the volume down. I can hear the low rumble of a voice, but thankfully, the volume is set low. "You going to go with Cornerstone?" I ask, pretending that message doesn't exist, stabbing some peas with my fork.

"Yeah." He casts his eyes down the hallway and back at me. "I booked time before I left." His eyes scan over his shoulder toward the phone and he rubs a palm along his jeans before inspecting me, gaging my response to the message. "I think it'll be the fresh start I need." His gaze holds mine and I swear there's more of a question there. He drops his eyes down and his shoulders lift with a breath as if to say something, but doesn't. When he lifts his gaze, they hold on to mine in a long pause. It looks like he wants to tell me something. There's *more* there, but I don't want to get into it.

Instead, I push the conversation forward. "What dates?"

He looks back to his plate and starts eating again, avoiding my gaze for a second. For all he knows, that message is from a client and I don't owe him an explanation. "March through September." When he looks at me, he's smiling again, the awkwardness dissipating in a breath. "I'll see where I stand at that point. I reserved the next six months, just in case."

"I was gonna say six months for you to lay down the tracks of an album?"

"I'm trying to get better at that. The last one only took me eighteen months."

"That's progress," I tease.

"Baby steps." He nods and crinkles his nose. "I don't like to rush these things."

I crinkle my nose back at him. "It's worked for you."

"Yeah, I think this music gig might work out for me."

"Like there was ever another option for you?"

He rests his fork down and looks out the window. "Yeah... no. I don't know what the hell else I'd ever do. It's the only thing I'm good at."

"I wouldn't go that far."

Tilting his head to the side, he seems to snort. "No?"

"You have your moments, Jeff, but you've always been very generous. You have an ear for hearing other people's talents and guiding them." I point to the hallway. "Case in point. Multiple Grammy-winning Fiona May, another." He drops his head to the side and curls his lip up in consideration. "I know you helped Gary buy that dairy farm because he made some poor investments." He arches an eyebrow at me before focusing on the pans scattered on the kitchen counter over my shoulder. "You have a good heart beneath all that ego and pomposity. It took me some time, but I figured out that you use that ego as your armor, keeping people at bay when they get too close."

"When *I'm* getting too close," he says in a whisper.

I smirk. "That, too."

"I didn't realize you knew that."

"Jeff, I lived with you. Anyone that's spent any time with you knows that. Some are better at waiting you out. Some, you just do an excellent job at pushing away."

"And regret it after I do, once I come to my senses."

I'm not sure how to respond to that. I know "a lady always accepts an apology." It's not that I doubt his sincerity, but I can't forget the pain, even after all these years. I know those eyes are gentle and soft now, but I've seen the disgust and hatred directed at me in them, too. I've seen his ugliness, and it took me too long to get over him.

Looking at him now, though, I wonder if I ever really did. I still want to be part of that world he draws me into with a mere glance. I want to buy into his magic. I *still* don't understand why he has this pull over me. He makes me want to be in his orbit and let him be the sun I revolve around. This time, I'm going to heed the warning flags, though. I don't need to avoid him, maybe, but I don't need to kick down the door and put out a welcome mat, either.

"We all have some regrets," I manage to say. "We need to forgive ourselves, too, sometimes." I give him a pointed look. "Both of us were doing the best we could, given our experiences."

He rests a hand over mine and smiles before he picks up his fork and starts eating again. "You're close to the beach?"

"A few blocks over." I rest back in my seat. "I like being nearby. Taking a walk clears my head after a long day. Where are you now? Malibu?"

"Nah. I moved up into the hills; Calabasas Canyon. Lots of privacy, tons of land, very woodsy." He lifts a shoulder. "No one is wandering up onto the property and asking for an autograph, you know?"

I want to say 'not really,' but nod. Our worlds are still miles apart. I don't know that we'll ever be in the same league, although I don't think I'm nearly as naïve as I once was about his.

"You should come by sometime," he continues. "Take a walk up there. It's a great place to find perspective after a long day of dealing with Hollywood, too. I still can't really cook a whole meal, but I'm pretty good at barbecue."

"You're a Texas boy, you'd better be. Don't they hang you or something if you don't do barbecue correctly?"

"Something like that, yeah."

"Then I can't wait to taste yours. Is there an official board I report you to if it's not up to snuff?"

"Yeah, write to P.O. Box Screw You." He laughs.

I remember how we used to be one-on-one without the pressures of being the people we were *supposed* to be. It was rare, but I hold on to the moments like finding a four-leaf clover among a patch in the grass. Sitting on our deck in the early morning talking about our days, the stories we'd tell about who we bumped into, the riff we came up with, the new melody that came out to play in the studio, that leisurely afternoon of walking around a flea market. When it could be *just us,* living our lives and sharing it, we were at our best. For just a moment, my heart aches for those people we were. When we lived for the discovery of what came next, in between the fear of losing what was happening and not knowing what was coming. There were flashes, for what felt as long as a lightning bolt, when we let ourselves be comfortable with who we were. I forget that sometimes when I only remember the heartache and loss.

"There's a reason you forget that," Hannah says over coffee the next morning in her kitchen. She's bouncing my Goddaughter, Suzie, in her arms, trying to keep her occupied as we talk. Even without a bunch of sleep and no make-up, Hannah still holds that natural California beauty.

"But why? Why do I only have to remember the crap?" I whine. I didn't sleep either. That floodgate of memories opened, and I spent much too long going over details and wondering about what I could have said, should have done, might have changed.

"To keep yourself from falling into the same trap over and over again."

I blink at her with a sigh. "Yeah, I think I failed this lesson several times."

"You do like your pretty bad boys." She giggles, shifting the baby to her shoulder.

"They're *so* pretty, though. And I'll be damned if Jeff didn't get better with age. It's just not fair."

"What do you think that boyfriend of yours would say?" She arches an eyebrow at me and tilts her head like a mother.

I take a quiet breath, not thinking all that much about Ken, if I'm honest. "He had impeccable timing calling in the middle of dinner."

Her bright blue eyes widen. "What'd Jeff say?"

I bow my head, puckering my lips. "I didn't answer the phone. It would have been rude. And it wasn't like Ken left a message like 'Hi, this is your boyfriend calling.' For all Jeff knew, it was a client." My finger traces a flower on the plastic floral tablecloth, avoiding her eyes.

"Well, now I really want to know what Ken said, since you didn't answer."

"I'll let you know when I *tell* him later tonight about Jeff coming by for dinner." I risk a glance at her with a weary grin.

"You didn't tell him?"

"He was in San Francisco with work." I shrug. "I don't talk to him every day. I'm not that co-dependent, and I don't think he'd appreciate me being that clingy."

"Sounds like true love," she teases.

"He's pretty." I tilt my head and grin. "And I didn't sleep with Jeff, so what's the big deal?"

"Did he try?"

Shaking my head, I lean forward to rest a hand on Suzie's back. "Not even a hint, no. He kissed my cheek when he left at a very respectable hour."

She hands the baby to me and laughs. "Careful. You sound disappointed by that."

Patting the baby's back as she rests against my shoulder, I lock eyes with Hannah. "God help me, I am. I wanted him to at least *try*. I went to bed questioning whether he found me attractive or not anymore."

"Well, you're not in your twenties anymore. You may have aged-out for Rock Wonder."

I nod before kissing the baby's head. "Sadly, you might be right. But, he doesn't come off as that party-boy, groupie dude anymore. He was... quieter. Reserved, maybe. Something changed. And I know that makes me sound naïve, and probably gullible, but I know Jeff Kingston. I might have ignored the warning signs, but they were always there. He has different signs now."

"Caution? Bullshit ahead?"

"More like, 'watch new adult at play.' I want to believe he was sincere. He could have just said hello and gone on with his life. He didn't have to come by and apologize."

"Did he do rehab?" she questions. "How many steps does he have?"

"No, I don't think so. They usually tell you if they do and talk about their higher power. I didn't get that, either. I just think he wants to do the right thing. Don't worry, though, I don't think there's anything to be cautious about. He apologized. I may never see or hear from him again. But it'll be nice to be able to say hello if we bump into one another somewhere. Maybe we can just be friendly now."

Hannah shakes her head and smirks. We both know what happened the last time Jeff, and I tried to be *friendly*.

Chapter 10

A week later, I'm packing up from my writing session at Cornerstone with a new British band. They're young, energetic, and boisterous, playing around and teasing each other filing out of the studio. I chuckle, remembering that kind of energy. Nights when we'd be out until two o'clock and then go into the studio to start work on a session. For a moment, it's quiet as their voices fade, but then there's a knock on the door. I lift my head, thinking one of them left something behind. Instead, it's Jeff poking his head in. "Can I interrupt?"

"Come on in. Nothing to interrupt. How's your session going today?"

I wouldn't be able to tell if he's been running his hands through his hair like I used to because those waves would remain as they are. He does look a little tired, though.

"They're coming along, I guess." He leans against the door frame and sticks his hands in the back pockets of his black jeans. "Not as easily as I had hoped, but we're working things out. How about you?"

"They're pretty talented," I say, sticking some folders in my bag. "They've got some interesting ideas about blending disco and punk, so who knows? I don't think they need me, but Columbia wants a babysitter. When they get stuck, they ask for help. That's half the battle."

"Smart." He comes in a little further to rest against the couch and crosses his arms, wearing an oversized gray sweatshirt. "They must know your reputation."

I glance up from arranging my bag. "What reputation?"

Laughing, he sits on the couch arm. "You have a reputation for being a musician's songwriter. Respect a bands dynamic, working yourself into their vibe, not overpowering them with your intentions. And? You'll readily tell a label to back off and let the band create. Real musicians *want* to work with you. I thought you knew that."

Where did *he* hear all that? From who? I don't know where to look, so I go back to arranging folders in my bag, pretending something isn't quite fitting, so I don't have to look at him. "I mean, I heard that some groups *liked* working with me…. But, you know, this whole business is built on word-of-mouth. I just wanted to make sure I was easy to work with."

"You are, and then some." He grins at me, and there's pride in his eyes, along with a tenderness that only makes me feel it stronger.

"Did you need something?" I ask, trying to distract myself from that look by slipping my oversized blazer on and checking if my socks were still scrunched over my leggings. Professional. We're professionals now. *Keep it that way, Cass.* When I ask, though, I sense something deflates in him.

His smile diminishes, and he crosses his arms again. "Not really… well, kind of, but…." He rubs his palm over his mouth for a moment, and I wonder if he's ever surprised to not feel his beard. It's strange for me to see his bare chin. When he pulls his hand back, he's smiling again, although not quite in confidence. "Thing is…" He scratches his head and takes a breath. "I'm having a few people over this weekend for a barbecue an' wanted to see if you'd be interested in coming by. I mean, I owe you dinner, after all." Those eyes turn playful, and his grin broadens a little. "If you aren't busy, that is. It's kinda last minute. Don't think you were an afterthought or anything because I really didn't plan…."

The poor guy is just bumbling his way through this, and I want to laugh. Where's that self-assured, confident rock star? This might be more adorable, even though I can't figure out why he's so nervous around *me*. I mean, it's *me*. "What day?" Like I have plans for either one? But he doesn't need to know that.

"Oh, uh, Saturday. About 3:30?"

"Sounds like fun, but…." It's my turn to hesitate. I have to tell him, right? "I should check with my boyfriend. We might have plans."

If he's surprised or disappointed by that, he hides it well. He merely presses his lips together and nods. "He's welcome, too, if you want to stop by. No big deal. I mean, it was a last-minute invite."

"You'll get me your address?" I've been to a few of Ken's work things and out with his friends. He can come along with me to this. It's sort of a work thing for me. There will be musicians and industry people there… right? I would think….

"You bet. Got a pen?" His smile breaks through, and his chest drops with a heavy exhale, which makes me wonder if he has been waiting to ask me. Maybe he needed to get up his nerve? Lady-killer, groupie king, Jeff Kingston? Needs to get up his nerve? Since *when*?

Saturday, as we turn onto the dirt drive, I look at the view. Open, overgrown fields sprawl on either side with mountains in the distance. I don't even see a house through the trees. It looks like another forgotten country road. I'd question if we were on the right path if I didn't see the single post with reflective numbers indicating house numbers—but that's all there are.

Ken doesn't have to say anything, but I'm sure he's freaking out about his fancy sports car on a dirt road. I also know Jeff, and it's fine for *his* fancy car, so he needn't worry. "How come you never told me you dated Jeff Kingston?" He glances at me from the driver's seat before focusing ahead.

I keep looking at the open fields. "It never came up."

"But he's famous."

I face him but look beyond at the view through his window. "That should make a difference? I don't know about all the girls you've ever dated, do I?"

He tilts his head to the side. "I never dated anyone famous until now."

"Who's famous? Me?" I chuckle and smooth the skirt of the dress I'm wearing. "I'm not famous. I know famous people. You never seemed to care before."

"You never asked me to meet any before," he mumbles. "Least they could do is live somewhere with paved driveways."

After a few minutes, there's a gate. Jeff wasn't kidding when he said people wouldn't stumble upon him asking for an autograph. The drive takes us through more woods and around a curve, which brings us to another view of the mountains, a clearing, and his house. It takes my breath away. The place looks like it's growing out of the ground, blending in easily with the woods with its rustic stone, wood siding, and porch. A few cars are parked in the circular drive, and Ken slips his car into a spare spot.

"So, this is how the other half lives?" Ken gawks around us with wide brown eyes, taking in all this solitude and space.

I rest a hand on his shoulder and chuckle. "*Half*? Try quarter."

We follow the music and voices when we get out of the car to the back of the house, where we're met with another panoramic view of the valley and mountains in the distance. A slate patio, a built-in pool, and a small manicured lawn where a huge brick barbecue greets us, along with a few tables and chairs set up on the property. People mill around chatting and laughing. Some lounge on picnic blankets laid out and held securely in the grass with large rocks on the corners. I recognize one peel of laughter immediately. Scanning the small groups, I see Teddy in a powder blue polo shirt and jeans. I'm shocked to see him with short hair and clean shaven. He sees me at the same time and breaks from his circle with arms wide, making his way over.

"He said you might come, but I didn't believe him!" Teddy wraps his arms around me, and I can't breathe for a second in his tight embrace. I don't mind it in the least, either. I close my eyes and break into a comforting smile like one of my stuffed teddy bears just hugged me. He releases me, holding onto my elbows and stepping back to observe me. "Did you just climb out of your time machine? How come you didn't age like the rest of us?"

I laugh. "It hasn't been *that* long, Teddy, geez. How much have you had to drink?"

He lifts a can of soda pop. "Been on the wagon for four years." He beams with a wide smile.

I hug him again, this time even stronger. "I'm so proud of you."

"Thanks, babe." I'd swear he's blushing.

"Oh, Teddy, this is Ken." I rest my hand on Ken's shoulder and offer a smile. Ken's wearing a pink polo shirt with the collar popped and white cotton pants, the kind with all pockets down the pant legs and that little loop for a hammer… I guess? Not that he would own one. I admit I'm nervous about introducing Ken to everyone. Most of these people will know me through work or possibly when I was Jeff's girlfriend. Maybe that's why this feels so stiff and awkward.

Teddy greets him with a handshake and welcoming smile, of course. I don't know if Teddy's ever not greeted someone with a welcoming smile. "Let's go find our illustrious host and get you two a drink." He wraps his arm around my shoulder and leads me through the yard. I wore a simple blue summer dress with a dark blue belt around the waist and white Keds. Stretching my hand back for Ken, he avoids taking it by slipping his into his pockets. I am not going to make a big deal out of it, but steal a glance over my shoulder at him before saying hello to a few people I know and introducing Ken to a few others as we make our way to the house.

Inside is just as rustic with wood floors, earth tones, and plain wood walls decorated with Southwestern prints and blankets, brown leather couches piled with burnt orange and deep red pillows, and a wall of acoustic guitars. We find Jeff in the kitchen stirring an enormous pot on the stove as others mingle near the kitchen table. Food is piled on trays all over the counter. "I found this one trespassing, Kingston. What do you want me to do with her?"

"We'll hogtie her and serve her for supper," Jeff says, walking around a few people. "Glad you could make it," he says in an embrace, pulling back to kiss my cheek.

My face grows warm with the sound of his voice in my ear, hoping no one will notice. Trying to recover, I brush my hair behind my ear and turn to Ken. "Jeff, this is Ken."

Jeff sizes up Ken in a fraction of a second. I don't even know if Ken sees him do it, but Jeff's gaze dashes toward me before offering his hand to him. "Welcome."

Ken shakes it, but his shoulders are stiff, and there's an equally stiff smile. "Nice place."

I know this is not Ken's kind of crowd. His friends are Yuppie, suburbia, pretentious, trying to one-up each other, dropping dollar signs like ice cubes into a glass for a watered-down rum and Coke. There's no way Ken can one-up Jeff on this level. This is *not* suburbia. This is pure, unadulterated fame, and Jeff now resides here unapologetically. He's earned it with long hours in the studio, years of touring, and giving up his privacy every time he walks into a public place. Jeff breaks free to introduce me to the other folks in the room. I'm handed a beer, and everyone chats around us.

"What's in the pot?" I ask Jeff.

He wiggles his eyebrows and grins. "Homemade barbecue sauce, of course. Can't have a barbecue with sauce from a bottle."

I lean over to peer in. "Impressive."

"Mom's family recipe. If people knew how easy it is to make this stuff, they'd never buy it again," he play-whispers. Then he glances over his shoulder, saying, "I slaved over the stove *all* day." He winks at Ken.

Ken offers a tight grin.

"Bullshit," Teddy replies. "I've been here since nine o'clock, and you were out there arranging picnic tables more than you were in the kitchen."

"You," Jeff points to Teddy with the spoon, "go away. Back outside. Go find other trespassers or something." He waves the spoon toward the door as the rest of us laugh. I missed their friendship. It's like coming back into a family I've been estranged from for years and forgetting I've been gone for such a long time.

"So, what did you do to get roped up with our Cass?" Teddy teases like a typical big brother, handing Ken a beer.

"Blind date," Ken answers, and Teddy arches an eyebrow at me.

"I never got that lucky with a blind date. *Damn!*" Teddy laughs. "Are you a musician?"

"I'm in sales," Ken answers.

"Oh. Is that your red Ferrari out there?"

"You bet. Want to take a look?" Ken puts the beer down and pulls the keys from his pocket. He doesn't like beer. That'll sit untouched unless I drink it after mine. Teddy starts for the door, all questions and curiosity. I grin, watching them, shaking my head. I don't know which one will do more talking because Ken likes to brag about that car, but he should loosen up anyway, especially with Teddy. A few people head outside with them.

Jeff watches them, standing in front of the stove and stirring the sauce. "I think you were just ditched for a car," he teases.

I drag my fingers through the back of my hair with half a grin. "It's quite a car," I mumble, not all that impressed by it. "Teddy'd talk to a tree stump, though, wouldn't he?" I chuckle.

Jeff tilts his head with that playful twinkle in his eye and looks toward the door. "D'you date a lot of tree stumps?"

I roll my eyes with a smirk before looking into the living room. Changing the topic, I continue. "I love your place. It's so earthy."

His smile warms as he follows my gaze. "Thanks. You want the grand tour?"

"Can you leave the sauce for that long? I don't want to be responsible for ruining your barbecue."

He turns the dial down on the stove and winks at me. "I think it'll be okay. Come on." He tilts his head. "So, obviously, the kitchen." We take our time as he leads me through the rest of the house. It's clear that he's proud of it, discussing how he's implemented changes to make it all more earth-friendly and energy-efficient. We stand in the doorway of three of the four bedrooms, but he strolls into the master and stops in the middle of it, clasping his hands in front of him. I stay near the hall and bite my lips together, trying hard not to imagine how much action that neatly made queen-sized bed with patchwork quilt smoothed over it has seen. Nothing is out of place. There's no hint of a dust bunny on the wood floor or a speck of lint on the large braided rug under the bed. As he heads back out, I notice an orange lamp on a small side table piled with books by an overstuffed leather chair.

"Is that?" I point to the corner.

He follows to where I'm pointing, and his smile brightens. "The lamp from that flea market, yes." He nods. "I think it suits the room, don't you?"

"I'm amazed you still *have* it."

"It was the first piece of furniture I ever bought. Once I settled here, I felt it needed to come out of storage." His eyes catch mine, and we both stand silent for a second. That was one of our good days. I wonder what he thinks when he looks at it and remembers that day. We wander through the rest of the house, and he shows me the study filled with shelves of books and his office with a huge mahogany desk. Of course, we linger in the music room because we have to discuss what he records on at home, which guitars are his favorite, and how his drum kit has grown before heading back out to the living room, which is open to the kitchen. He heads back to the stove to stir the sauce since it's been left for almost twenty minutes.

"My little hallway would fit in your music room six times over," I say, following him into the kitchen. The music room also has a wall of gold records and a shelf full of Grammys and other awards.

"I've been in the business six times longer, darlin'," he replies before taking a sip of his beer. "Besides, most of those are a group effort, you know. I didn't win Expedition awards on my own." He stirs the sauce, dismissing his accomplishments.

"Still something to be proud of, Jeff."

"That's why they're on the wall," he says, turning to me. "But, like you, I don't claim to have done it all on my own."

I smile before sipping my beer, noticing a mason jar filled with daisies on the counter. "Where'd they come from?" I motion to the flowers with my chin.

He looks over his shoulder and grins. "Backyard." He reaches over to grab one, taps the stem to get the water droplets off, and then tucks it behind my ear.

I look down, and my stomach tenses, but I glance back up at him with a grin. Somehow, we have become the only two people in the house. My stomach tightens more with the realization, and I head over to the counter, pick up Ken's forgotten beer and take a sip. "So, do you want me to bring anything out for you?"

He hands me some bowls and bags of chips, which I take and place around the tables. It reminds me of a dad's backyard barbecue instead of a mega-rock star's party. Food is placed out once everyone comes back from gawking at sports cars.

I mingle, chatting with Teddy and several other people I know before grabbing another beer, and another hour goes by when I see Ken off on his own again by the side of the pool. I head over to sit by him and look around at everyone else enjoying themselves. "The ribs were good, weren't they?" I ask, brushing a hand over his shoulder. He lifts it. I'm not sure if it's to brush me off or his answer to my question. "What'd Teddy say about the car?" I ask. That should get him going, but he tilts his head. "What's wrong?"

He turns his head to look up at me. "How much longer do we have to stay?"

"I don't know. A little bit, I guess. Give them a chance, Ken. They're fun people."

"Hmm." He turns away.

"Come on." I stick my hand out for his, but all he does is look at it. "Let's go talk to people. I'll introduce you to...." I glance around the patio, but I am pretty sure I've introduced him to everyone. "I don't know. We'll just mingle."

"I really don't feel like it, Cass," he sighs. "We have nothing in common."

"You have cars in common. Did you see what's in the driveway? We all work in L.A. There's got to be *something* in common there." I rest my hand on his shoulder again. "Can you try? You're not going to have any fun just moping around here on your own." Why do I feel like I'm coaxing a kindergartner into going to school? It's not like he's glued to my side when I go to these things with his friends, so I didn't think I needed to babysit him. He's a businessman. He *should* be able to talk to anyone. "Come on." I take his hand, tugging him into standing, and give him a quick kiss. "Pretend you want to sell them a suite at the stadium." He rolls his eyes at me. "Teddy likes sports. He's probably a Dodgers fan."

I lead us over to where Teddy and his fiancée sit near the barbecue. She's got a stick and is roasting a marshmallow in the dying embers. "Teddy, you're a sports fan, right?"

"You bet. Football, baseball, basketball, golf."

"Did Ken tell you he works for the Dodgers?"

"No kidding? *Man,* that's a gig! D'you ever get to go to batting practice?"

"What do you think of that kid, Orel Hershiser?" someone asks.

"You tell that guy, Brock, he'd better snap out of his slump and *soon*!" someone else adds.

Ken should be fine now. He just *might* end up selling something tonight. I step back and let him talk, taking a breath before sipping my beer. Jeff pops in and out, making sure people have food and drinks. I follow him inside to grab a drink for Ken and tell him the ribs are out of this world as he begins cleaning up.

"So, when did this happen?" I ask him, helping with some of the mess.

"What?" He holds the garbage bag open while I toss used paper plates and cups in.

"Domesticity."

He laughs.

"Seriously. I didn't think you knew how to make toast. But…" I motion to the table of food in front of us. He's even made the potato and macaroni salads himself.

"I picked up a few tricks over the years."

"What other tricks have you learned?" I giggle.

Uh oh. I'm flirting with him.

He leans forward, and I almost expect him to kiss me. Instead, he moves closer to whisper in my ear. "Where's the fun in *telling* you?" He winks and offers a smile that's part tease, part mystery as he pulls back. *Damn it.* He's flirting, too. Someone draws his attention away before anything else can be said.

I take Ken's rum and Coke to him, where he's, thankfully, still with some of the guys.

Teddy comes up behind me, pressing his hand at the small of my back, and leads me further into the lawn as the sun starts setting. He folds his arms and smiles at me. "So, when did you and Jeff start speaking again?"

"Didn't he tell you he apologized?"

"Not until today when I showed up, and he was all in a tizzy and flustered."

"What for?" I laugh.

Teddy fixes me with a stare before breaking into a tender smile. "You." He arches an eyebrow and drops his chin a bit. "The one that got away."

"Oh, come on." I roll my eyes.

"When have you ever known Jeff Kingston to apologize? For *anything*?" He gives me another steady look, those deep brown eyes reminding me of another honest conversation when he watched me cry from across a kitchen table.

It makes me uncomfortable to think of that, and I quickly clear my throat. Taking a sip of beer, I scan the yard for Ken and find the daisy patch, which makes me smile. I shake my head and look for Ken again, finding him sitting on his own, looking at his fingernails. Jeff's in a plain blue tee-shirt that makes his eyes bluer, looking casual and relaxed by the patio door, laughing with friends.

"When have I known Jeff Kingston to cook? When have I known Jeff Kingston to be modest or humble even? I don't know who this guy is." I motion to Jeff. "Since when does Jeff Kingston wear *shorts* or *shoes,* for that matter? We lived on the beach, and I never saw him in shorts. Maybe he's the kind of guy who apologizes now. I don't know."

"Sure, he's learned a few skills. I guess he couldn't eat out *every* night of the week for the rest of his life. And, well, after his mother got sick...."

"His mother was sick?"

"He didn't tell you? He went back to Texas and stayed *months* when his mom got sick. When he came back, he had his act together. Hasn't touched coke in three years. I don't know that I've seen him stoned more than twice since."

"Is his mom okay?"

Teddy tilts his head to the side and puckers his lips. "Better. He got them a caretaker to help his dad take care of her. Took some time for her to regain use of her arm and be able to speak again after the stroke. She's better, but not a hundred percent."

I glance over at Jeff again as he laughs. "He didn't say anything about it."

"He did the typical Jeff thing and took care of it without speaking much about it to anyone." Teddy runs a hand through his hair. "I don't know what went down while he was there. Maybe someone said something... I don't know. All I know is he straightened up. I thought he told you, and *that's* why you're here."

"He just apologized for being a dick. Didn't say anything to me. Well, he did tell me you punched him when we had that fight."

Teddy smiles at me and wraps his arms around me again. "Which one? I slugged him on several occasions."

"You probably did, but you know which time, and you did it for me. So, thanks, many, many years after the fact."

"Doesn't matter s'long as you guys are friends again, and we get to see you more often. I missed having you around."

"I've missed you guys, too." I forgot how much I enjoyed being around him, how much I missed feeling like his kid sister. We had a lot of mutual friends back then and grew apart. Today feels like a homecoming.

Well past midnight, the party begins dying down. Teddy and his fiancée, myself, Ken, Jeff, and a few studio guys are the last remaining guests sitting around the patio talking shop. Ken's silent, sitting off to the side and brushing his fingers through his neat short brown hair that never falls out of place. Teddy and I pull guitars off Jeff's wall and play off one another, doing Expedition songs, Beatles tunes, some of their solo stuff, some of mine, which I'm surprised Teddy knows, and anything that comes to mind. Then, I begin a simple melody, and Jeff perks up from the lounge chair and watches me. "Do that again."

"Do what? This?" I play some progression, and he nods, rolling his hand in a small circle to keep me going. "What?"

"Just… keep doing that a second," he says, watching my fingering. I keep playing, watching his face. I know that look. That's his creativity sparking. "Is that something you're using?"

"Just something I play around with. Why? You want it?"

"Wait here." He pushes himself up and heads inside while Teddy starts playing along, his eyes watching my fingering until he's picked it up. Jeff comes out a minute later, holding a notebook, and sits, holding a pen. "Start again?" As I do, he sings the words on the page like the melody was written for them. "I've had this for two years and couldn't find the melody."

"I've been fiddling with this for just as long," I tell him with an easy laugh.

"That's amazing," Teddy's fiancée murmurs. "Is that how songs happen?"

Teddy leans over and kisses her forehead with a chuckle. "With him? Not usually, no."

"Can I…?" Jeff asks me, his gaze searching my face. "I mean, you'll get writing credit, too, of course, but…."

"*Yes*!" I press my hand against my chest. "I'm happy to have somewhere for this thing to land, finally."

"Right?" Jeff laughs, leaning forward again.

I start over. Before I know it, I look up, and it's just Jeff and I left on the patio. He's got a few pages of lyrics, some things scribbled out, more words added. I've added some. He's suggested a chord progression change. It's all written down, and I have happy fluttering butterflies in my stomach from the energy of it all.

"Do you know where Ken went? I should go," I say, handing him the guitar and standing. I scan the yard for Ken, but don't see him before heading inside to check. He's not there either. I wander to the front of the house, lit with small lamp lights, and find him sitting in his car with the door open, looking into the woods ahead of him.

I make my way over. "What're you doing?" I question. Around us, crickets and katydids hum in the woods, and a cool breeze rustles the leaves.

His gaze shifts to me, but his face remains stiff. "You noticed?"

"Noticed what?" We're interrupted by Teddy and his fiancée saying goodbye. The others come out behind them and say their goodnights. Once they leave, I turn back to Ken. "Come say goodnight, and we'll head back."

"Why?"

I do my best not to roll my eyes. I drank a lot. Maybe I'm not following this line of conversation very well. "Just come say goodnight, Ken."

"I'm not going to make him jealous for you."

"Who?" I look to either side of me. "What are we talking about? Why are you pouting?"

He pushes himself out of the car and puts his hands on his hips. "I'm not *pouting*!"

I arch my eyebrows at him and snort. "No? What would *you* call this?"

"He's hung up on you, too."

"*Who* is?" I open my empty hands and shake my head again. "Can you just come say goodnight?" I point a thumb to the house.

He sets his perfectly square chin and puckers his lips. "No."

I exhale and close my eyes, but the ground feels shaky under my feet, so I open them again. "Fine. Stay here, then. I'll go say goodnight for the both of us. I'll be back in a minute. *Okay*?"

He drops back into the car with a petulant sigh. The door stays open, so I don't get the sense that he will leave me stranded as I head back inside, but I'm not sure.

Jeff collects glasses from the patio and looks over with an easy grin. His eyes are bloodshot, and I wonder what I look like right about now.

I sigh. "Ken's in the car. I wanted to come back in and say thank you and goodnight."

His smile dims when he catches my expression. "Everything okay?"

"It will be." I wave a hand and take a step but miss the rise onto the patio and almost trip. He reaches his hand out to steady me. I snap my head to where he's touching me, remembering that last time he grabbed my elbow. I look up at him with a straight face.

He seems to have caught the same memory and releases me with a mumbled, "sorry."

"No, I tripped." I brush my hand over his forearm.

He takes hold of my fingers and squeezes, lifting his gaze to mine.

I look at him and lick my lips. I don't trust myself with how he's looking at me. The way his eyes dart between mine, I don't feel he's checking if I'm okay. It's that look again, that unasked question. Hope, perhaps?

Or, maybe that's me...

I don't move when he leans forward. I don't move as his eyes search mine. I don't move when I notice the slight tilt of his head as he comes closer. I don't move as I close my eyes, waiting to feel the press of his lips against mine, taking a sharp breath when I do. I slip my hand behind his neck and hold him against my mouth in a kiss I've been longing for since seeing him again. I savor his hand slipping into my hair to hold me against his mouth. My tongue recognizes the familiar dance it played with his so long ago, and we don't miss a beat.

When we pull apart, we both blink, waiting for the other to move… say something… apologize. I touch my lower lip. He bites his together in anticipation. Our gazes locked, trying to figure out what we do next, what any of this means. *I don't know what it means.*

"I'm um… I didn't… ah…" he stammers. "I'm sorry."

"Yeah, that's…." I swallow, feeling my chest rise with quick breaths.

Do it again! Please do it again!

"Um…." He keeps blinking at me, anticipating something. Is he as taken off guard by it as I am?

"So, I'm gonna go." I point over my shoulder and offer a weak smile.

"Yeah, okay… right…." He clears his throat and wipes a hand over his shirt. "Ah, thanks for coming."

"Yeah, sure. Of course. Thanks for the invite. I'll, um…."

"…See you around the studio," he interjects.

"Right. Yes." I nod.

My stomach twists in either confusion or anticipation. I can't decide which. I'm petrified of a kiss. It was only a kiss, though, right? Not time travel. Is this what Ken's talking about? Did *he* see something between us? I desire Jeff. I've always known that. That was obvious. There's always going to be an attraction, but that doesn't mean it's healthy. Besides, it was just a kiss at the end of a party where, maybe, we both drank a little too much, right?

A simple…

Aw, hell, who am I kidding?

Nothing with Jeff is simple.

In my bed, my tee-shirt twists around my torso, and my sleep shorts ride up while thoughts of Jeff's kiss run rampant. Somehow, having the blankets pulled up beneath my chin will keep me grounded in this life as Ken snores beside me. But in my head, I'm replaying those six months with Jeff like an old vinyl record, and get waylaid by the blank wax at the end when I'm supposed to turn it over. Around and around I go, listening to the scratching pop and static of the needle on dead air.

We had no right getting together. We had no right falling in love or thinking whatever that was *was* love. What happens to the one that gets away? Are they gone for good? Isn't that the point of getting away? Who'd want to go back to that, anyway? That fear and fragility, the self-doubt, his arrogance, and anger. But *did* I ever actually get away? He's everywhere. When I least expect it, his face is on a magazine cover, his songs drift from speakers inside shops and on car radios. One note, and I know what's coming. I know his voice will invade my core, and those memories I tried to bury swirl in my head.

But like turning over a record, the good memories play, too, like the deep cuts rarely heard in public. The times when we'd giggle half the night in bed together; walks we took on the beach, holding hands. The way he'd look across the studio from behind his kit and give me a wink to make me feel like I was the most important person on the planet. And the sex.… Some days, I *still* miss the way we moved together, the way he knew how to please me, how solid his arms felt around me, the quiver of his belly when I reached for him, the sound of his breath as he tried to calm himself after orgasm. The tenderness in those faded denim eyes, how they crinkle when he laughs. His soft, tired voice whispering, "goodnight," in the darkness as he drifted off to sleep.

Then it's time to change the record, but I'm still hung up on the blank scratchy silence, wishing the side was longer, wishing there were more songs to play. Around and around I go, turning over the album, dissecting the notes and lyrics that made up our relationship, straining to hear something different in them, some kind of whisper buried in the scratches and blank wax.

In the morning, when Ken comes into the kitchen, I'm at the table with a mug of cold coffee, staring out the window. I turn my head when I hear him and attempt to smile, but he's already seen my other thoughts. He doesn't return the smile.

"Sleep okay?" I ask him, ignoring his look.

"Not really." Pouring some coffee into the mug left out by the coffeepot, he turns to me. He's wearing what he wore last night, and it's not even very wrinkled somehow, aside from the creases on his pants from sitting. "You tossed and turned all night."

"I'm sorry. Must have been the alcohol."

"Or seeing the ex-boyfriend?" He sips his coffee, keeping his dark eyes on me over the rim.

"Why would that make me toss and turn? It wasn't a shock he'd be there. It's his house."

"Yeah." He takes a breath before his mouth forms a flat line. How is it he doesn't even have stubble in the morning? "It was mentioned a few *thousand* times last night. I know."

"By who?"

"Everyone there. Raving about this. Raving about that. The view, the house, he *recycles*...." His eyes widen as he tilts his head side to side. "Big deal. He sorts his trash. I'm supposed to be impressed by that?" He smirks.

"Well, it *is* better for the environment."

"Cass, I don't give a shit."

I glance at the table and run a hand along the side of my neck. "Apparently," I mumble.

"What was I supposed to do, anyway? Make him jealous or something?"

I snap my head up, furrowing my eyebrows. "You said that last night, too. Why?"

He ignores my question. "Guys like that aren't the jealous type."

"Guys like what?"

"Good looking, self-assured, arrogant."

"Arrogant? What did he do last night that was arrogant?"

Ken talks over me, continuing to ignore my questions. "Whatever guys like that want, they buy. They don't get jealous of guys who they think are *below* their stature."

"Below their...? Where is this *coming* from? Were we at the same party? Did someone insult you last night? Is that why you were so pissy?"

"*You* insulted me. Do you realize you never once introduced me as your boyfriend? Not once." He folds his arms and blinks at me.

"You don't walk around introducing me as your girlfriend to your friends, either. You've always introduced me as your *friend*."

"You didn't even say that. 'This is Ken.'" He motions with his hand to the side like he's introducing an imaginary person. "Some random guy who walked in with me."

I flip my hair over my shoulder. "Give me a break," I sigh before taking a sip of coffee. "Is that why you acted like a child and wouldn't say goodnight to Jeff? Because I didn't introduce you as my date? Newsflash, pretty sure they all figured it out."

"That's not my point. I thought this was going pretty well until yesterday. Suddenly, I'm competing with some super-rich rock star ex-boyfriend I didn't even know about for your attention. Like I don't know who's going to win *that* battle."

I draw my head back and glance around the room. "When did this become a battle? We've been dating for three months. Now there's a battle for my virtue? Do I get a say, or are you going to randomly challenge every guy you meet to a duel?"

He leans back against the counter and folds his arms again. "I thought this was good between us."

Staring at the table, I hope I hide my eye roll well enough from him. "I don't know why yesterday would change anything."

It's his turn to sigh. "Because I can't compete with that."

"I didn't ask you to compete with *anyone*. You're all up in arms about this. If I wanted to be with Jeff, do you think I'd bring you to his *house*? You're twisted in knots over something...."

"He's not over you. Don't you see the way he looks at you? And I don't know what that was at the end of the night. The two of you with the guitar and the pad and all 'try this. No, no... what about this?' It's like you two were the only people on the patio."

"I'm a songwriter. That *thing* on the patio is what I do for a living. It was spontaneous. We were writing a song."

He arches an eyebrow. "You write like that with everyone?"

"Sometimes it's on a piano," I tell him, sticking my chin out. "I don't know what you want me to say, Ken. I'm sorry if I made you feel uncomfortable. It wasn't intentional. I was close to those guys once. I haven't seen them in a while, so if I ignored you...."

"Why?"

"Why did I ignore you? I told you...."

He shakes his head, arms still folded across his chest. "No, why haven't you seen them, and why are you seeing them now?"

"Jeff and I had a bad breakup. We avoided each other for a long time and bumped into each other last week. He asked if we could talk, so I invited him over for dinner...."

"You *what*? He came *here* for dinner?" His arms drop and he points to the table, and his neck stretches with shock. "Where was I?"

"San Francisco. We don't live together. I have people over my house lots of times without checking in with you first. Don't start getting possessive. It's been three months. I have a life outside of us."

"No, I know that, but... you invite your ex-lover over for dinner and don't bother to mention it? At all?"

"I wasn't *hiding* it. I don't tell you about everything I do every waking moment of my life. Neither do you, for the record."

"So, you'd be okay if I had some chick over for dinner and didn't tell you?"

"You get to do whatever you want to do." I wave my hands slightly as I shake my head.

One thing I learned after Jeff is that I have no say over someone else's actions. They're going to do what they want to do, but it is not my job to approve at the end of the day. I also don't think three months is all that long for anyone to have a say in anyone's life. Jeff also taught me that. I take more time before giving my heart to anyone. I am more cautious, and I don't let myself get as involved. Maybe I wanted to a few times, but I promised myself I wasn't going to go through that kind of pain again.

I don't necessarily want to tell Ken outright, but I'm not going to fall in love with him. I didn't think he was all that hung up on me either until last night. This jealousy thing isn't doing him any favors, either.

"What's gotten into you?" he asks me, grabbing onto the counter behind him with his fingertips.

I shake my head and try to smile. "I don't think anything. Ken, I've never been clingy.

"But you were with him, I bet."

"Clingy? Probably." I scoff. "I was also twenty-three years old and in way over my head. I have no desire to go back to that."

"Do you have a desire to be in this, though, with me?"

Well, hell… how am I supposed to answer that? I don't need to continue dating him to know he's not forever. He's a nice guy. We had fun when we went out. He can carry on a decent conversation, and it wasn't all about the celebrities I've worked with. He's traveled. We could talk about the places we've been. He was considerate in bed, but the best part was that the next day, he'd go on with his life. I'd go on with mine.

"Wow, okay." His eyes widen, and he sighs. "That answers that question."

"I didn't say anything!"

"You didn't have to. That look of dread on your face said it all for you." He shakes his head and turns to the hallway.

"Ken, stop. You're blowing last night way out of proportion. Three months isn't long enough to know anything."

I turn from the table to the hallway, where he's stopped, arms folded, with his back to me. When he doesn't turn around, I continue, "when did this suddenly become exclusive? When did it become so *serious*?"

He shakes his head as he faces me. "I'm not sure. But I wasn't expecting to be dismissed like that last night." He sticks his hands into the pockets of his trousers and drops his shoulders. "I was okay with giving us time to get to know each other until last night."

"What *happened* last night?" Aside from a kiss he doesn't know about, and I'm doing my damnedest to forget. Did he see it? Is that what this is about?

"You're never going to look at me the way you look at him," he says after a quick breath. "I sensed something when you kept introducing me as Ken. But I knew, from the second we walked into that kitchen, that this was going to be over sooner rather than later. You came to life when he looked at you. No guy stands a chance with him around. I guess I just wanted to hear you say it, but you won't. You won't even admit it happened."

We're interrupted by a knock on the door, and we both glance down the hallway. When I open it, there's a delivery man on the other side. "Cassandra Taylor?"

"Yes."

"This is for you."

He hands me a single daisy.

Chapter 11

After a restless night, I sit at the kitchen table, looking at the stupid daisy in a vase. Ken left when I walked in with the flower. I doubt I'll hear from him again. I can't talk to Hannah because I don't know what I would tell her yet. I can only imagine what she'll say about the kiss. *I* don't even know what to think about it.

One thing is certain, though: Jeff.

It's like he's come from behind to tap my far shoulder for me to turn, and find him grinning on my other side like it's some funny surprise joke. Only, I'm not laughing. I square my shoulders, clear my throat, and pick up the phone. I will not let him play games with me this time.

It takes a few tries, but I get his home number from an assistant and call. As the phone rings, I wonder if I'm playing right into him and I'm annoyed with myself. I want to click off, but he answers, calm and easy before I can and I forget to speak when I hear his voice—until he says "hello" again.

"What do you want?" I blurt out, my eyes filling with frustrated tears. I hate that he gets me this worked up and confused. Realizing how harsh I sound, I stutter. "I... I mean..."

"Who *is* this?"

I reply, slow and quiet, trying to pull the rush of emotions from my voice. "I got your daisy."

"Oh." He's silent a moment, but I swear I can hear his smile when he says, "Good morning."

"You can't play games with me, Jeff."

"I have no *intention* of playing games with you, Cass."

"What's with the daisy then?"

"I was thinking about you."

I sigh, closing my eyes, willing myself to scrounge up resistance against his charm. "Please, stop."

"Not sure I can." He chuckles.

"You can't do this to me. I can't fall for you again."

He's silent for a second, and I hear him exhale.

"I have a boyfriend," I inform him. He doesn't need to know I'm lying.

"That guy you brought to the barbecue?"

"Yes, that guy I brought to the barbecue. He's not thrilled I'm getting flowers from another guy."

"You barely paid attention to him the whole night, and then he went to sulk in the car. You don't have patience for that kind of thing."

I bite my tongue and scowl at the refrigerator. "I don't have patience for this kind of thing, either."

"Give me a chance to win your trust back."

"Trust isn't won. It's earned."

His voice softens, "then give me a chance to earn it. I'm willing to put in the work this time."

I scoff, unable to hold it back. "Why? Why now? What's changed?"

"I have. And I'm finally ready to face up to the shit I put you through and try to make amends for it."

"Why *now*?" I want my voice to sound stronger than it does. "You couldn't have done this before now? Where the *hell* have you been all this time?"

He's silent, like he's hesitant, before he says, "Can we meet somewhere?"

"No. What is left to say?"

"Please?" There's that tone in his voice, gentle and scared, like in that dark New York hotel room so long ago. It's the vulnerability in his tone that makes me consider his request. "Let me... I can't explain over the phone."

There's a silence between Jeff's words that I innately understand. Somehow, I always did. "Some place public."

Despite my understanding, maybe *because* of it, I don't trust us alone.

We meet later that afternoon, so I don't have time to back out. At this point, I wonder if I ever *could* back out when Jeff was concerned. I choose a local coffee shop that's usually not crowded. Since the owners know me, I'm confident we won't be disturbed should a customer get curious or star-struck and attempt to interrupt. By the time I arrive, Jeff's already at a small corner table. I offer a weak smile and wave, order my coffee at the counter, and head over to sit with him. He stands and leans over to kiss my cheek, motioning to the cushioned chair across from him with an awkward smile, looking drawn with nerves.

"Find the place, okay?" I ask.

"Yeah. Easy enough."

"They have good coffee."

"Yeah." He looks at the cup in front of him, barely touched.

I don't know why I'm talking about coffee. He doesn't care. "Have you been waiting long?" The server brings my drink over and slips away.

"Not really. Just sat down." He wipes his palms over his thighs and takes a breath that lifts his shoulders. "Thanks for this. Meeting me."

The spoon *'tinks'* lightly against the side of my mug as I stir. My shoulders stiffen, feeling his anxiety, and I don't know where to look.

He sits back with a tense, forced smile. "Man, this is awkward. I don't know where to start." He's going to wear a hole in his jeans with how hard he's wiping his palms down his thighs.

"Since when are you awkward around me? It's just us, Jeff." He glances around the empty cafe, landing on the staff behind the counter, chatting and cleaning. It's not very big, only about seven tables in all. "They know me. They'll give us space. It's why I picked it."

"It's not that." He shakes his head and closes his eyes for a second. "I just don't know where to begin now that I've got the chance."

With a quiet sigh, I offer a slow shake of my head and look at the coffee still slowly swirling around the cup. "You already apologized…."

"It's more than that. You want to know what's changed. *How* I changed. If it's real." He rests his arms on the table and clasps his hands around his mug with white knuckles, looking down. "It happened when I went home." His blue eyes widen and lift.

I don't know if I've ever seen him scared. I've seen him try to *cover* it with arrogance or cockiness, being rude and dismissive, or hidden away in the dark with a whisper. But this isn't hidden. I know he can pile on the bullshit, but this is too much to pretend, even for Jeff.

"What happened?" I ask, doing my best to keep any kind of judgment from my voice.

"My father called when Mom had a stroke, so, of course, I went right home. And, I showed up at the hospital loaded off my head, so coked up my entire face was numb, my *brain* was numb. I pushed through the door, saw Mom lying there, and started demanding doctors do something, cursing the nurses, demanding she get better care, ranting that I was going to take her back here with me." He looks at me, holding my gaze. "So, as I was attempting to yank my mother out of bed, a nurse tried to stop me. I shoved her aside. Thankfully, she landed in the chair by the bedside, but that's about the only good thing about any of it. Not only was my mother watching me with these huge, frightened eyes, crying, almost cringing away from me, but my father was right there, too, mouth gaping open at my wild behavior."

I'd seen that anger build in him and remember being on the other end of it. One look could make me feel insignificant and stupid. I've taunted that anger, too. Maybe I wanted him to lash out, so I had a definitive excuse to leave, especially toward the end. He was unpredictable, and I knew it was only going to get uglier. Part of me is thankful I didn't have to watch him deteriorate any further than I did.

He works his bottom lip with his teeth for a moment as his chest rises and falls. "Security threw me out. Then, as I'm doing another bump, my father came outside and knocked my head into next Sunday… slammed it into the side of my car…." He pauses with a slight shake of his head, biting his lips together again as if he can see it happening, and his eyes tear up. "… just trying to make me feel *something*, I think. My nose was bleeding, but I didn't know if it was from the coke or the car. But then… he grabbed onto me and *wouldn't let go*." His voice is so low and soft that it's hard to hear him.

"I kept hearing my father's voice in my head. '*What the hell are you doing? We raised you better than this!*' Every time I rolled over, I heard that disapproving tone." He runs his palm over his mouth and chin. "Every time I reached for a bump, just to get myself through the night, I started asking myself, '*what the hell am I doing?*'"

He lifts a hand, fingers pressing against his temples. "Falling apart." His hand drops to his lap. "The next morning, he sat me down at the kitchen table like I was twelve and read me a riot act like I'd never heard before. I wasn't about to tell him that I was a grown-up and could do whatever the hell I wanted. I couldn't tell him I'd done lines that morning just to get my sorry ass out of bed, then two more bumps in the bathroom because I was shaking so bad I couldn't brush my damn teeth." He tries to chuckle, but it's forced. It's disgust. "Thing is, everything he said was true. I couldn't argue with him. He gave me a choice to either continue what I was doing, leave and never come back, or straighten up, get my vices under control, and have his help while I did. So, I left."

My hand tightens on my mug as my mouth and shoulders drop. "You *didn't*."

He rubs a hand over the back of his neck and nods, his gaze cast to the floor. "He needed to help Mom, not deal with my issues. So, I talked to Jace, and he found someplace close by that was willing to help me detox."

With a sincerity I haven't seen from him before, those deep blue eyes lock with mine. "That was the last time I touched coke. I knew it wasn't going to be easy, but..." He bites his lower lip again with an almost indiscernible head shake. "It was absolute *hell* stopping, which I don't want to go into detail about. I will if you need me to"

I don't even speak, only shake my head and I see his relief as he closes his eyes for a second, dropping back into his chair.

"After that, *so much* shit cleared up. I was finally able to get my head on straight and see what I'd been doing to everyone around me." He wraps his hands around the coffee mug again. "The longer I stayed away from it, the more I realized how destructive it was, how many people I *hurt* along the way. That last day in the studio... I was so out of my head I barely registered what you said. Too busy calculating my next hit." He spits the words out, his face twisting. "It took me a hell of a long time to figure out just how petrified I was and come to grips with... *everything*." He closes his eyes a moment as if he's still bewildered by it.

"The fame, the money, the drugs, the stress, trying to control the chaos, attempt to keep up when all I was doing was falling further behind, and more and more scared. It all came at me like that." He snaps his fingers. "So worried I would lose it just as quickly. Become some has-been and have people come up and say, 'didn't you used to be...?' Figure out that I didn't have *any* talent." He drops his shoulders and hunches over his mug. "I have no fucking idea how any of it happened... all those people looking at me and thinking I had it all... but in truth, I didn't have the time to enjoy *anything*."

He lifts his chin and shakes his head. "I tried to show you. At least, I *think* that's what I was trying to do sometimes. You would look at me sometimes... and I could *feel* your confusion and didn't have the words or the strength to explain it."

I never understood the pressure he was under until I had a sliver of that kind of success. After two weeks of traveling between New York and Los Angeles, I remember dealing with different artists' personalities, hotels, waiting for things to happen, people to show up, getting to meetings across town, and endless phone conversations. After dropping into my bed at home, it all clicked. I understood the allure of that false energy or the blissful relief of taking a pill to not have the capacity to think about anything for a few hours. I realized then how, some nights, Jeff probably wanted to come home and collapse, too. Instead, he found me clueless on the couch, wanting more from him when he had nothing more to give.

"It's part of why I cheated on you," he says in his quiet voice, sounding remorseful.

I lower my eyes. Sadness balls in my stomach with his acknowledgment, but it's far from a surprise.

Shifting in his chair, his unease about this admission is almost palpable. "It felt easier to screw a groupie than be present in a relationship. I didn't have to care about them. I could just fuck 'em and kick 'em out. And I did. And I'm sorry about that, too."

"I'm sorry I was so…" I whisper, my chest tightening as I try to take a breath.

"This isn't about *blame*." He interrupts me, leaning forward and pressing a palm flat on the table between us. "And you weren't to blame for that. I was excessive, and out of hand, and *selfish*. I needed to come back to reality at some point. Unfortunately, coming back was a rocky, fiery crash landing with very little of my ego intact once I stopped spinning. But being able to walk away from it with some kind of career? Hell, with my fucking *life*? Realizing there are plenty of things more important than some fucking single or getting an album out for the Christmas sales. I lost that perspective living the way I did."

"It wasn't just you, though, Jeff. There was so much being asked of you"

"*Stop*." His gaze holds mine, and I swear I can see our past swimming within them. All those memories stirred up and settling like mud, thick and deep on the floor of a still pond. "*Stop* making excuses for me." Jeff shifts in his chair again, pulling the coffee mug closer with both his hands wrapping around it. "You walked into the middle of it all. I expected you to make sense of it and clean it up for me. God only knows how hard you must've tried, but you only had half of the pieces you needed to survive that relationship. You stood beside me, loving me at my *worst*. Who the fuck could love *me*? Even *I* hated me."

Staring at him with tears in my eyes, my breath quick and shallow, I whisper, "but I *did* love you."

"And I was painfully aware of it, too. I didn't want to let you down and looked anywhere to find fault except at myself. I *wanted* to be that guy you loved. I *tried.* "

"I know you did." I offer as much of a smile as I can muster for all those 'could haves'… all those possibilities…. "It was *because* you tried that I lasted as long as I did."

He takes a deep breath as if to gain the courage to continue while dread pools in the pit of my stomach. I'm unsure if I can keep going down this heartbroken path. Reeling with all this, I'm not ready to hear more about what could have been. With a pause, he shifts again, tilting his head. "*So*, a few months ago, I was doing this radio thing. They asked me that boring question, 'What regrets do you have?' And I gave them the patented answer of not having any because then I wouldn't be where I am now, blah, blah."

He rolls his eyes and waves his hand in the air, sitting back. Sliding the chair out further to rest his ankle on his knee, he then rubs his palms over his thighs again. "When I got home, Teddy called to rag on me about it, started singing that Sinatra song '*regrets… I've had a few….*' I flat-out told him I lied. I told him I have quite a list." He sets his gaze on me and holds it steady. "And at the top of it—was you." He dips his chin, still not looking away from me.

My breath catches and I look down at a stray piece of a straw wrapper under the table. I don't think I could take a breath if I tried. Blinking, I try to pass all this off in some calm, collected manner, but my insides vibrate with fear, wonder, satisfaction, and disbelief.

Jeff rubs his hands on his jeans again and clears his throat. "I told myself that if I bumped into you, I'd apologize." He bites his lower lip and waits until I look at him. "I am sorry I used you. I'm sorry I lashed out at you. I'm sorry I laid my hands on you when I was angry. I'm sorry for not appreciating everything you did. I'm sorry I wasn't there for you when you needed me the most.

"And one final confession," he pauses before continuing, "I knew you were at Cornerstone. It's why I put it on my list of places to check out because after being back and never seeing you, I had to force it. My stomach was in knots the entire time Mike was talking during that tour that day. I was just trying to figure out something to say to you, trying not to stare at you… After our dinner that night, I realized I wanted more than forgiveness. I wanted to try again because I *missed* you, and it hit me just how much I fucked up."

Every guy I've ever dated was happy to share with me why I failed them and how I was the reason for the relationship not working. They could always *explain.* It was never *them.* If only I tried harder, supported them more. If I *truly* loved them, I would have known what they needed: give a little more of myself, be more assertive, more submissive, more independent—and know when to be what so as not to interfere with their plans. It took me long enough to realize that *because* I did all that, they could blame me. I was the only one changing in the relationship to suit their needs. Not one guy ever owned up to their shortcomings or made *themselves* vulnerable.

Not *one*... until now.

He sips his coffee, which must be as cold as mine by now, but he licks his lower lip, and his chest rises. "After that kiss the other night, I needed to see if I stood a chance. I know you're dating that guy...." He waves his hand over the table and shakes his head. "I don't think he's going to last because, well," a half-smile touches his eyes, a hint of that arrogance still flickering, "you kissed me back."

I bite my lips together and look into my mug, but don't say anything. I think he's waiting for me to interject something, but my mind is going over our kiss. I can't contradict him. I did kiss him... and wanted to kiss him more.

"So," he exhales and shifts again in his seat, "I'm going to write and record my album and wait for *you* this time. Ask for an opportunity to earn your trust and show you how serious I am. Right now, all you have are words, and I know my word doesn't mean a whole lot to you." He cocks his head to the side and offers a slight grin. "I get that. If you don't think we have a chance and want me to take a hike, just say so." He sits back and lifts his palms to me before resting them back on his thighs. "I'll go away and wish you all the best. I just needed to give it one more shot to see if maybe, somehow, I stood a chance in hell...."

I grip my coffee mug and try to take a few breaths to get my thoughts together. What I want to do is jump into his arms and kiss him until neither of us can breathe, but I learned my lesson doing that with him. Possibly the hardest thing right now is saying, "I need some time. It's not completely take a hike. Just time to figure out... everything."

There's a whisper of a smile in his eyes, and his face relaxes when he gives me an easy nod. "I can do that."

Looking at my mug again, I nod and take a sip. He does, too. Then we sit in silence for a moment. "What do we do now?" I ask.

He lifts a shoulder. "I'm content to sit and have coffee with a friend. Tell me about... you. Working with Linda Ronstadt. I know she was someone you wanted to collaborate with. Was it everything you thought it'd be?"

I can't help but feel flattered that he remembers little details about me, like my favorite flower and who I most wanted to work with. Can this really be who he is?

"You in a rush to get home?" I ask when we step outside. The sun slips below the buildings and the streetlights have turned on.

"What do you have in mind?"

I motion to the beach. "Take a walk?"

He gives me an easy smile and nods.

Taking his hand, I start across the street to the sand. He rolls up his shirt sleeves. The wind blows his hair back, and he pulls me a little closer as we step onto the beach. I take my shoes off to feel the cool sand on my bare feet and roll the ends of my jeans up as we head closer toward the surf, hearing the hiss of the foam from the waves receding before the next crash drowns it out. The wind blows from the shore, so they're a little tamer than usual, but still, I love the roar as they splash and sprawl over the beach.

"This brings you back, doesn't it?" he asks.

I drop my head against his shoulder as I used to during our beach walks. I can smell the spice in his cologne and want to close my eyes, taking it in. It reminds me of a moonlit summer night with its earthy scents, and a memory of rumpled sheets and our naked skin flashes through my mind.

He chuckles. "So does that." His lips press against my hair as we walk.

"I loved living on the beach. I still miss that house sometimes," I confess, lifting my head.

"That deck... I wish I took advantage of it more when I lived there."

"How long did you stay after I moved out?"

He lifts a shoulder. "I didn't. I lived on Jace's couch for a few months. One of the studio girls grabbed my things. I never went back."

I stop and drop my chin. "You're joking." He shrugs at me and starts down the beach again. "You didn't even go back to get... how do you know they got everything?"

"We were renting most everything. I remember asking the girl to grab that lamp, whatever instruments were left lying around, and my clothes, but the rest? They were just things."

My forehead creases in bafflement. "How much have you left behind with random girlfriends?"

He slips his hands into the pockets of his trousers and tilts his head. "You were not random. I was interested in you before we even had sex."

"It's what brought us together." I switch my shoes to my other hand and watch the beach ahead.

"No, it wasn't." He shakes his head, looking forward. "Your talent brought us together. You forget we were friends with Curt. He kept going on about his session players and this chick who blew him away. We came to hear it for ourselves. Why do you think Teddy grabbed you when we needed an extra guitar that time?" He looks over at me. "I'll let you in on a secret. It had nothing to do with the way you kissed me or what you looked like. When it came to our music, we wanted the best. *That's* why he grabbed you. *That's* what drew me to you. Didn't hurt that you were one of the prettiest things I'd ever seen, but it was Curt that brought us into the studio to hear you."

I stop in the sand and draw my chin back, blinking at him. "How come no one ever said anything? You... when did you...?" I glance to the surf as another wave bursts over my thoughts before looking at him.

"We were in the booth. You were in the live room working out some piece with one of the other guys, and we were mesmerized by what you were playing." He reaches over to brush my hair back, but it blows forward again. "Then you flipped your ponytail over your shoulder, leaned forward to help him with his fingering, and I heard you laugh." He keeps his gaze forward and smiles as though he were watching the memory play through his mind. "I was smitten from that moment on."

Fixing my gaze on him, I don't know what to say. "I had no idea."

"Because you always insisted our meeting was that joint and doughnut."

I fold my arms. "No, it was when you were a drunken ass and thought I was the receptionist, keeping the takeout menus from you."

He dismisses my comment with a wave of his hand and a sheepish grin. "That doesn't count. I was too wasted to have any recollection of that exchange."

"It does count. *I* remember it."

"I wish you'd forget it," he says with a slow release of breath. "I wish we could start where I'm not an ass behaving badly. So..." He reaches out again to let his fingers slip through a strand of my hair. "Can we start right this time, you think?" He tilts his head to the side with a questioning lift of his shoulder.

I press my lips together, thankful for the shadows as my emotions scatter over my thoughts like the crashing waves, uncovering feelings

I thought I had buried. I blamed myself for being vulnerable. I blamed myself for being dumb enough to trust him. I lied to myself, rationalized his behavior because I didn't want to be that hurt, diminished my fears, and hid my sadness, trying to protect myself from them. But the lies I told myself made no difference, and that pain resurfaces as he stands in front of me, almost as if he's a shadow I'm confronting from the past rather than a reality.

"You *broke* me," my voice cracks, finally admitting my whole truth. "Not just my heart. *Me.* I want to believe you when you look at me or say you're sorry, tell me you've changed… that you loved me." I take a step back and hold my hair off my face. "How do I know? How do I know you won't get bored again? Get too busy to care? I don't need you to take care of me anymore. I can take care of myself now."

He licks his bottom lip and shakes his head. "*You* took care of *me.* All I gave you was a place to live and some introductions. You didn't need me to take care of you. You needed me to *care*." He stops walking and glances to the horizon for a moment, but turns to face me. "I'm still attracted to who you are, Cass, not only your looks. I'm still blown away by your talent and creativity. And, I haven't been in a serious relationship for a solid two years because I don't want to go through the motions. I want this to mean something."

I turn my face to the waves. White foam spreads on the shore, showing me outlines of a wave as it rushes in. Its salty scent lingers in the air between us. My walls try to build back up, but they're like a sandcastle left in the surf and keep getting washed away into soft, rounded mounds of sand.

"You have no idea how much I want to believe you" Wrapping an arm around my waist, I'm unsure if it's to protect or comfort myself. "… how much I want to give in and let myself fall for you all over again. Any other guy in the world, I am cautious. But you?" I turn to let the breeze blow my hair from my face. "I don't know how to trust you."

His chin dips down with his nod.

"I don't know how to trust myself around you."

He shifts his foot in the sand, hands still in his pockets.

I watch the next wave rush in. "But I don't know how to walk away, either."

He lifts his head.

Another wave scuffs along the shoreline, and I follow it with my gaze and decide to stop standing in the surf with him and choose whether I'm willing to move forward or not. I turn my face to him with a determined stare. "We start fresh, starting now."

He reaches a hand out to brush over my arm. I think he's uncertain if he should hold me or not.

I step forward, wrap my arms around his waist, and rest my cheek against his chest. His arms wrap around me, and I close my eyes against him, taking a breath. It's the first time I've ever felt like I could breathe around him.

Sitting in my kitchen a few days later, Hannah bounces my goddaughter, Suzie, on her knee. After Hannah found out she was pregnant, we swore to meet weekly so she could keep in touch with the "real world" and I could get baby time. We've been fairly steady in keeping the appointment for the last year, too, aside from the few times I've been away on business.

Hannah widens her eyes and murmurs 'no way' every few minutes as I tell her everything that's happened with Jeff and Ken. She chuckles when I tell her I woke up to another daisy on my doorstep.

"He sends one every day." I motion to the vase on the table with six other daisies. Hannah's mouth drops open with a short laugh. Rolling my eyes, I try to chuckle with the absurdity, but honestly? I'm too touched by the gesture to pull it off. "I know." I sigh.

"How could you not tell me this?" She motions to the flowers. "I talk to you almost every day!"

"I didn't have time to go into the explanation. It's more than a quick five-minute phone call to explain."

"Have you heard from Ken at all?" she asks.

I shake my head and pucker my lips.

"Does Jeff know he's not your boyfriend anymore?" She laughs while I keep shaking my head. "Atta girl!"

"I don't necessarily want to lie to him, but I want him to know I've got options, too. I want him to see that I'm not that hung-up, starry-eyed kid anymore."

She hands the baby to me and stands up to pour more coffee into our mugs. "Well, you're not."

I look at Suzie, grinning and shaking my head. "Won't hurt for him to think he's got some competition, though, will it?" The baby, sucking on her fist, smiles a toothless grin at me. "Suzie agrees with me."

"So does Suzie's mom. I think you're doing the right thing. Take your time with him, and, you know, there is no shame in walking away if he pulls his bullshit. You did it once, you can do it again."

I shift a squirming Suzie onto my lap and glance over to Hannah sitting back at the table. "I don't know what I'm supposed to do, though. I am *not* one of those women who's going to play games and test him. Neither of us have time for that."

"Aside from the daisies, has he gotten in touch with you?"

Dropping my shoulders in defeat, I press my lips tight. "We talk every day," I groan and close my eyes. "I see him at the studio almost daily. He pops in when I'm taking a break... lunch a few times. It's all been so... easy. Again." I lift my chin to look over Suzie's head at Hannah. "I am so freaking scared, Hannah."

"Honey...." She frowns, tilting her head to the side with gentle eyes.

"It feels so much like the first time. How can I be sure it's not going to end up the same way? We've always been...."

"*You've* always been," she interrupts, lifting a finger. "You lost yourself back then, Cass, and you haven't let anyone get close since. Each new boyfriend, Paul and I take a bet on how long they're going to last."

My mouth drops open, releasing an indignant grunt.

Hannah arches an eyebrow and smirks. "I know, we're awful. But neither one of us bets over six months. You don't give them a chance."

"I've been in relationships." I counter, trying to remember if I dated anyone longer than six months recently... maybe in the last few months... years...? I sigh. "Okay, but it's not like I have a mass of boyfriends to choose from. I've been busy."

She nods and curls the corner of her mouth. "You don't give yourself the chance, even if you had a plethora of boyfriends to choose from. I mean, the guys are attractive and all, but they aren't anyone you'd ever share your life with long-term. Hell, half of them could have been cardboard cutouts and been more interesting. It's no wonder you didn't keep them around."

I can't argue with what she's saying. I dated some guys because I was, at *most*, attracted to them, hoping for something deeper once we got to know each other. We never did. I avoided dating musicians as much as possible for fear that we'd only end up in competition with each other or worse; he'd try to tell me how to write my music or get jealous of my accomplishments. In my business, it's hard to meet someone that *isn't* a musician.

Hannah drops back in the chair, lets her hands fall into her lap, and rests her gaze on me. "I can't believe I'm going to say this, but hear me out. Maybe, instead of looking for the ways Jeff can hurt you,

you let yourself look for the ways he can love you. Rock Wonder is *not* perfect. He's going to fuck up at some point. I am certain of it. But if he's come back to make amends and own up to his screw-ups? See if he can. Maybe you can give him the chance you never gave anyone else all this time. We both know you never stopped loving him, don't we?"

"I just feel like…." I bite my lower lip. "It's like Jeff was teaching me how to ride a bike, you know? Encouraging me to keep pedaling while I was learning, only I never knew when he let go. I only figured it out when I looked back and saw him standing with his hands on his hips and a proud smile on his face, and I'd get distracted and fall. Sometimes, he was willing to kiss my skinned knee and tell me I was brave. Other times, he'd stand there, shaking his head, asking why I took my eyes off the road."

Hannah tilts her head side to side and squints, crinkling her nose. "You forgot one significant part in that scenario, though."

"I did?"

"You already knew how to ride a bike. You were riding a bike for years before he even showed up."

I bob my head from side to side in reluctant agreement.

"He gave you confidence, Cass. He saw something in you that even you didn't see until he pointed it out. And when he saw it, you believed him."

"Yeah, he gave me confidence in some weird, twisted way. I'm still not sure if that's part of what I loved or loathed about us." I groan. "God, I'd get so angry at myself for feeling like I needed his approval or something—but I'd still crave it."

She snickers and a smile breaks across her face. "I know one other thing you craved with him, and I'm *dying* to know if he's just as good in bed as he was back then."

I burst into a laugh and shake my head at her. "Well, you won't be disappointed when I tell you he at least still knows how to kiss." I keep going over that kiss on his patio last week. How simple it was. How easily we fell into it. How many times I keep thinking about it. "It's the rest of it I'm unsure about." My shoulders tighten as my stomach hardens, and I look over Suzie's head at Hannah in my hesitancy. "He's always been so damn charming and charismatic. I don't know if I trust myself not to fall for it again."

She relaxes back into the chair and arches an eyebrow at me. "Oh, honey, I hate to break it to you, but you already have. Now, he has to live up to the promises. See if he can. If he hasn't changed, you're a strong, smart, capable woman who can live without him.

Whatever happens, you'll be able to say you tried, right?"

Chapter 12

A week later, I'm finishing up in the studio with a new artist when there's a knock on the door. New guy opens it with wide-eyed excitement, letting Jeff inside. After a quick introduction and his stuttering about Jeff being an idol, he heads out, leaving Jeff and me alone. He glances at the closed door, suppressing a laugh before turning to me.

"How'd your session go today?" he asks.

I tilt my head from side to side and curl my lip. "I've had better. It's gonna be hard living up to his standards now after meeting you."

Jeff scoffs, rolling his eyes. "He knows you've written a gazillion hits, doesn't he?"

"Not as many as you."

"I had a lot of help," he dismisses with a wave of his hand.

"We all need a lot of help." I start collecting some papers from the coffee table in front of me. We're not working in a full studio, more a break room with a piano, couch, chairs, and some end tables. "It's only our second meeting, though. He hasn't completely given up on me yet."

Jeff smiles. "It'll come if he knows what's good for his career."

I crinkle my nose and lift a shoulder, dragging my work bag across the couch toward me. "I'm not that concerned. He needs to be less guarded and trust me a little more. If it doesn't happen, he'll find someone else to collaborate with, that's all. I've got a few other people who can fill his spot if necessary."

Jeff rests against the door and folds his arms, surveying the room. The walls are painted burgundy and a brown throw rug covers the floor. A thesaurus, dictionary, and a bunch of out-of-date magazines lie on the coffee table for inspiration or assistance in writing. In the corner, a coffee pot sits on top of a mini-fridge. "We never had rooms like this in the 70s." Jeff chuckles.

"No. Because we know what would happen in rooms like this in the 70s, and it had nothing to do with making music."

"You're right, but what's stopping it from happening now?" He laughs.

I point to the corner of the room where there's a surveillance camera mounted.

He looks over and snickers. "All that takes is one well-placed tee-shirt."

Laughing, I shake my head. "Where are you going so dressed up?"

"Radio thing," he answers with a casual shrug, looking down at his jeans and a gray tweed blazer. "I wanted to ask you something."

"Shoot." I stand up and put my guitar in the case.

Cocking his head to the side, he grins, pointing at my guitar. "Is that…?"

Looking at the case, I smile. "The Bicentennial you gave me? Yes." I lift it back out and hand it to him. There are a few scratches on the back from wear and tear, but overall, it's still in prime condition. It was stuck in the corner of my music room, hidden behind a music stand and some other acoustics I had because just looking at it made my stomach clench with too many emotions. But, one day, I made myself take it out of the case and fell in love with it all over again, the pain seeming to disappear with each note I played on it. "I love the way it sounds when I'm writing. It just has that perfect resonance."

He admires it, holding it up to inspect the stenciling.

"It's one of my favorite guitars, in all honesty."

His smile reaches his eyes as he hands it back. "Glad to hear it. Wasn't sure if it ended up battered against a brick wall after everything."

I rest the guitar back in its case and shake my head. "I would never do that to an innocent instrument." I glance up. "I didn't use it for a long time, but in the end, her sound won out."

"Well…" Clearing his throat, he shifts, sticking his fingers into the front pockets of his jeans as I turn to close the case. "I wanted to ask you… There's an industry thing next week, a new talent showcase or something? Bunch of bigwigs, agents… that sort of thing. I got roped into going, and while it'd probably be good for both of our careers to schmooze, I'd kind of like to… well… um… take you… as my… uh… date?"

I turn to face him and arch an eyebrow, puckering my lips to keep from giggling. He blinks at me, biting his bottom lip in anticipation. When did he get so nervous to ask a girl out? "You planning on going anywhere afterward? Any tours or something planned that I should know about?"

"Geez, Cass. I *swear*, I *called* you!" We both laugh as he shakes his head. "But, no, no plans. Maybe a farmers' market in the morning, depending on how early I wake up, but I promise it's in the same zip code."

"What day?"

"Friday, about 7:30?"

"It's a date." I smile with a quick wink.

Friday night, I'm standing in front of a full-length mirror staring at myself wearing a sleeveless burgundy mini dress with a low-v back, black stockings, and short burgundy suede boots. I've laid out an oversized black blazer and will roll up the sleeves once I put it on, but I still need to fix my make-up and curl my hair. I'm pretending not to care, but really, how am I not supposed to be thinking about that other first date almost a decade ago?

At least this time, I've been to events like this, so I know what to expect, how to dress, and probably also know quite a few of the people that will be there. I'm not a starry-eyed pup, but my sweaty hands betray my nerves. I keep staring in the mirror, wondering if I'm trying too hard to impress him while reminding myself that if I were going to an industry party on my own, I'd be wearing the same outfit.

My make-up stays simple with just a pale-pink eyeshadow, some mascara, a quick swipe of blush, and some pink lipstick. The brand and name of the color have long been worn away. My hair hangs below my shoulders. I twist in some curls with a curling iron, fluffing them out with my fingers to give them some volume, then lift and spray with hairspray, hoping it'll hold for a few hours, anyway.

Just as I'm finishing, Jeff rings the doorbell. He's in a pair of tan khakis and a black shirt with the sleeves pushed up and black loafers, sunglasses still covering his eyes. His smile broadens when he sees me, and he hands me a bouquet of colorful flowers with daisies among them in abundance.

"Aren't they pretty?" I press my nose closer to take in the fragrance.

"Not even a contest next to you." He leans over and kisses my cheek. "You look fantastic."

I roll my eyes at him but smile. "Thank you. Let me put these in some water, and then we can go. Do you want something to drink?"

"Nah, I'm good." He follows me into the kitchen, lifting the sunglasses into his hair. It may not be curly, but there's still plenty of volume with his waves, parted neatly down the middle and brushed back. He sits at the counter as I rummage to find a vase and get the flowers situated. "I got us a table at Spago for after, so we have an excuse to leave if we need one."

"Oooh, Spago. Aren't you fancy?"

He presses his lower lip out. "I figured I'd go all out and try to impress you with my wealth and fame in case my charm and good looks fail me."

I laugh. "Because that happens to you often?"

He lifts his shoulder and cocks his head to the side.

"Yeah, that's what I thought. Go ahead, Kingston, impress me," I tease.

"I'm trying. It's not as easy as it used to be."

I give him a wink. "You'd be surprised." I rest my hands on the counter, standing in front of him. "Somewhere in the back of my head, a tiny little voice is saying, 'you're just a session musician.'" I laugh.

He opens his palms before letting his hands drop to his thighs. "I'm still a nerd trying to impress the girls at the high school dance."

"Well, this session player thinks you're pretty cool for a nerd."

"And this nerd can't *believe* his luck getting to be seen in public with you."

He may think he's a nerd, but nothing about him shows it. When we arrive, we have to walk through photographers. I forgot this part about being out in public with him in an official capacity. Handlers assist by guiding the media to the new talent, pushing them in front of the cameras so we can be ushered inside. Of course, Jeff still demands attention because of his star status, and some onlookers behind the red velvet ropes cheer and call his name.

I hold my breath until he looks over, offering me a smile and squeezing my hand in a quick, playful gesture as though he sensed my nerves—or maybe my sweaty hands. As soon as his head turns to me, shutters fly, and a handler rushes over, putting her hands up to the media.

"Mr. Kingston, hello. This way, please," she says in a quick, clipped tone, charging down the sidewalk to open the door. She frantically waves at someone as we make our way behind her, cameras still clicking, but he ignores all the commotion.

I do my best to follow suit, keeping my head forward, reminding myself to hold my chin up and not duck into my shoulders. I didn't consider this part when I agreed to come with him and realize we may make the gossip columns in the morning editions. Back when we were dating, I was usually 'Jeff Kingston's date' or on occasion, 'girlfriend.' They never used my name, probably because they didn't know or care who I was. With my own success now, I'm fairly certain they'll use my name this time. It makes my heart thump heavier against my chest. I forgot he could be *this* famous. He's only been just Jeff when we've been together.

"Right this way, Mr. Kingston," a new handler says, greeting us with a smile and clipboard.

"How're you, Gen?" he says with a calm smile. "Everything going as planned?"

Her eyes bulge in response before she looks at her clipboard. "It never does," she groans. "How was it out there? They didn't bog you down, did they? They were supposed to grab you…"

"I've survived Grammy night. This was a piece of cake. Don't fret. Where are we supposed to be?"

Like the rock'n'roll royalty that he is, Gen ushers us to a separate bank of elevators where servers hold trays of beverages and passed hors d'oeuvres. Down the hallway, there's a bigger crowd, and the chatter echoes over to us. They're in a general reception area with their own bank of elevators where they'll check credentials and only allow a chosen few into the actual showcase. I'm usually on *that* side of the rope when I come to these things. Not anyone the media wants to talk to, but where the networking happens with the agents and label reps. Jeff doesn't need to do that, either.

Taking it all in stride, Jeff continues holding my hand, his other stuck in his pocket, sunglasses still in place. I smile at the server standing beside me and glance away, thankful when the elevator doors open. We step inside and Gen turns a key and presses a button. It's quiet in the elevator and he glances over at me.

"Too bright for you in here?" I tease in a whisper and arch an eyebrow. It's like he didn't even know they were on, murmuring a quick, 'oh,' and pushing them up on his head. "There you are," I say with a grin.

He leans over and kisses my cheek. "Thanks for coming with me."

Moments later, the elevator doors slide open, and we're met with a buzz of voices and laughter. "Have a good night, Mr. Kingston," Gen says.

"You too, Gen." He gives her a wink. "Grab a drink."

"I *wish*," she laughs as the elevator doors close in front of her.

Jeff scans the room, and his chest rises with a breath. "Rock star reporting for duty," he mumbles before plastering a smile on his face. Putting his confidence on, almost as though it were a blazer, Jeff's transformation is complete, and he wears it well. He greets people with a sturdy handshake or kisses the cheeks of the women he knows. Holding my hand, he introduces me to the handful of people I don't know. I introduce him to a few people, which surprises me. I figured he'd know everyone by now. During small talk, he's attentive and asks questions. A few trays of drinks come around, and he sips on a glass of red wine until we find our seats at one of the tables.

Where people are seated reflects the hierarchy of popularity. The closer to the front, the higher you are in the food chain, and we're sitting in the first row of tables. His face will be in any photos taken of the performances—mine, too. I should have tried harder with my make-up. Glancing around the room, I check to see how many photographers there are milling around. These won't make it into the gossip pages, but some will be distributed to the press. I wonder if Jeff's considered this at all, or if it's just another minor detail in his world. He can't possibly pay attention to every picture taken of him.

I recognize a lot of the women, most recording artists. I've worked with a few. They're dressed in skin-tight outfits and oversized jackets like me, but even so, I feel like they've been let in on that Girl Secret. Their hair and make-up are perfect and stylish. They seem more comfortable in their skin than I will ever be.

But then I wonder if maybe they're looking at me and thinking the same thing. I've just watched Jeff go through his transformation. He's the epitome of cool, and because I know him so well, I can tell he's putting on an act in here. Maybe, just maybe, most everyone else is doing the same, and we're all just looking at one another, feeling inadequate.

The first act is announced. It's a trio; a singer, a synthesizer player, and someone on keytar. They're dressed in futuristic pantsuits made of gold lamé and what looks like white cotton bibs. Even their knee-high boots are gold lamé with chunky heels. All of them have the same bleached-blond hairstyle. One side brushes fully back, one side brushes straight up, and the back brushes forward and shaped into a triangle. Each has a blue triangle drawn over one eye and a pink triangle on a cheek.

The outfits are bad enough, but halfway through the set, the keytarist begins a solo by going to the other side of the stage and getting on his knees, playing to the table in front of him. Our table is opposite on the other side of the stage, and I know he's going to repeat his trick by coming to this end. I will not be able to maintain a straight face while some guy in gold lamé plays a miniature keyboard on a strap like it's some new-age guitar. Before he can come serenade us, I touch Jeff's arm and excuse myself to stand in the hallway.

A moment later, Jeff comes out. When the door closes, we burst into laughter. I lean against the wall with my arms over my stomach, trying to catch my breath.

He's beside me, his head down. "You can't make this shit up." He laughs, dropping his shoulder against the wall, and glances at the door.

"A *keytar* solo?" My voice lifts in another fit of giggles. "Of all the acts… *keytar*?" I keep laughing. "I can't…."

"More power to 'im," Jeff chuckles, catching his breath and shaking his head.

I glance at the door. "Think they'll notice our empty chairs?"

He rests his shoulder against the wall beside me and crosses his arms. "I don't think they'll notice anything but that keytarist."

I squeeze my eyes shut a moment, giggling. "Got anything to erase *that* vision from my brain?"

He grins, the corners of his eyes crinkling. "How about this?" Leaning forward, he tilts his head slightly and presses his lips against mine, keeping his arms folded over his chest. I reach out to rest my hand on his wrist and respond. His hands move to rest on my waist as he tilts his head the other way to come back in for another kiss, longer and deeper.

Again, my body recognizes his. I press my fingers against his jaw, my finger hooking in one of the belt loops on his khakis. We linger in the hallway, kissing until the door opens and there is applause inside.

"We should head back in there," he murmurs, motioning toward the door with his head.

"Yeah." As I smile, I press my lips together, reaching up to wipe some of my lipstick from his bottom lip.

He leans over to give me another quick kiss, reaching for and squeezing my hand before we head to our seats.

I never thought I'd be disappointed by a keytar solo ending, but as he leads us through the tables to our seats, I'm wishing for another excuse to go back in the hallway to kiss again.

We're stuck in traffic pulling up to the restaurant because someone famous showed up, and cameras flash like fireflies as they get out of the car. Jeff watches it unfold with a tight expression on his face. The cameras at the event had boundaries. It wasn't a feeding frenzy like this is—photographers out to make a quick grand by selling someone's privacy. I can see his mind whirling with how to get around that.

"You know, I know this great little place by me in Santa Monica." He snaps his head towards me as I watch the photographers through the windshield. "Pretty sure there're no photographers outside."

"You don't mind?" he asks.

"They'll have food. Besides, I think there are plenty of pictures documenting our date tonight, don't you? Let's not saturate the market." I'm trying to laugh this whole thing off. If I'm going to go out with Jeff Kingston, this is part of it. He can't escape it when he's a *Rock Star on Duty*.

"Well, I wanted to be fancy. You know, show off."

"Show off another time. Make a right at the light." I motion to the road with my chin, grinning. As he drives off, I settle back in the seat and glance at the mayhem on the sidewalk, just as thankful as he is to avoid that. "And since when are expensive meals and paparazzi impressive?"

As I look over at him, he grins, checking the traffic before turning. "I didn't expect paparazzi. They're not usually that bad, so someone huge must be dining inside. Dinner out was the only thing I could think of. It's been a minute since I really cared about impressing a date. I'm still trying to make a good impression." He sneaks a glance at me with a raised eyebrow. "How'm I doing so far?"

"Very impressive. Now, relax," I say, making him chuckle. "Make a left up there. You forget, Mr. Kingston, I lived with you. I know beneath this very cool exterior of yours lies a man who checks the inside of a cup for spiders when he takes it out of the cupboard." I laugh.

His smile breaks wide. "You never know when a spider might make itself at home."

"Don't you think it'd drown, or you'd notice it's in there by the time you took a drink?"

He waves a hand at me. "Don't pester me with details. It's worked so far. I haven't had a spider in my drink yet."

"Psst, me neither."

"So, it's worked for you, too?" he teases.

"You can't possibly get away with impressing me. I know your secrets. You're a nerd just like me."

"You're not a nerd," he says with another glance my way.

"Sure I am, but thanks."

He stretches his hand out for mine, and we drive in silence for a few minutes. "Neither of us is as nerdy as that triangle keytar group," he chuckles, which sets me off again.

"I'm just glad we got out of there before I had to talk to any of them. I don't know if I would have been able to hold it together. How do you have a conversation with someone who has triangles painted on their face?" I question with a shake of my head.

"Worked for Bowie," he offers with a tilt of his head.

"Number one, Bowie had a lightning bolt. Number two, he's *David Bowie*."

"I still wouldn't have been able to take him seriously with a lightning bolt covering his face. I think he's got more credibility without it."

"Well, of course, because you're Jeff Kingston, and you have that voice. You didn't need a gimmick to get noticed."

"None of us did, and there was still a hell of a lot of talent in my day...."

"Yes, Grandpa, in *your* day," I tease.

"In *our* day...."

"Are you calling me grandma?"

He looks over at me and winks. "You're ageless and timeless."

I snicker, glancing out my window. "Oh, that charm gets you out of so much trouble."

He nods and purses his lips in consideration. "It usually helps when I step in it, yeah."

"Don't I know it. Turn right at the light."

"Where are you taking me, anyway?"

"Nervous?"

"Should I be?"

I don't reply, but grin and wiggle my eyebrows at him.

About ten minutes later, I take his hand and lead him across a parking lot to a clapboard building with neon signs and tacky, oversized plastic lobsters hanging over the doorway. He arches his eyebrows at me, but I tug his hand and walk into the bar. There's a pool table in the corner, more neon signs, and a few tables with mismatched chairs. Open doors in the back lead to a covered deck with more tables. It's not super busy, but it's a good crowd, and a band sets up by the small stage near the bar. I head to the deck and wait for the bartender to lead us to a table outside. Only two other tables are occupied out here, and I point to the corner. The bartender gives me an easy smile and motions to it with his hand. He has no problem with giving me some privacy since I've been coming here for a few years.

It's a warm night, and the ocean breeze is refreshing. I'm sure several people recognize Jeff, but no one comes over. When the bartender walks away, leaving us with menus, Jeff sits back and looks out over the sand and the water lit up with floodlights.

"Come here often?" he asks, glancing at the menu.

I put my hand on the menu and gently push it back to the table. "Trust me."

He nods with a quiet laugh and settles back in his chair. "You got it. I'm pretty hungry."

"You'll be well fed," I promise. The bartender returns, and I order the bar burger with the works for both of us and beer. "I've been coming here for a while. It's just a fun, casual place to hang out. No frills, but good food at reasonable prices, and he generally books decent bands. It's too far out of the way for the tourists to venture, so it's sort of a local's best-kept secret, so, shhh." I press a finger against my lips. "Keep it to yourself."

He mimics turning a key near his mouth and tossing it over his shoulder before looking at the beach a minute longer. "You really blossomed, Cass."

"I have?" I laugh.

He shakes his head. "No, I don't mean... not like... You are so much more comfortable in your skin. Confident. You really..." He pauses and takes a breath. "I'm not saying it right...."

"Thing is, Jeff, I was always pretty easy-going." I motion to the surrounding bar. "This? This is who I am. I was never comfortable in the big crowds, trying to get noticed, fancy dresses, loud nightclubs."

"It's not me, either, I guess, but I think I made a wrong turn somewhere."

I shake my head. "It's your job. It's not who you are. I know that. I always knew that even when you were trying to live that lifestyle. You did the same thing tonight that you did back then, and I don't even know if you noticed it."

"What'd I do? Reservations at Spago?"

I lean my elbows on the table, resting my chin in my hands with a smile. "'Rock star reporting for duty.' It's like you psych yourself up to be famous. I get it. I go through the motions sometimes when I have to work with someone I admire. But this is who I am when I walk out of that room." I open my palms and glance up. "I think only a select few ever get to see who you really are, hiding out in that canyon of yours."

He squints at me in consideration, and I watch his chest rise. Just then, the bartender comes back with a pitcher and two glasses. "Burgers will be out in a minute," he says, eying me up and down. "What got you all gussied up tonight?"

"Fancy-pants party," I answer, lifting a shoulder and dipping my chin down. "I needed to blend in with the hotshots."

He looks over at Jeff and then me. "Sweetheart, you're too pretty to blend." He winks at me and heads inside.

"You've got a fan," Jeff says, watching him.

"He keeps an eye out for me."

"Think he might have a crush on you?"

"More like he'd have a crush on *you*."

He nods and squints in his direction. "Oh."

"Thought you might have some competition?"

"Don't I? Aren't you seeing that guy from the barbecue?"

I pour our beers and settle back into my chair. "Well, truth is... he pretty much dumped me when your first daisy arrived."

His eyes widen. "Should I apologize?"

I crinkle my nose.

He cocks his head and gives me that rock star smile. "Good. Because I don't think I'm sorry."

"What makes you think there aren't others?"

"There should be. There should be hundreds vying for your attention."

"Ah, that charm." I bite my bottom lip and tilt my head at him. "You're so good at that. I almost believe it."

He folds his forearms on the table in front of him, leaning in. "In order for it to work, there needs to be truth in it. And I meant what I said. There should be. I fucked up, and you have no idea how much I want to be the one you end up with." He drops his chin a bit but keeps his gaze steady.

I'm starting to figure it out.

Chapter 13

Coming into Jeff's studio, something sounds a little *off*. With his hand on his hip facing the band, Jeff holds some papers in one hand and his mic in the other. I'm pretty sure he's trying to hear them, so he's singing softly as they slog along.

He waves his hand with the paper. "All right, all right… stop." Shaking his head, I watch his shoulders come up. "It's not… coming together."

"Gerard needs to play an F major seventh chord," I say.

Jeff turns to look at me, then back to the band and asks them to try it again. Gerard adds the lower C to his chord, and Jeff nods, offering a smile at me. He gives me a wink, and I nod back at him.

They continue playing, and I head into the sound booth, kissing Jace's cheek as he stands in front of the soundboard. For all the years I've known him, he hasn't changed at all. His hair is still shoulder length, but now it's a steel-gray color instead of the dirty blond he once had. He spends a lot of time shaking it off his face, and I wonder if he ever did cut it if he'd continue to shake his head out of sheer habit. He rests a hand on my waist as he steps back with a smile. "Cass, have you met Cole Hammond? He's with *Rolling Stone*."

I swallow and glance through the glass at Jeff. He said nothing about there being a reporter here today. We haven't discussed what we're saying about one another—if anything. The only time we've been out in *public*-public was that once for the industry party. He's kept a low profile working on the album, so it hasn't been an issue. All our other dates have been low-key or just hanging out at one of our houses. Jeff might stop over for a drink or a cup of coffee if I'm between clients, but we're both working crazy hours.

When I don't see him, we talk on the phone. If it's longer than three days, he sends me something—a cd with a song that reminds him of me, some flowers, a bottle of wine and bath salts to unwind after the day. He's been open, honest, realistic, and, much to my amazement, made me feel like an actual priority. All his actions make it harder and harder to keep this slow and casual, but I remain firm and refuse to rush ahead.

Our picture made the paper after the industry thing, but Jace's team was able to control the message. There was one picture of us walking up to the building with Jeff holding my hand, both of us looking forward with barely a smile on our faces. The caption read *'Jeff Kingston and Cassandra Taylor attend Capitol Records Evening of New Talent Event.'* Plain. Simple. Nothing remotely salacious or scandalous about it.

But *Rolling Stone*? I wonder if I should have said something just now. Did I insert myself into his album and the reporter can write about that? At least, for now, Jeff isn't paying attention, but I don't want another *Creem* magazine scenario.

Plastering a smile on my face, I stretch my hand out to shake Cole's. "Haven't met, but I've read your articles. Nice to meet you."

"Cassandra Taylor, right?" Cole says, his smile widening.

I feel my cheeks burn with a sinking feeling. "Yeah."

"Lady, I love your work," he says with a slow shake of his head, still grinning and shaking my hand.

"Oh, thank you." My heart races with both excitement and dread. Someone from *Rolling Stone* knows who I am and likes my work! But I can't shake the feeling of this becoming *Creem* all over again. I glance to Jace and over to Jeff, still hoping to get some insight into what the party line is supposed to be, and get nothing from them. Jeff's busy with the band, and Jace continues smiling at one of his cash cows in action. "I didn't think anyone would really know...."

"I'm a rock journalist." Hammond tilts his head to the side. "We *know* these things. Well, if we're going to be a *good* rock journalist, we know these things. Did you help out on this album?"

"Well, we just stumbled into a few things and they worked out." I lift my shoulders, trying to be vague.

"I didn't realize you two were still friendly."

I swallow. If a deer in headlights could smile, I think it'd look a lot like me right now. "Oh, sure."

"Rock legend has it that the two of you had a pretty rough breakup back in the day."

I keep smiling and flick my gaze over to Jace, still watching Jeff. I want to kick him. I wonder if they ask guys dating questions or if they're reserved for girls, and the boys get the hard, rock'n'roll musical questions. But without talking this over with Jeff, I'm hesitant and need to figure out how to avoid responding to his comment.

"Really?" I cock my head to the side and blink at him. "Rock legend, huh?" Now, I force a skeptical laugh. "That's your rock legend." I point to the live room. "Would you excuse me?" I lift a finger and step back toward the door. I can pretend I'm going to the ladies' room or something and hide in the reception area to avoid answering more questions.

Before I reach the door, however, the band stops playing. Jeff gives a little more direction before releasing them for the night. It's another thing that's different this time around. Jeff doesn't go on into the early morning wearing everyone out. He's been much calmer and saner these last few weeks than I expected him to be. He's even met me for dinner and was on time!

When I return, all three of them are still standing around the soundboard, chatting. Jeff has his hands stuck in his back pockets, and his shoulders are lifted, making me wonder if *he* knew this guy would be hanging around this long. Maybe he *was* asked a dating question? I step up beside him. His smile warms as he rests a hand on the small of my back, and then he shocks me by leaning over to give me a quick kiss. "Hey."

"Hi." I stare at him, my smile stuck in place.

"Cole was just asking us to dinner. You up for it?" Jeff blinks at me and tilts his head, hardly noticeable, but I see it.

I respond with a slight arch of my eyebrows, hoping he can read my *'what's the line, bub?'* whirling in my brain.

Next thing I know, he intertwines his fingers with mine. "I didn't think we had anything planned, did we?" His shoulders relax as he gives my hand a quick squeeze.

I squeeze his back. "No... nothing planned."

On the way to the restaurant, Jeff glances at me as he drives. "You're okay with this?"

"Just so you know, I stuttered through answering a question about writing some songs, but played it down."

He glances at me from the traffic. "Why would you play it down?"

I widen my eyes and swallow a laugh. "Well, the last time I was around for a reporter, Jace called me Yoko Ono and sent me home to get me out of the way, remember? After the article came out, I overheard you telling him that singling out my song was dangerous for your album."

He crinkles his forehead. "I did? Well, that was a shitty thing to say."

I gaze out my window, seeing the whole scene play back in my head. "You said it. So, it was like a knee-jerk reaction when I saw this guy today. I just didn't want you thinking I was trying to steal your thunder again."

"You deserve credit for your work, Cass, *then* and now."

"I'll take it, too, but I didn't want you thinking I was trying to show off for the press. He asked me outright if I wrote anything on the album, and he'd find out when he did his fact-checking. I just…"

He chuckles. "Babe, it's *okay*. You wrote on the album. You are the last person in the world I'd accuse of trying to steal my spotlight. And, while I think you are a hell of a lot more interesting and talented than I am, I don't believe *Rolling Stone* would ditch my cover story for yours, pompous and egotistical as that sounds."

"I didn't think *Rolling Stone* would even know my name, but he did."

"*Plenty* of people in the business sing your praises. They're aware of who you are."

I smile over at him. "I guess I knew that. It still boggles my mind that people know who I am. I always feel like I'm lurking in the shadows, you know? It's weird when people point out that I'm not as far behind the curtain as I think I am."

He stretches his hand out for mine. "I don't think you've *ever* been as far behind the curtain as you thought you were. And if you're okay with it, I have no intention of hiding our relationship. I get in trouble when I try to hide shit, and it's too hard to keep track of who knows what. But, if you'd rather not…."

"Paparazzi won't be taking up residence in my driveway, will they?"

He laughs. "*Highly* unlikely. I doubt anyone will give a shit."

It's my turn to smile at him and squeeze his hand. "Oh, honey, you're going to be on the cover of *Rolling Stone*. D'you really think that'd happen if no one cared? You sell magazines for them. That's the point of being on the cover."

I see his chest lift with a breath, but he just watches the traffic for a moment. "But, anyway, really, I don't want to force anything or assume anything… I mean, if you'd rather keep this quiet…"

"You don't think I'll have groupies going through my trash, do you?" I giggle.

He laughs. "If they do, you're welcome to hide out on my mountain with me for a while."

"Yeah, and when would that happen? Between your schedule and mine?"

"I dunno. Let's take a look at our schedules and get you up on that mountainside to hibernate with me." He wiggles both eyebrows and gives me a devilish grin.

I don't *think* he's hinting at taking me to his bed… not *really*… maybe…? I've thought about it… *if* I would. I was close a few times but then gave myself a break, came back, and chickened out. I talked myself out of it by making up excuses like the sheets weren't changed, or I didn't shave my legs. To his credit, Jeff hasn't pushed, hasn't once put a hand out of place, or groaned when I pulled away. That cocky arrogance of his former self doesn't seem to exist anymore, or if he does, he's stuck in the way-back and bound with duct tape to his seat—but, *oh!* I remember that grin, and one more barrier of my reserve melts away.

We pull into a parking spot. He shuts off the engine and cracks his door before turning to me. "So, we're on the same page here?" In the overhead car light, his eyes are that beautiful light blue I love, and he looks at me with curiosity and hopefulness.

I'm distracted by thoughts of my hand reaching out to unbutton another button on his denim shirt… and then another… and pressing my lips into the crook of his neck…

His smile widens, and an eyebrow lifts in curiosity. "Going public?" he prompts.

I lean over, placing my hand on his jaw, holding him against me a moment in a warm kiss, and pull back. "Yeah." I brush a lock of his hair from his forehead. "Let's go make this thing public."

A few weeks later, I stick my head into his studio after finishing one of my sessions down the hall. He's in the live room with his band, his back toward the booth as they work out a section of his song. Although his hair is shorter, I can tell he's been running his hands through it by the way it sticks up in sections. It's a bad day when it looks like that. His guitarist sits on a stool, and Jeff keeps shaking his head.

"I don't…." Jeff sighs, resting his hands on his hips. Whatever he's hearing, his guitarist isn't getting. "I mean, *yes*, but I need it more… syncopated, staccato… disconnected" The guitarist looks up at him with his eyebrows furrowed. "… but connected, yes. I know I told you connected—but not *that* connected."

"Dude, you don't know what you want," he tells Jeff, trying to laugh it off, but everyone is frustrated.

"I *do* know what I want. Not *that*." Jeff motions to the guitar and turns away. He swings back around to him. "I need it more…." He sings the piece with a hand accentuating certain notes. His guitarist plays what he was playing before, only now accenting a note, and it's not *flowing*. I motion to the sound engineer for permission to enter.

He drops back in his chair and shakes his head. "You're brave," he mutters.

Jeff turns to the door when he hears it and his shoulders drop when he sees me. He motions to the guitarist as he steps over to me, kissing me quickly. "Hey, babe. Sorry… I'm running behind."

"Can I?" I point to the guitarist, and he pulls his head back in question.

Jeff opens his palm out. "Give her the damn guitar."

"I think I know what he's trying to do," I explain with a grin.

He hands it over with a doubtful look, giving up his stool. I sit and ask Jeff to sing it again. He stands before me and starts singing the notes in '*da-da-da's*.' As he sings, I pick up his thread and start playing, watching and nodding along until he stops singing and my fingers play it the way he wants. He drops his head back, and his arms open wide in relief. Then he turns to his guitarist and arches his eyebrows, pointing to me. "*That's* what I wanted," he tells him.

"That's not what you were singing," the guitarist says.

"No, but that's what I wanted."

"How was I supposed to know if that's not what you were telling me to do, man?"

"You needed to *listen* to what I was asking for, not just mimic… You know," Jeff lifts his palms, closing his eyes and shaking his head. "…never mind. Just learn what she's playing, please?"

After another hour, Jeff breaks for the night, and his band disburses. He stands in the middle of the studio after they all leave, arms limp at his sides, blinking at the ceiling. I head into the studio and slip my arms around him, resting my head on his soft gray sweatshirt.

"Rough day?" I ask as he wraps his arms around my shoulders.

I pull back, and he gives me a few quick kisses before resting his forehead against mine. "It'd have been a lot rougher if you didn't help out. Thank you for that."

"I speak Kingston," I say, winking.

He lifts his head and looks at the door. "I don't know how much longer I can use him. He's so *stubborn*. He hears what he wants and doesn't want to listen to what I want."

"Sounds familiar," I tease.

He smiles, still looking at the doorway a second longer before looking at me. "Yes, but it's *my* album. When it's *his*, he can do whatever the fuck he wants to do."

"For the record, I think you're both wrong."

He drops his chin. "What does *that* mean?"

"Listen." I go over and pick up an acoustic. "He was playing this." I play back what his guitarist was doing. "You want this." I finger the section the way he wants. "But, *I* think it should tie in that front section, and if you do something like this...." I strum what's in my head, keeping my eyes on him. "... you'll emphasize the melody a little more, and then when you head over to your bridge...." I switch into the song's bridge. "It's already there, waiting to be picked up."

He comes to stand in front of me, nodding along, watching my fingering. "Wait, instead of that..." He rolls his hand for me to repeat what I did. "Play the A, then the C. Hold it for a beat..." I do as he asks, beginning to hear what he is. "Yes... *yes*! That's... *yes*!" He leans over to kiss me. "*Finally*!" He kisses me again. "Stay here a minute."

I think he's going to go get his guitarist. Instead, he returns, and I see the sound engineer settling behind the board in the booth. "Do you mind staying to play with it for a bit?"

"Sure," I say, dragging the word out as my eyebrows furrow. "But don't you want your guitarist to do it for you in the morning?"

"I want *my* guitarist to do it now." He gives me another quick kiss. "Let's just play with it a minute."

"All right." I settle on the stool and check my levels.

We spend the next hour recording the song with just him singing and me on acoustic. Since he's been working on it for the last few weeks, I knew much of the song. I also draw on my time watching him in the studio with Expedition, so I know *how* he works and fall into step with his vision. Getting swept up in the piece, my doubt and insecurities drop far below, and I let the music drip from my fingertips and course through my blood. It's how I know a song is working. The faster that creative current takes me, the longer it takes me to wade out of it, the better the song. When we finish the last take, he wraps his arms around me with the guitar poking into his chest. He kisses me, swathed in the adrenaline from our session.

"I take it you like that version?"

He twists to the booth. "You got all that?"

"Got it," comes the engineer's godlike voice over the speakers.

Jeff turns back to me. "That's it. That's a keeper. *That's* going on the album." He sets his words off with a quick nod. "That's better than even what I heard in my head—how it should have been from the start." He leans over and kisses me. "I will pay you *double* the going rate to use it."

"All right then." I chuckle. "Except I think you know the going rate better than me. I haven't been a session player in years."

"Well, you're getting that and writing credit," he says with another quick kiss and a gentle tug of my hair.

"I'll take 'em and..." I shift the guitar as he steps closer, "I'll take another kiss, too, please." I forgot how sexy he can be when he's working with that energy directed into his music. There's nothing like that feeling, and it doesn't always happen with the artists I work with. This is the second time it's happened with Jeff.

"With pleasure." He leans in, and I hold him against me to lengthen the kiss. My hand slips up the back of his neck into his hair. If I weren't holding a guitar, I'd have my hand against his chest, too. I release him, holding his gaze once he opens his eyes with a smile.

He clears his throat. "Dinner?"

I brush back those errant, weary-pulled strands with my fingers and grin. "My place?"

During the drive home, I try squelching the flock of butterflies doing an Irish jig in my stomach and not think too hard about what might happen. I avoid looking in my rearview mirror the whole way in case I catch his expression at a stoplight or something. I look at my own eyes instead and suppress a giggle, feeling like a giddy teenager. Part of me wants to glance back, make sure it's real, or see if the moment has passed, but I'm too scared. Something in the studio today changed our dynamic, but I'm not quite sure what it was. Our music is how we reach others. Tonight, it reached us. Maybe it was the music, the concentration, the interaction... but somewhere in it, I found our trust.

No matter how calm I act, when I get out of the car and wait for him on the walk, inside I'm craving him. Once the front door closes, we both know what's going to happen. I reach for him, bring his mouth to mine for a kiss, and open to him. Instead of thinking of an excuse to walk away, I'm thinking of where I want him to touch me. Without a word, I take his hand and start down the hallway to my bedroom, glancing back at him with a grin.

He watches my face with wide eyes. Hesitant? Expectant? Both? When I turn and kiss him again, this time pulling him against me and stepping back to the bed, I feel his chest rise in a heavy breath beneath my fingertips. I lift his shirt to feel the warmth of his skin and run my fingers over his belly in a deeper kiss, remembering how it used to make his whole body shudder with anticipation.

"You're sure?" he asks, pulling back, his hands firm on my hips.

I close my eyes and take a breath before I nod.

"Words, Cass. Are you *sure*?"

I open my eyes to look into his, a dark sunset blue looking back. "Positive."

He leans forward and kisses me, letting it linger. I think he's giving me another chance to back away, but when I don't, his hand buries into my hair to hold me against his mouth like he's finally been released.

I take hold of the hem of his sweatshirt and tug it over his head, anticipating the feel of his skin beneath my fingertips. He's not the kid of twenty-five before me. His chest and shoulders are broader, but I remember how they felt beneath my palms. His kiss trails down my jaw and neck. Taking hold of my shirt, he tugs and tosses it alongside his before sitting beside me on the mattress. With another kiss, his fingers unclasp my bra. As I fling it aside, his hands press up against my breasts. I drop my head back, releasing those butterflies from my stomach in a soft breath as his kisses lower to explore.

It isn't long before he's unbuttoning my jeans. I help slide them and my panties off, then cast the blankets aside. He undresses and comes back to me, his hand sliding along the inside of my thigh until his fingers reach between my legs. In a kiss, I close my eyes as he pleases me while his mouth explores my breasts, then the crook of my neck. I take heavy breaths, inching closer to orgasm, and cling to him in a kiss, riding out my pleasure.

Then, I explore him. I touch him in places I never expected to touch again. Placing kisses on his palms, the crook of his elbow, his neck, chest, and belly. I take my time to savor each one, listening to the intake of his breath as I do, and let my fingers graze over the trail of hair that leads down to his arousal.

Before we go further, I sit up and rummage through my nightstand, placing a condom in his hand. Sitting behind him and kissing between his shoulders, my hands run up the inside of his thighs as he rolls it on. When he's ready, he twists to kiss me, and we drop back to the mattress. I take him in my palm, guiding him inside me, and hear him groan in my ear with pleasure.

We move together like we do when we're writing. I shift. He

bends. He moves, and I follow. It's instinctual and natural, like it has always been between us. He's still skillful in how he touches me, but now there's more of an awareness of my response to him. It's not only about the orgasm but wanting to continue pleasing. Once he comes, he holds me tight against him, his breath heavy and quick against me. I brush his hair back, damp around his forehead and temple. He brushes his lips against my shoulder as he lies beside me. His fingers reach out to intertwine with mine to keep touching, checking in, taking in my response. "You still okay with all this?"

"I wouldn't have invited you in my bed if I wasn't sure."

He watches my face, those eyes darting between mine with a hint of a smile on his lips.

"What? What're you thinking?" I ask with a grin, my fingers still in his hair.

"This was not what I was expecting to happen today." He chuckles, kissing my shoulder again, an arm draping over my belly.

"Me either." I close my eyes to the way that feels. It's not a memory. He's here. It's real. I turn my head as he shifts again. This time he kisses me, long and deep. I play with his hair as his head presses into the pillow, still studying my face. "*What*?"

"I'm not sure if it's time."

"Time for what?" I lift my head to glance at the bedside clock: 10:34 pm. "Dinner?"

He closes his eyes before he shakes his head, still smiling. "I...." He leans over and kisses me. "... could eat. Yeah, dinner sounds good."

"I can probably find something." I sit up but immediately lean over to kiss him.

He's here. He's in my bed and, if anything, more skilled at making love than the quick-flash satisfying romps we had so long ago. I just want to stay here a moment longer, feeling his arms around me, my skin against his, seeing that soft look in his gaze watching me.

"You don't have to rush off anywhere, do you?" I ask.

His eye crinkles return when he smiles. He reaches up to pull me back against him for a kiss as his answer.

Jeff's honey and wheat-colored highlights intensify in the morning light through his walnut waves. Sheets wrap around his waist with the blanket kicked off as he sleeps. I close my eyes and listen to his breathing, slow and heavy, with his arm draped across my back. I never thought I'd feel that again, and part of me doesn't ever want to move, so I can feel this content for the rest of my life. His eyes flutter open into a squint from the sun before closing again with a breath. He still wakes up slow, his smile a small, soft shadow in his stubble.

"Go back to sleep," I whisper, waiting another moment simply to watch him.

I leave him in bed and sneak into the bathroom to freshen up and slip on a short terrycloth bathrobe. In the kitchen, I open the back door to the flowers bursting with color around the patio, sending a soft fragrance to blend with the smell of the coffee.

When he comes out a few minutes later, he's wearing his jeans, barefoot and shirtless, like a faint vision of the rock god I once lived with. He's still trim, and already I want to feel his chest beneath my fingertips again.

"Good morning," I say with a smile, sitting at the kitchen table with my coffee. "Sleep well?"

He nods, coming over to kiss me and rubbing his nose against mine. "Morning," he mumbles, his voice heavy with sleep. Heading to the counter, he pours coffee into the mug waiting for him. "I slept just fine. You?"

"Yeah, I did. I half expected to wake up and find you rushing out the door for an interview or something, though." I chuckle.

He snickers and takes a sip of coffee. "Not yet, but soon enough, I'm afraid."

I sit up a bit, wrapping my hands around my mug, feeling the warmth sink into my fingers. "Oh?"

He lifts a shoulder and sits at the table. "Album's almost finished. That means drive-time radio interviews and summer tour."

My stomach clenches. How long will he be gone? Has he been on tour since he's clean?

He takes another sip and slouches in his chair next to mine, stretching his legs out, ankles crossed in front of him. "*Interview* magazine is starting to sniff around, and Jace thinks it'd be a good idea for them to come out to do a feature-length piece. Maybe hit a few tour dates, possibly highlight all of our tours in one piece since Teddy's looking to tour this summer, too... I dunno." He glances out the window and takes another drink. "He's still working out logistics. I just have to focus on finishing the album right now. We're looking at that studio in Culver City for tour rehearsals. It's not far to commute every day and won't be crazy with expenses. What do you think?"

"Tour?" My brain is stuck. He's a working musician. Of *course,* he needs to tour. Of *course,* he's going to head out on publicity tours, do radio interviews, have magazines poking around.

"Well, someone's gonna have to sell the damn thing once it's released. That's usually how it's done." He winks at me, waking up a bit more. "They're shorter these days. Probably no more than thirty dates. That's why the label's been on my ass to finish. They've been securing dates and greasing up the publicity machine, although why anyone's interested in some old '70s rocker these days. Who knows what Jace'll want me to do to prove that I'm still relevant."

He's rock royalty, regardless of how much he wants to play it down. If his last solo album is any indication, his tour will sell out in a day, too. He's anything but an old '70s rocker.

"You put a keytar on your album; we're through."

He laughs, his eyes crinkling.

"How long before you're done, do you think?" I hope I sound casual and not panicked. Do I have a right to be panicked? I'm getting so far ahead of myself.

"We're close." He lifts a shoulder. "With last night's song, maybe one more, then I can start final mixes. I'm guessing by the end of next month I should have something to shop around."

"You know," I tilt my head at him, "you make all this sound so old-hat."

He grins down at his mug and nods. "It is. I don't let the label push me around like they used to. When they start putting pressure on, I remind them my contract is up after this album, and I can start looking to sell my talent to another label. They back off a little. Besides, Jace starts running interference for me, and they *really* hate when that happens. They don't get to talk to me for weeks, running in circles."

"It's good to be king," I say, "or Kingston."

He lifts his shoulder again.

I laugh. "Are you practicing humility? You think other artists get to pick and choose their time frames?"

He tilts his head side to side, puckering his lips. "I guess not."

"Bullshit, you guess." I shake my head at him, curling my lip up. "Are you nervous about the circus starting back up? Is that it?"

"Less circus, more carnival these days. Just one ring in the big top when I'm solo." He sips his coffee and glances out the window. "Still just as colorful and chaotic."

I know he's commenting on touring, but the same could be said for my garden, or heck, our track record. "You okay with that?"

He looks at me for a long moment, his eyes a stormier blue. "I guess I'm about to find out, aren't I?"

I reach my hand across to rest on his, wondering how much courage it took for him to admit that.

"I'm sure it'll be fine." He purses his lips before turning his head to look back outside.

"You worried?" I ask.

A flicker of a smile crosses his lips. "I'm always worried when it comes to touring. Too many moving pieces, just my name on it. I don't have the other guys to fall back on, so if it sucks, it's me."

"If it's awesome, it's you, too."

He looks at me and nods. "That too. I won't lie and say I'm not concerned about doing it drug-free. I've never been on a tour where that wasn't an option until now, so…" He presses his lips into a line and arches both eyebrows. "I mean, it's not like I don't think I *can't* do it, but I'm pretty sure it's gonna be different. New band. New album. *Sober*." He sips his coffee. "I can't drink when I'm out because I can't carry off interviews and sound checks with a hangover. Never mind what it'll do to my voice. I'm not gonna risk getting caught with weed after Paul McCartney's Japan ordeal and get stuck in jail and the publicity and everybody freaking out. It's a new era of touring, I guess, and I'm not sure what that's gonna look like."

"I'm sure it'll be smoother than you think. You'll over-prepare. You'll have every detail ironed out. I watched you do it when you were half-baked with Expedition. I can only imagine how much better it'll be when you're clear-headed. Are the lobbies still swarming with fans?"

He laughs. "Fans grow up, too."

"Do they? Or can they just afford to book rooms in the hotels and wait in the bars instead of the lobby?"

He furrows his eyebrows and smiles at me. "They won't be bumping into me if that's what they're doing. I haven't been in a hotel bar in years."

How can I be insecure about this? Glancing down at the table, I brush a few lingering crumbs into a small pile. Scenes of 1976 are going off in my brain like flashbulbs. But it's 1983, and he's done none of that in the months we've been together. I've only seen him drink, and even that hasn't gotten out of hand. So, why would I have any reason to believe he's going to do that now? Didn't I want to stop looking backward? I lift my chin to look at him. Here. In my kitchen. After getting out of my bed. It's not 1976.

"You okay?"

I smile and take a silent breath. "Yeah. I guess I didn't realize how close you were to finishing. I thought we had more time."

He rests the mug down on the table. "What do you mean?"

"Before I lost you to the industry again."

Turning his wrist, he takes my hand and squeezes my fingers. "That's not going to happen."

"It's kind of in the job description, Jeff. You belong to them when you're out there."

"But in here," he points to his chest, "I belong to you."

I tilt my head to the side and smile. "Do you?"

He nods. "I tried to tell you last night, but then it would have sounded like I was saying it because we just finished being intimate, and I didn't want it to sound like that. I wanted you to know it was real." He leans forward. I lean in and let him kiss me. He doesn't pull back all the way. "I love you. Again."

I drop my forehead against his and smile, hearing those words from him. "Love you, too. Again."

"Come with me."

I give him a quick kiss and sit back in my chair. "Where? On tour?" I drop my chin and scoff.

"You never got to go on tour, right? Come be my guitarist on stage and groupie off it." He chuckles.

"You know, Yoko still has that reputation of breaking up the Beatles and ruining rock music forever. No one wants to be the Yoko."

He tilts his head from side to side. "Well, I see you more as Linda McCartney. You know, a real part of the band, playing an instrument, involved in the actual music. Not caterwauling through the tracks. You'd make my band a hell of a lot better."

I chuckle. "I'm glad you think so. It's flattering, but I like my job, and I've got a full schedule through October. I'm gonna keep it."

"Understandable. Definitely my loss."

I rest my elbow on the table and put my chin in my palm with a devilish grin. "The groupie part, though, is very tempting."

He arches an eyebrow. "Yeah?"

"Can I still audition for the part?"

He gives me his rock star sexy smirk. "What kind of audition do you have in mind, darlin'?"

I lower my eyes to his groin and take my time to scan up over his bare chest with a slight grin on my face. "Got any suggestions?"

He shifts in his chair and bites his lips together, looking away in pretend thought. "I could probably think of one or two if pressed."

"Hmm." I slip from my chair and crouch in front of him as he shifts again, uncrossing his ankles. Moving between his knees, I rest my palm on his groin. "Pressed like this?" I rub the heel of my palm over the denim seams. "Or maybe… more like this?" He exhales slowly, his gaze locking on mine. "Maybe, something more like…." I undo the jeans as he shifts again, spreading his knees a little more. He's not wearing his boxers, so his growing arousal is evident.

I lower my head and slide the tip of my tongue along its length, hearing him take a ragged breath. "Like that, maybe?"

"Yeah, maybe something along those lines." He's grinning at me when I look up at him, those eyes locking on mine. "Maybe we should take this back into the other room?"

I reach into my bathrobe pocket and pull out a condom with a grin.

His eyebrows lift with his laugh as I open it. I think he's enjoying my taking the lead, and possibly catching him a bit off guard with it, too. *Good.* I enjoy surprising him. It keeps him guessing. Once it's open, I tug at his jeans until they're around his ankles, rolling the condom on for him. When I finish, I give him a sly smile, untying my robe to reveal my nakedness and straddle him. He holds onto my waist as I guide him inside me with a long, deep breath. *Oh*, how I missed the way his hands feel on my skin.

Even in this playfulness, we read each other's needs, shifting together, his hands on my waist, bringing me down against him in his desire. He bites his lower lip as he watches us move together, at first, slow and steady. I rest my gaze on his chest, rising and falling with his breaths, holding onto his shoulders as his pleasure builds. My thoughts scramble with being able to touch him again like this, remembering how good we used to be together, all those mornings we would wake up and just start touching each other, listening to the ocean outside our window. Watching his face now as he lifts his chin to look at me with a hint of a smile again makes me want to laugh with joy. That look is fleeing, though, as he pulls me against him with faster thrusts until the chair legs rattle against the floor and his head drops back with his orgasm. Drawing my hands down to rest on his chest, I lean forward to place a kiss on his shoulder with a giggle.

I kiss his mouth, but he surprises me by grabbing my waist and slipping off the chair until I'm lying on my robe on the floor. He dabs his tongue along my belly before circling and sucking my breasts briefly on his journey lower until he's using his tongue to please me. My hand rests in his hair, and I blink up at the ceiling, almost wanting to laugh at where we're doing this, but he feels too good, and I am too close to my orgasm to consider it for long.

When I moan with my release, he makes his way back up, kissing and licking until he reaches my mouth to kiss me deeply. "How about I become your groupie?" he questions with a quiet, seductive tone.

"You're hired."

Chapter 14

"What the hell is that supposed to be?" Jeff barks as I come into the rehearsal space.

His band stands on the makeshift stage with Jeff facing them in the center. "We're three weeks in, people. I thought you were fucking professionals!" He waves a dismissive hand as he turns and runs it through his hair before circling back to them. "Let's do it *again,* but this time, how about you pretend like you've heard the damn song before?"

I step over to the sound engineer and place my bags on one of the stools. "Ouch," I whisper as the band breaks into an older Expedition song.

The sound guy glances at me with warning and a slight shake of his head. "He's been a bear all day," he mumbles, looking at the soundboard.

I wince at him, knowing all too well how Jeff can be. To be honest, I've been waiting for his rock star to make an appearance ever since they started tour prep a month ago. I know he's stressed and concerned, but until now, he's handled it all fairly well. Sure, he's been frustrated and tired some days, but he's kept it in perspective.

Jeff waves his hands in the air, stopping them again with a string of curses, shaking his head. "Go the fuck home. On your way, go buy the album and listen to the *damn* song, and don't come back until you've figured out the friggin' *notes*!" He storms away with another wave of his hands. No one in the band moves. They keep eying one another in confusion, unsure if he means it. At the edge of the marked-off stage area, Jeff stops and turns. "Get the fuck out of here! I mean it!" They drag their straps over their shoulders, watching him and glancing at the other band members. "Figure it out, or I'll find someone who can."

He heads toward the bathroom as everyone wanders out with whispers and wide eyes. This is the rock star I remember, and I'm more than a little frightened to encounter him again. The sound engineer writes some notes down and takes a breath. Giving me a blessing sign while arching his eyebrows, he grabs his gear and heads out. I'm left alone on the sound stage, waiting for him, wondering if he'll even come this way or head straight to his car. I'm not sure if he saw me.

"Hello?" I call out after a minute, my voice echoing in the empty space. I hear a door open. "It's safe. Everyone left."

"Not everyone," he grumbles, crossing the expansive warehouse and stopping to face the stage.

"I brought you dinner."

"Hmm." His arms fold over his chest, distracted.

"Sounds like you're having quite a day," I continue, trying to coax him out of this mood.

He comes over to the soundboard and checks over the notes left by the engineer before his mouth forms a thin line, reviewing the empty stage again. "Where the hell did I find these assholes?" He picks up the pen, crosses out what's written, and scribbles something else. It's illegible in his fury.

"Jeff, calm down." I reach out to put my hand on his arm, but he pulls it away. "What's *wrong*?"

He motions to the stage. "They're assholes!"

"They're *not*, but you're acting like one."

He fixes me with an icy stare. "You can go, too."

I nod. "Yes. I can." I pick up my purse, step around him, and leave.

On the drive home, I tell myself that I don't have to put up with his tantrums as I fly around slow traffic, taking my anger out on the drivers by cutting them off. When I get home, I slam a few doors. I don't care that he said he loves me; I don't have to stand there and let him take his bad day out on me.

Changing into a pair of shorts and a baggy tee-shirt before heading into the kitchen, I stare into the refrigerator. It's not like I *want* any food, but I don't know what else to do. I keep seeing that anger in his eyes, that cold fury he can summon like a demon unleashed from the deep. Slamming the refrigerator door shut, I open the freezer. Nothing in here I want, either, so I open the fridge again, grab a wine cooler, and flop onto the couch to watch *The Facts of Life*.

By the second commercial break, there's a knock at the door. I glance out the window at Jeff's BMW in front of the house. Taking another long swallow from the wine cooler, I head into the hallway, taking my time, peering through the glass in the door before opening it.

Jeff lifts his palms, and his shoulders rise and drop with a breath, his mouth open. "I'm an asshole, and my mouth runs three times faster than my brain sometimes. I'm sorry." He drops his hands and shakes his head.

"Do you want to talk about it?" I ask, taking a sip of wine cooler, letting him stand on the porch. "Or do you want to pout like a spoiled brat a little more?"

He glances down to his feet and rests his shoulder against the door frame. "Are you busy right now?"

I glance over my shoulder. "I might be."

"Do you have time for a drink while I tell you what happened last night at that industry thing Jace dragged me to and explain why I've been an ass all day?"

I glance toward the living room where I can hear the laugh track and turn back to him. "Well, I am in the middle of a very important episode of *Facts of Life*. I think Tootie might be jealous of Jo's boyfriend."

Furrowing his eyebrows, he asks, "What's a Tootie?"

"It's too late to explain now." I step back and motion for him to come inside with a tilt of my head. I tell him to sit in the living room before grabbing a beer and another wine cooler from the kitchen. He's blinking at the TV when I come in while the actress, Kim Fields, is on screen. "That's a Tootie." I turn off the TV and sit on the other end of the couch, a cushion between us, as he pops the beer top. "So? What happened last night?"

He rests an ankle on his knee and sits back with a sigh, sipping his beer. "I should have known," he starts. "The second he told me it was at some producer's house, I should have known."

"Known what?" I fold my legs beneath me and sit back into the corner, facing him.

He shifts to face me, his eyes a crisp fall-day blue in the lamplight. "Drugs would be everywhere, and with the long hours I've been doing, the upcoming tour prep... I should have known...."

There's a flutter of panic in my stomach as I study his face, trying to see if he's clenching his jaw or chewing the inside of his cheek. It would explain that demon making an appearance. It would also mean we're done. I'm not putting up with that anymore.

He notices what I'm doing and turns away, biting his lower lip. "I didn't do anything," he continues with a hush in his voice. "You don't need to inspect me."

"Do you blame me after the way you were snapping at everyone?"

He grimaces, dispirited, as his shoulders drop. He picks at the seam on his jeans. "I suppose not," he mumbles.

"I believe you... that you didn't do anything."

He furrows his eyebrows at me, almost surprised when he faces me again.

"You're not fidgeting and licking the skin off your lips. But if you didn't, what's the attitude about?"

His chest rises with a breath. "I didn't want to *want* it. But my God, Cass..." He blinks at me and then squeezes his eyes closed, his hand resting on his forehead to squeeze his temples with his fingers. "I thought I had a better handle on it. I've been to plenty of places where it's there. Hell, it's fucking everywhere... but last night...." He swallows and takes a mouthful of beer, blinking forward at the empty room. "That voice in the back of my head kept telling me...."

"Telling you what?"

"I could get so much more done if I did just one little bump." He lifts his hand and pinches his fingers together. "I'd get that energy to get through all the bullshit with one quick hit. No one would have to know...." Closing his eyes again, he continues, "... and I won't lie and tell you I wasn't tempted." He gazes at the ceiling and takes a breath. "There's still so much to do, and I'm running out of time. I mean, next week, Jace has me back-to-back-to-back with interviews—the first one? Johnny Carson. I always did something to take that edge off before an interview, so I didn't over-think what I was saying or *try* so hard to say the right thing. And my first time out sober, Jace books me on Carson? What was he *thinking*?"

"Maybe getting the big one over with so you can relax for the rest?"

He groans. "The *rest*...." He closes his eyes. "That's what scares me. I keep waiting for that little voice to stop screaming at me that doing a quick bump makes me feel like I am king of the world and can just...." He strangles the air in front of him. "... grab it by the throat and *make* shit happen. "

"Except you waste more time spinning your wheels than getting anything done. And you know that, or you'd have taken a hit and not been this disturbed by its presence. You can't have a tantrum because you were around some coke and wanted to do a line. You've been around it before now. What made last night different?"

He releases a heavy breath and drops his hand to the cushions, reaching over to pick up his beer again and taking a sip. "I don't know," he sighs. "I thought I was stronger."

"But you didn't take anything."

He shakes his head, almost as though he's embarrassed to face me. "Wanted to. All fucking day."

"So, why didn't you?" I question. "What stopped you?"

He faces me with another heavy breath. "I was going to prove to myself that I didn't need it. I want to be *done* with this bullshit. I wanted to be done," he repeats softly.

"You walked away from it," I remind him.

"And what did I do? I've been on a rampage today." He lifts his hand to the door and drops it on the cushion. "I took it out on everyone around me. I'll be shocked if any of them come back tomorrow. And I… truly didn't mean to snap at you like that. I regretted saying what I did the second I said it."

"I know. Otherwise, I wouldn't have let you in my house again. And I hate to break it to you, but you're going to be an asshole sometimes, even without the drugs. But you're not a full-time asshole anymore. You did apologize."

Now, he lowers his chin and holds my gaze. "Because you're the most important thing in my life."

Turning my head, I take a sip of my drink and slip my hand down my ponytail, trying to hide the shock of his words. Those few simple words send a flash of giddiness through me like some silly teenager.

"And I didn't want to fall back on *that* old habit, either," he continues.

"Which old habit was that?" I question, glancing into the wine cooler.

"Taking *you* for granted," he says as I look at him. "I don't want to screw us up again because of my attitude and ego." He scowls, dropping his head back to the couch. "I'm a dick sometimes, but I'm trying to be better."

"You are better." I stretch my leg out to nudge him with my toe. "You apologized. You can apologize tomorrow to whoever comes back. I'm pretty sure they'll all show up and are probably memorizing every song on every album Expedition ever made right now. Question is, Jeff, ask anyone that's tried to kick it; that craving doesn't go away. What're *you* going to do when that desire strikes again?"

He angles his head in disappointment, not even bothering to lift it from the cushions. "Probably the same thing I did—walk away but maybe not let it haunt me all day afterward—hope it doesn't happen when I'm in the middle of freaking out about my album dropping and tour prep."

I tilt my head to the side and offer a gentle smile. "Your single is amazing. Your album is great. Your dates are selling out."

He stares at me with wide, frightened eyes, and I stretch my hand out on the cushion between us. "You'll be amazing, baby. I know it sounds counterintuitive, but what I really think you need? Is a day off." He takes another drink and shakes his head, releasing a sigh. I can virtually see his 'to-do list' scrolling before his eyes. "How about a *night* off, then?"

He arches a doubtful eyebrow at me.

"Have a beer. Put your feet up. Watch mind-numbing TV with your girl and leave everything you need to do at the doorstep. It'll be there in the morning. I promise."

He pauses but sits up to untie his sneakers and kicks them off, then drops back into the couch, leaning closer toward me. I let my fingers run through his hair, and he closes his eyes. I wonder if he needs his dark tour cocoon to close everything out. It's been a non-stop array of auditions, rehearsals, album mixes, photo shoots, merchandizing.... There are a million details he's losing sleep over.

Reaching behind me, I turn the lamp off to soften the light in the room. "I think I have some bubble bath. Want to tune the world out for a little while?"

A slow, tired smile spreads over his face, and he closes his eyes again for a moment. "You'll join me?"

"You go find as many candles as you can. I'll draw the bath."

"How do you do it?" he asks as we sit up.

"Do what?" I ask, standing up and finishing my wine cooler.

"Still know me so well after all this time."

I lean over and kiss him gently, tugging at the ends of his hair at the nape of his neck. "I just pay attention."

"One day, I'd like to be able to provide you with comfort like this. Turn your day around."

Stretching my hand out to him, I wiggle my fingers. "Who says you don't?"

When he stands, he pulls me into his arms and replies with his voice a low rumble. "I do. But I'll figure something out to make it up to you."

"There's nothing...."

He presses his mouth against mine and kisses me.

"Okay, you can try."

I open my eyes to my overnight bag sitting on a chair across from the bed in Jeff's bedroom. Next to the chair is a small table with the lamp he bought at that flea market so long ago. Shadows dance on the floor from leaves swaying in the breeze, the sun still low enough to cast them through the trees. Jeff places a kiss between my shoulders, and I close my eyes with a deep breath. He moves and pulls me closer to kiss a spot below my neck, and I smile into my pillow.

"I have a plane to catch," I mumble with my eyes closed.

"Catch another one," he says, his lips against my skin as he speaks.

I chuckle and run my palm over his arm wrapped around me. "Doesn't work that way, baby." I roll onto my back.

He lifts on his elbow and brushes my hair back. "You sure? I can...."

I put my finger over his lips and nod into the pillow. "Places to go. People to see. For the both of us."

He groans and closes his eyes, but puckers his lips to kiss my finger. "You'll call me with your number when you get in?" He pulls his head back before smiling and then playfully bites my finger with a nose crinkle.

"I will call you when I know which hotel they're putting me in, yes, but you'll be at work rehearsing for *Saturday Night Live* and won't get my message until late." I pull my finger back but slip my hand into the back of his head and draw him closer. "Call me anyway."

"I'll call you anyway," he says, his lips against mine as he does. "Are you *sure* you can't get a later flight?"

"We'll make up for it when you're back from New York." I slip my arms down and push his shoulder back reluctantly. When I sit up, I lean over and kiss him, pressing him back into the mattress with it.

He chuckles as his arms wrap around my waist. "What about your flight?"

"I know." I pull back with a sigh and brush his hair off his forehead. "You make this very difficult when you're this sexy and scruffy, you know." But I force myself from his arms and slip out of bed. I *do* have a plane to catch.

Two hours later, as I walk through the airport, I glance at one of the kiosks and see Jeff's pale denim blue eyes peering back at me from the magazine stand. His issue of *Rolling Stone* is out. Of course, I grab a copy for my flight. The blood drains from my face when I read it.

In the 70s, Kingston reached out for songwriting help
when Expedition couldn't find the words to make a decent
song themselves. This album is no different, although it's

just Kingston's. Also, like the 70s, Kingston hasn't reached very far for assistance: his latest girlfriend and multi-gold songwriter, Cassandra Taylor. You might remember her as a prior lover and live-in girlfriend of Kingston's in 1976, or maybe you remember her song off their platinum album Desert Sage, "I'm Always at Home." Maybe you remember some of her other songs: "Morning Do," "Saying Goodbye," "Late in the Night," and "Love Keeps Coming." You should. They're all top ten songs by artists she's worked with.

Kingston wasn't playing around when he tapped into her talent for his album. Was it because he's still competing with band mate Teddy Derricks for the solo crown glory? Was it because she was sitting beside him, ready to offer help? During the interview, they made it very well known that they were a couple to be reckoned with and quite cozy. Even the great Jeff Kingston gets smitten and lets his lady rule the roost.

That's not to say the album doesn't shine, or that Kingston isn't talented in his own right. There are some gems. They're not the songs your dad listened to fixing the car in the garage with a beer like Expedition songs. I suppose some people call it maturity, and if you have to mature, you want to do it Kingston's way with a lot of money and a bunch of groupies before writing some slick, catchy songs about growing up and getting older.

My gaze dashes around as though someone might point and laugh at me, but it's just my inner voice snickering; *I told you so.* I close the article with a queasy stomach, understanding why Expedition griped about having to do interviews. Cole Hammond seemed nice when we were at dinner, very personable, and funny. But reading this, I'm surprised it's the same guy. The article is basically about how Expedition should remain as a group and not bother doing their side solo projects because of how mediocre they are individually.

This is worse than the *Creem* article. I can't believe he could get away with panning Jeff's album like that. There's no rhyme or reason to it. It's not Expedition, so it's boring? Why is a slick and catchy song a *bad* thing? And Jeff deferring to me? *Smitten?* Am I that blind? Or were we *that* nervous? No matter what, our going public does not seem to have sat well with Cole Hammonds of *Rolling Stone,* and I can only imagine how Jeff is going to react.

By the time I land in Nashville and check in at the hotel, it's past midnight, but I call. His machine picks up, so I leave my room and phone number and get ready for bed, expecting to be woken up by his call at some point when he got home.

I'm not woken up.

When I come back to the hotel after my session the next day, no messages are waiting for me, and now that queasiness returns. He saw the article, too, obviously. Probably second-guessing going public, right? *Creem* all over again.

Then I take a sharp breath and shake my head quickly. *No.* I refuse to get freaked out by this and jump to conclusions. He's busy. He's performing on *Saturday Night Live* and has a bunch of finishing touches for the tour.

He's *busy.*

I sit on the bed, and his machine picks up again when I call. "Hey… just got back to my room—crazy day. Just wanted to check in and see how it's going. Umm… Room 512." I leave the hotel number and hang up.

Then I sit and stare at the phone on the nightstand before chastising myself for doubting this. I draw a bath, grab my book, and relax in the tub.

The phone never rings.

By the third day of not hearing from him, I'm convinced I'm both overreacting and broken up at the same time. I wonder if he's had some kind of relapse and fell off the wagon. Is he detoxing somewhere and can't call me? I've called Jace's office and left messages but can't get any information out of the girl answering the phone, and Jace isn't in to take my call—supposedly.

Maybe Jace is taking care of damage control and can't take my call. But they are still promoting his being on *Saturday Night Live*, so I'm pretty sure he's okay. He's fine. He's just cutting me out of his life again over a stupid magazine article that neither of us had any control over. But somehow, it always seems to bite me in the ass, doesn't it? If this thing isn't over, I am never letting either of us do another interview ever again.

But what if something happened to him…?

My thoughts flip back and forth like one of those toy hand clappers.

Resigning myself to flying back to LA, tears threaten my eyes most of the flight. His face stares at me from magazine racks in both airports, and the person across the aisle from me leaves it on their tray table, so he watches me the entire way home. I don't go back to my house, though. Instead, I ring Hannah's doorbell, leaving my luggage in the car. In my backseat, I see the case Jeff's guitar rests in. This feels much too familiar, and my stomach tightens.

"Hey!" Hannah says, swinging the door open. "Come in. When'd you get home?"

"Only about an hour ago. Got any coffee?"

"Of course, I do. You look tired." She heads down the hallway, and I follow, closing the door behind me.

"Baby sleeping?"

"For the time being. She's teething. It's been a nightmare. That's why *I* look like crap. What's your reason? I hope it's more fun than mine." She chuckles, fixing me with a smile before setting the coffeepot to brew.

As the comforting scent of coffee fills the room, it's in direct contrast to my nerves. "I'm kind of... freaking out."

"Why? What happened? Weren't you in Nashville? Work okay?"

I nod, dropping into a seat at the kitchen table. "Work's fine. Had a great session. It's not work that I'm freaking over."

"What'd Rock Wonder do this time?" she asks with a grin, folding her arms and resting against the counter. She's in a pair of powder blue sweatpants and an oversized pink tee shirt and looks anything but crappy. She is still the sunny California chick, although her hair is a little darker these days.

I explain my week as we sit at the kitchen table, drinking coffee. "He's due to leave for New York today, and I had half a mind to fly there instead of home just to see if he's all right. But Jeff, New York, and me? Not a good track record, and if he's cut me out of his life again, I don't want to look like a fool showing up. I'd look desperate, wouldn't I? Like I didn't trust him."

She leans her arms on the table and dips her chin at me. "*Do* you trust him?"

"That's the part that's pissing me off. Because I *do*. I *want* to believe there's a reasonable explanation, but we haven't gone this long without touching base since he's back in my life. We might go three days, tops, but not a week. And to not even get a call? What am I supposed to think?"

I swipe my fingers over my cheek, trying to get to the tear before she sees. "I'm disappointed in myself that there is still part of me that believes he'd dump me over a magazine article. That he'd dump me without so much as a phone call, just as I felt like we were on the verge of sharing and trusting each other enough to let me into his world and see everything for what it is. The good, bad, ugly, boring, tiring, mundaneness that it is. But now, radio silence for a week."

"But over a stupid magazine?"

"It wouldn't be the first time, but I thought we were beyond all that." I tap my spoon against the napkin and sigh. "We *were* beyond all that. This isn't *him* anymore."

"Then what is this?"

I fix my gaze on her, unable to keep the tears from welling. "I don't know," I whisper, "and I'm so scared to find out. Hannah, I didn't think I could love him again. Not like this. Did I get too comfortable? Did I trust him too soon?"

She sits in the chair next to me and leans over, resting her hand on mine. "Cass, did you ever think that maybe he's not dumping you?"

"I keep trying to tell myself that. That I'm jumping to conclusions, but it's *Jeff*. He's so methodical with everything. Can *you* think of one good reason why he wouldn't return my calls all week?"

Sitting back, she folds her arms. "Didn't you say he was preparing for a summer tour?"

My shoulders drop in a sigh. "Yes."

"So?"

I drop my head back with a groan. "Am I overthinking it?"

"You've got history. I totally understand that some things are going to make you nervous. But you said yourself; he's not gone this long without talking to you since he's been back. I don't believe a few paragraphs in a magazine at this stage in his career will mean squat. If he were injured or hurt, you'd know about it by now. I think there's going to be a very reasonable explanation, and when there is, you're going to sit down and have a talk with him and let him know how you feel about all this—and him."

I fold my arms on the table and drop my cheek to them. "This is why you're my best friend. That ledge seems much further out than it did half an hour ago."

My answering machine is blinking when I walk in the door. I drop my keys on the table beside it and press play, leaving my bags in the doorway.

"Hey Cass, it's me," Jeff's voice sounds tired. "I think my plane may have passed yours. Jace got me set up with some interviews, and I had to fly out a few hours after you left. I'm gonna miss your call with your hotel info. Uh... I checked, but there're like fifty studios... and thirty hotels and not a whole lot of time for me to call to find you." He exhales. "I'll give you a call when you get home, I guess. Love you, babe."

I sit on the chair next to the table as the next message plays, biting my lips with tears of relief in my eyes.

"Hey, babe, so the girl in the office must have gotten the information wrong. I called the number she gave me, but it was a Piggly Wiggly. Pretty sure you weren't staying there. Just wanted to call and say I *tried* to call. I didn't disappear this time, either. I think you might have, though. Thinking of you, babe. I'll talk to you when you get home. Love you. Bye."

I smile at the answering machine. He *did* try to call me. Twice. I take a breath when the next message starts.

"Hey... I know you're not home. I just wanted to say... hey. It's weird. We didn't talk for seven years—and four days seems like an eternity now... All right... Um, love you... bye."

Now, I laugh through my tears, telling myself I should have trusted him. *Us*. My shoulders finally release the tension that's been holding them up against my ears for days, but I know Hannah's right. I have to let him know how I felt about this... and him.

When he steps onto the stage, he's nervous. I can tell by how he presses and rubs his fingers together, looking side to side, then back to his guitarist to start. He steps up to the mic, grabs hold, and his gaze lands on me sitting in the front row. I smile at him and blow a kiss with a giggle. I'm sure the person next to me thinks I'm a freak, but I know that wink and the wide grin he gave were for me. In the end, when the cast comes out to say goodnight, he steps off the stage to grab my hand, takes me in his arms, and kisses me like we've been apart for months.

"We'd better get used to it," I tell him when we get back to the hotel after a late dinner.

As I say this, his arms wrap around me from behind, and he nuzzles into my neck with a quiet moan. "Not yet. You're here now."

I turn to face him and am greeted with a kiss. "I missed you."

He smiles against my lips before kissing me deeper. "I missed you, too. Can we pick up where we left off?"

I revel in his touch, and when we finish, I cling to him, listening to his heartbeat as I rest my head on his chest. His fingers slip through my hair, giving me goosebumps as it tickles my back when it falls away. His lips press into the top of my head, and I want to hold tighter.

"How was your week?" he asks me.

"Awful," I murmur and close my eyes.

"Why? What happened?"

I lift onto my elbows to blink at him. "I convinced myself you dumped me over that stupid article in *Rolling Stone*."

His head presses back into the pillow as he knits his eyebrows. "*What?*"

"When I didn't hear from you… I read that awful article… I thought you were pissed about what they said about us and didn't want to talk to me."

His face softens, and he pulls me against him, mumbling a gentle, "Oh, Cass. *Why?*"

"It seems irrational *now*." I wrap my arms up to hold on to him and close my eyes. "But I jumped to every conclusion you could possibly think of, back and forth."

"Baby," he says before kissing my hair again, "don't you know by now? Haven't I made it clear to you yet? I'm not going to let anything or anyone come between us again."

"I know," I mumble. "It just felt like *Creem* all over again. Didn't you read it?"

He chuckles and holds me tighter. "No. I don't read what they write anymore. Someone calls to fact check, but they talk to management about that bullshit."

I lift my head. "It…"

He puts a finger over my lips. "I don't care," he says with a gentle smile.

"But if they fact-checked…."

His finger taps my lips. "Facts were probably right. I have no control over opinion, and I don't care. The thing I care about is right here in my arms right now. Baby, if we're gonna make it, *we* have to believe in it. Believe in *us*."

I nod and feel the tears fill my eyes. "I do. I guess I was scared that I was getting more invested, that you'd change your mind somehow."

He shakes his head against the pillow with a soft smile. "Not a chance. I lost you once. I'm not gonna do it again." He wipes an escaped tear from my cheek as I return his smile. "We're okay, Cass," he whispers. "I'm not going anywhere."

"You're going on tour," I tease with a breath.

"But you'll come to visit. It's only a few weeks at a time, and I'll make sure you have the phone number for every venue and every hotel we booked." He arches his eyebrows at me and nods. "It's safe. You can trust this. We're both invested. I'm not changing my mind. I love you, remember?"

I lower my head back to his chest and take a deep breath against him, closing my eyes. "I remember."

"Now," he wraps his arms tighter, "believe it."

It's been three weeks since the last time I met Jeff on the road with his tour this summer. The delay in the airport on my way to Lexington makes it feel more like three months. Once I finally get to the venue, I've missed most of the show, and the crew mills around the hallway bored, waiting to break the stage down. Jace sees me as he wanders through, and his arms open wide with a smile on his face.

"Oh, will he be happy to see you!" he says, kissing my cheek and walking with me toward the stage.

"There were thunderstorms over Idaho." I groan. "Delayed my flight. I almost didn't make it at all."

"He's been doing nothing but talking about seeing you all week. I think he'd have walked to Idaho to carry you back here."

"I'd have met him halfway. How's it going?"

The show echoes through the hall as we get nearer the stage, its sound flattened and dense falling against the cinderblock walls. "I'll tell ya, I've never seen or heard him any better. Have you met his new tour manager? He's keeping everything on the ball." He snaps his fingers in quick succession.

"Not yet. Jeff told me about him, though." Like how he's been through detox himself. Jeff's been talking to him if things become overwhelming with cravings or temptation. He's taken control of his environment and walks away if he's concerned about his sobriety. At the start of the tour, he'd call me when he felt weak, which wasn't very often, surprisingly. I expected it to be worse, but since he's made backstage drug and alcohol-free, temptation has been kept at bay, for the most part. He still checks in with me every night, though. Even if it's just five minutes to say goodnight before he drops into bed.

The reviews have been phenomenal. His album has been on the Top Ten list all summer, and the single has been holding on to the number one spot for the last three weeks. All those doubts and fears he had were for nothing, but I knew that. Just like all those doubts and fears I had about him touring were for nothing, too. I should have known that. I do know how hard it can be to put your blood, sweat, and tears into a song and hand it over to the world, so it's not like I didn't understand his concern. I'm so proud of him… for all of it and for figuring out how to handle it.

We reach the side of the stage, and Jace rests a hand on the small of my back and leans in to be heard over the noise. "This is where I leave you. I need to go talk to a vendor about tour shirts."

The venue is packed, and there is energy in the crowd as I watch Jeff perform. He commands a presence center stage as opposed to that fluffy curly-haired rock star hiding behind his drum kit a decade earlier. Before me is the Rock God and veteran musician, the stoned, exhausted kid, and the older, wiser, sober professional all at once. He clasps his hands together in front of him as he bows to the applause, a humble grin on his face. Rising, he offers an appreciative nod to the audience before turning to walk offstage with an easy wave.

His gaze lands on me in the wings as he's handed a towel, and his smile grows brighter. He's a sweaty mess with his hair sticking to his forehead and his button-down shirt stuck to his chest, but he wraps his arms around me in a tight embrace before realizing and stepping back. Heat radiates off him, and I laugh, wiping his sweat with my fingers from my neck and cheek; occupational hazard, but it reminds me that I get to make him hot and sweaty in a few short hours after we get back to the hotel. He kisses me, both hands on either side of my face, adding a few brief pecks before he pulls back and offers me the corner of his towel.

"Hi! I got to…." He points over his shoulder to the stage and a thunderous audience calling for an encore.

"Go!" I laugh, taking the corner of his towel and dabbing at some of the sweat beading on his forehead. "I'll wait here," I tease, crinkling my nose at him.

He gives me another quick kiss before rubbing noses with me. "So glad you're here." His hand slides down my arm as he steps backward toward the stage. With a wink, he turns and jogs out, waving to the audience as he and his band take their places. The crowd erupts even louder with whistles and applause, and he grins over at me in the wings. With another wink, he looks out at the crowd.

"I'd like to do something if you'll indulge me." The response is louder cheers, and he looks back at me. "In honor of a very special guest, I'd like to pull out one of the old songs I used to do with that other band I'm in. Would that be all right with you?" The place erupts again. He lowers his mic and steps over to the guitarist to speak in his ear, then to the other guys on stage. I can't hear what he's saying, but the rest of the band nods. "All right. We haven't done this one a lot, so if it sucks... be kind." He arches an eyebrow and lowers his chin. Then, the chords to the song I contributed to Expedition's album, *I'm Always at Home,* begins. I haven't heard him do this since that day in the studio in 1976.

Jeff gives me a sly smile and starts singing as the fans go wild. When he gets to the chorus, he lifts the mic over his head, and the audience sings to him, loud and clear—every word.

My mouth drops, and I rest a hand on my chest. Thousands of people are singing my song. Lighters appear over their heads, swaying to the music. People knew of it because it was on that album, but they never released it as a single. He holds the mic out, and the band plays, but without prompting, the audience sings every word into the second verse without Jeff singing.

He looks over at me with a twinkle in his eye and a broad smile on his face. With his free hand, he points to me, nods, pats his chest, and points back at me. He pulls the mic back and joins in, but the audience keeps singing loud enough for me to hear them over the band.

I stand with my hands over my heart, watching, each note filling me like a cup left outside in a downpour. He must have known he'd get this reaction from the crowd to show me just how much of an impression I've had. I may be here in the wings, but my music is center stage. He found a way to demonstrate my influence in a manner that is undeniable and authentic, showing me where I fit in this industry when I've always told myself I was only on the fringe.

As the song plays the final chord, Jeff lowers his hands to his side and looks out over the audience, holding the last note. He's smiling, taking in all that energy and enthusiasm like sunshine. He bows to them in appreciation, coming up with a nod. "Thank you," he says, putting the mic into the stand before him and lifting a finger as if saying 'one minute.' "If you'll indulge me once more...." He glances in my direction and jogs over to me.

I don't know what to think. My heart pounds in my chest with dread, thinking he's going to pull me out on stage. We're off to the side so no one out front can see us, but his band plays the beginning of his single and watches us. He's oblivious to any of it, breathless and wide-eyed in front of me. Sweat pours down his temples from the heat of the stage lights, probably adrenaline, too.

Then he looks at me, and it feels like it's just the two of us, face to face.

"Will you marry me?" he asks before biting his lower lip and arching his eyebrows.

In a blink, he's standing at the end of the studio hallway in bell bottoms and a Hawaiian shirt, one of the most handsome guys I'd ever laid eyes on, taking me on a journey that showed me how naïve I could be, and broke my heart. Simultaneously, he forced me to realize my strength and value. He's allowed me to see how scared and vulnerable he could be, too, holding on to my hand for courage and validation. The thought of having him beside me for the rest of my life makes me breathless and overwhelmed.

I swallow and blink at him, my heart racing.

"Cass?" he asks. The audience still roars in anticipation, waiting for him to return, but he lets them wait... for me. "What do you say?"

My memory shows me flashes of his smile. My heart focuses on how he made me feel that first time he kissed me. My mind reminds me of how thrilled I was when he kissed me again on that patio in the hills.

I break into a smile and release a shaky breath. "Yes." I nod, throwing my arms around his shoulders. "Yes!" I feel his heat against me, and his sweat dampens my bare arms, but none of it matters. I want to cling to him and remember exactly how this moment feels forever. His arms wrapped around my waist, his deep seductive laugh in my ear, and his warmth pressed against me as an audience roars in the distance, oblivious to any of this.

He leans back and kisses me, pulling further away to look me in the eye, curiosity, and hope looking back at me in their deep blueness, as though he wants me to repeat myself.

I laugh and nod again. "Yes," I tell him, loud and clear, my gaze holding onto his as sure as my love for him.

"I have to get back out there," he says.

I lean forward to kiss him. "I'll be here when you're finished."

He takes a few steps toward the stage but returns to give me another kiss. "I love you."

"I love you. Now go!" I nudge him toward the stage with a laugh.

As he walks out, he looks over his shoulder at me with a wide grin, and the corners of his eyes crinkle with it. I realize then that smile belongs to me.

It always did.

Other books by
Heather J. Bennett

Letting Go

Expecting to Fly

Available on Amazon.com

Follow
Facebook: heatherjbennettnovelist
Instagram: @heatherjbennett_author

Find short stories and more
www.heatherjbennett.com